DISCARD

Peabody Public Library
Columbia City, IN

Praise for the
Double Feature Mysteries

It Happened One Knife

"Reading Cohen's book is like hearing a great story in a bar—conversational, amusing, and you just want to buy someone a beer when you are done—and then ask for more. Cohen creates wonderful characters and Elliot Freed is a guy who's right on the edge of nuttiness, but is so kind and bighearted that it's easy to forgive his obsession with old comedies . . . Lots of laughs, some nice red herrings, and a perfect way to spend a summer afternoon."   —*BookBitch*

"Everybody knows Jeff Cohen writes wonderfully funny, well-plotted mysteries peopled by characters more human than most humans, but did you know Cohen also knows how to write love? No? Well, this book showcases all his many skills. Including love. And, of course, love lost."

—Linda Ellerbee

"Cohen's greatest strength is his characters . . . Cohen creates characters with heart. *It Happened One Knife* combines great characters, humor, and suspense, with a little slapstick, in the tradition of the best movie comedies. You can't go wrong with Cohen's Double Feature Mysteries."   —*Lesa's Book Critiques*

"Cohen shows why he is a wonderful mystery author with his humorous yet action-packed investigative tale. *It Happened One Knife* is fast paced but contains a quirky cast that insures the audience will believe they are at a comedy show instead of in an amateur sleuth novel. Elliot is the terrific star in this comedic cozy."   —*Genre Go Round Reviews*

"Jeff Cohen is the class clown of the mystery world. *It Happened One Knife* has it all: a puzzling mystery, characters to love, and nonstop rapier wit. Cohen is truly a class act!"

—Chris Grabenstein, Anthony Award–winning author of
Tilt-a-Whirl

D0912192

Some Like It Hot-Buttered

"Cohen fires up the gag reel for a new tongue-in-cheek mystery . . . Freed solves the mystery and earns his amateur sleuth credentials, promising more comic adventures to come. Cohen develops his lively characters almost as effortlessly as he delivers jokes—and the occasional guffaw—and manages to sneak in some suspenseful twists besides." *—Publishers Weekly*

"A light, funny murder mystery . . . The start of a wonderful new series." —ReviewingTheEvidence.com

"A wonderful treat for cozy mystery lovers! A smart and witty protagonist leads a dynamic cast through a vibrant first-person narrative filled with satisfying twists and turns. The first of what promises to be a wonderful series . . . Funny and exciting, I simply cannot wait to read more."

—Romance Readers Connection

"You're in for a treat, that is, if you like good mystery written with great humor, as well as warmth and wit . . . Solving the mystery and finding those responsible for the crimes is only part of the fun in this wonderfully entertaining book—Mr. Cohen's writing and wry sense of humor is a delight . . . I can't wait to read the next one!" *—Crimespree Magazine*

"Cohen has begun a new series featuring another nice, *schleppy* hero with a heart of gold. This seems to be his specialty and I, for one, couldn't be happier . . . This new book has, at its heart, an everyman who just happens to get involved in murderous doings, and we, thankfully, get to go along . . . Not only is the book funny, which you would expect from Jeff Cohen, but it is also well-plotted (also expected), and loaded with plenty of misdirection. Plus you get to meet another terrific bunch of characters." *—Mystery Ink*

"Readers keep coming back for more [of] Cohen's delightful sense of humor and ability to create main characters who shine with sly mirth, bubble with self-deprecating humor, and zing one-liners nearly every time they open their mouth or even have internal dialogue with themselves . . . If you enjoy humor in any form, you'll get a kick out of *Some Like It Hot-Buttered.* If you like comedic mysteries, you're in for a

real treat. And, if you happen to like comedic mysteries and are a fan of classic comedy movies, you've hit the jackpot."
—*Curled Up With a Good Book*

"A twisty mystery with lots of laughs and lots of heart. This is the first in the Double Feature Mystery series, and hopefully it won't be too long a wait for the next." —*BookBitch*

"Those looking for a few laughs will find plenty to enjoy with this offering." —*Roundtable Reviews*

"A very entertaining read." —*New Mystery Reader Magazine*

"A delight to read and Elliot quickly joined the ranks of my favorite cozy heroes. The plot was fresh, the writing sparkled . . . Film buffs and readers who like to laugh should read this book." —*Mystery News*

"Will keep you laughing till the end. It is a book I highly recommend." —*I Love A Mystery*

"A little bit of mystery heaven—don't miss it." —*Aunt Agatha's*

"Even if you're not a movie buff, you'll love this first book in a new series . . . The author doesn't go for the zany approach here; Elliot, who narrates, has a very dry and sarcastic wit. The mystery . . . will keep the reader guessing until the end." —*CA Reviews*

"A witty, enjoyable mystery . . . Perfect for anyone who needs a 'Comedy Tonight.'" —*Lesa's Book Critiques*

"A hilarious read, with quips and asides to movies and movie people. The plot is very believable and provides a great insight into the comedy genre niche, which is sorely ignored all over the country." —*Love Romances and More*

"Grab a bag of popcorn from the microwave, find a comfortable seat, and prepare to be entertained." —*Chattanooga Press*

"A very funny mystery . . . The characters are well-defined, the dialogue frequently laugh-out-loud funny, and the plot adequately complex without being overly complicated . . . A terrific debut." —*Mysterious Reviews*

"The plot is nicely twisting, with enough action to keep the reader entertained . . . This is the book for anyone who wants to relax, chuckle a bit, and get involved in a good mystery."
—*Front Street Reviews*

"Something for everyone! . . . Bursts with mystery, action, romance, and laughs . . . A sure thing smash-hit. Jeffrey Cohen is the Dave Barry of the New Jersey Turnpike."
—Julia Spencer-Fleming,
Edgar® Award nominee and
author of *I Shall Not Want*

"Movies, murder, characters who are real people, laughs, danger, and damn good writing."
—Linda Ellerbee, television producer,
journalist, and bestselling author of
Take Big Bites and *And So It Goes*

"Knock, knock. Who's there? Cohen. Cohen who? Cohen buy yourself this most entertaining book."
—Larry Gelbart, writer of *M*A*S*H*, *Tootsie*, *Oh, God!*,
A Funny Thing Happened on the Way to the Forum,
Barbarians at the Gate, etc.

Berkley Prime Crime titles by Jeffrey Cohen

SOME LIKE IT HOT-BUTTERED
IT HAPPENED ONE KNIFE
A NIGHT AT THE OPERATION

A NIGHT AT THE OPERATION

Jeffrey Cohen

Peabody Public Library
Columbia City, IN
DISCARD

BERKLEY PRIME CRIME, NEW YORK

THE BERKLEY PUBLISHING GROUP
Published by the Penguin Group
Penguin Group (USA) Inc.
375 Hudson Street, New York, New York 10014, USA
Penguin Group (Canada), 90 Eglinton Avenue East, Suite 700, Toronto, Ontario M4P 2Y3, Canada
(a division of Pearson Penguin Canada Inc.)
Penguin Books Ltd., 80 Strand, London WC2R 0RL, England
Penguin Group Ireland, 25 St. Stephen's Green, Dublin 2, Ireland (a division of Penguin Books Ltd.)
Penguin Group (Australia), 250 Camberwell Road, Camberwell, Victoria 3124, Australia
(a division of Pearson Australia Group Pty. Ltd.)
Penguin Books India Pvt. Ltd., 11 Community Centre, Panchsheel Park, New Delhi—110 017, India
Penguin Group (NZ), 67 Apollo Drive, Rosedale, North Shore 0632, New Zealand
(a division of Pearson New Zealand Ltd.)
Penguin Books (South Africa) (Pty.) Ltd., 24 Sturdee Avenue, Rosebank, Johannesburg 2196,
South Africa

Penguin Books Ltd., Registered Offices: 80 Strand, London WC2R 0RL, England

This is a work of fiction. Names, characters, places, and incidents either are the product of the author'
imagination or are used fictitiously, and any resemblance to actual persons, living or dead, business estab
lishments, events, or locales is entirely coincidental. The publisher does not have any control over and doe
not assume any responsibility for author or third-party websites or their content.

A NIGHT AT THE OPERATION

A Berkley Prime Crime Book / published by arrangement with the author

PRINTING HISTORY
Berkley Prime Crime mass-market edition / April 2009

Copyright © 2009 by Jeffrey Cohen.
The Edgar® name is a registered service mark of the Mystery Writers of America, Inc.
Cover illustration Andy Ward.
Cover design by Annette Fiore Defex.
Interior text design by Kristin del Rosario.

All rights reserved.
No part of this book may be reproduced, scanned, or distributed in any printed or electronic form
without permission. Please do not participate in or encourage piracy of copyrighted materials in
violation of the author's rights. Purchase only authorized editions.
For information, address: The Berkley Publishing Group,
a division of Penguin Group (USA), Inc.,
375 Hudson Street, New York, New York 10014.

ISBN: 978-0-425-22815-9

BERKLEY® PRIME CRIME
Berkley Prime Crime Books are published by The Berkley Publishing Group,
a division of Penguin Group (USA) Inc.,
375 Hudson Street, New York, New York 10014.
BERKLEY® PRIME CRIME and the PRIME CRIME logo are trademarks of Penguin Group (USA)
Inc.

PRINTED IN THE UNITED STATES OF AMERICA

10 9 8 7 6 5 4 3 2 1

If you purchased this book without a cover, you should be aware that this book is stolen property. It was
reported as "unsold and destroyed" to the publisher, and neither the author nor the publisher has
received any payment for this "stripped book."

This book is dedicated to
Rhoda Cohen,
my mother,
who taught me not only how to read, but why.

ACKNOWLEDGMENTS

I'D like to thank the Academy, but they've never done anything for me, so that will have to wait for another day.

Screenwriters like to say that if you want control over your work, you should write a stage play. Playwrights, however, say the way to maintain control is to write a novel. It's a question of degree, really. There's no such thing as total control over a creative work, unless you write, edit, and publish that work yourself.

So even though it seems like I just keep thanking the amazing editor of the Double Feature Mysteries, Shannon Jamieson Vazquez, there's a reason behind it. With this novel especially, you would have read something considerably different—and demonstrably worse—had it not been for her. If you have enjoyed any of the Double Feature books so far, you have Shannon to thank, but most of you don't know her, so I'll do it for you. Thank you, Shannon. Every author should be so lucky, but that would really increase your workload.

For supporting the efforts of Elliot and his cohorts, thanks to booksellers and librarians truly worldwide. All those I've visited have been amazing, and I hesitate to single any out for fear of inadvertently leaving someone out. So if you're a bookseller, and I've met you, assume you're the one I'm talking about. Because you are.

The author's support group keeps growing: thanks to my blogging buddies at Hey, There's a Dead Guy in the Living Room: Janet Reid, Lynne Patrick, Sharon Wheeler, PJ Nunn,

Robin Agnew, Abby Zidle, Deni Dietz, and Gordon Aalborg. And to my book tour companions, Chris Grabenstein, Ken Isaacson, and Jack Getze.

And of course my dedicated and tireless agent, Christina Hogrebe, and the many talented people at the Jane Rotrosen Agency, who look out for all the things I completely don't understand. Thank goodness for you.

But the backbone is always my family, and they make it possible for me to sit around and think of stories to write down. To Jessica, Josh, and Eve: You are the best a man could ever hope for, and far more than I deserve.

Old situations, new complications
Nothing portentous or polite
Tragedy tomorrow—comedy tonight!

—STEPHEN SONDHEIM,
A Funny Thing Happened on the Way to the Forum

1

Man does not control his own fate. The women in his life do that for him.
—GROUCHO MARX

FRIDAY

Sullivan's Travels (1941) and *Train Trippin'* (this week)

"SHARON is missing."

I looked up from what I'd been doing—playing an addictive little computer game called MacBrickout—and that resulted in a double punishment for me. First, I lost the ball that was knocking out a series of increasingly-hard-to-hit bricks on my computer screen. Second, I was now looking at the face of Dr. Gregory Sandoval, my ex-wife's soon-to-be second ex-husband, who was standing in the doorway of my office, uninvited.

"What do you mean, 'missing'?" I asked. I actually do know what "missing" means, but I was caught off-guard and hadn't really been listening to Gregory. I try not to listen to Gregory whenever possible.

The thing about Gregory is . . . I have tried, on numerous occasions, to pretend he doesn't exist, but there is scientific evidence that he does. The man is an irritant, like a tiny speck of dust in your eye that won't wash out, no matter how much Visine you use.

Of course, he was wrong. Sharon was *not* missing. I'd seen my ex-wife only the day before

Peabody Public Library
Columbia City, IN

It hadn't been a pleasant experience, but I couldn't blame that on Sharon, nor, even more surprisingly, myself. The fact is that after the age of twenty-two or so—and maybe even before—it's just no fun to get a physical examination.

I go to my ex-wife's medical practice for a number of reasons. First, I know that Sharon and Antoinette Westphal, who started the practice, invite only the best doctors to join them. Second, it is conveniently close to where I work and where I live. Third, I get to see Sharon, with whom I had a cordial divorce, whenever I go there.

And last but not least, I still get the family discount. A man paying for his own health insurance worries about such things.

But that doesn't carry much comfort with it when you're a man in his late thirties and another man is checking you for signs of testicular cancer. It's hard to think of much at a time like that.

"I don't see anything," said Dr. Lennon Dickinson, Sharon's rather disturbingly handsome partner. Lennon, who was not named after Paul McCartney, George Harrison, or Ringo Starr, had dark hair, blue eyes, and the kind of look that makes Dr. McDreamy look like Dr. McDumpy, I'm told. Now, he was simply reporting the facts. He hadn't been named after Jack Webb, either, but his sensibility was similar to Jack's.

"That's a little worrisome," I told him. "Maybe you should get glasses."

Lennon looked up, which, under the circumstances, was something of a relief. "I meant, I'm not finding any nodules or striations," he said. Lennon is as funny as an Ingmar Bergman festival.

"I know, Lennon. I was just kidding."

He nodded. Yes, that was the price one pays for having a patient who owns a movie theatre that shows only comedies. You have to deal with the occasional joke.

"I think you're just fine. Get dressed," Lennon said.

"If I had a dime for every time I've heard that," I said under my breath. But I followed his instructions, and, luckily, Lennon didn't try to banter back.

Dressed and dismissed as healthy, I followed Lennon out of the examination room and into the hallway, where doors to four other such rooms were located. One of the doors was closed, with the color-coded "patient inside" flag showing, and that was where Toni Westphal was, I assumed. Sharon was right in front of me.

She smiled her professional smile when she saw me, and spoke in Lennon's direction. "I assume his heart is still beating," she said, gesturing at me.

"I didn't find anything wrong," Lennon answered. The man's a carnival.

"That's only because you're not a psychiatrist," she told him, grinning at me a little too hard.

"You married me," I reminded Sharon. "What does that say about *you*?"

"I divorced you, too. That speaks volumes."

I gave her my "droll" face, and moved on. "C'est Moi! on Monday?" I asked. Sharon and I meet about once a week for lunch at a badly named restaurant in Midland Heights, near my theatre and her practice. It's part of our ongoing effort to not have an acrimonious divorce. Some times are harder than others, like when she orders a steak sandwich for lunch and I try to mooch the french fries. The woman is vicious in defending her fries.

Sharon considered my lunch proposal. "Monday. I'm not sure. Yeah, I guess Monday will be okay."

"Don't be too enthusiastic, or I'll think you're harboring feelings for me," I said.

"Keep dreaming," Sharon said. She knocked on the door of the exam room next to her and walked inside before I could think of a witty response, but then, she could have stood there waiting for an hour. I had nothing.

Sharon and I had divorced when she'd decided she'd rather be married to Gregory, a choice I've never fully understood, but came grudgingly to accept. She had since come to her senses, and was now in the process of divorcing Gregory. But Sharon and I had remained friendly. One night, a couple of months before, we'd gotten *very* friendly, but that had only reminded us of some of the reasons we'd divorced to begin with, and it hadn't happened again.

Not yet, anyway. A man can dream.

The following Friday, eight days hence, would be the ninth anniversary of our wedding, and even though we were no longer married, we'd decided to get together that evening. It makes more sense to us than celebrating the day we were divorced. We'd had a better party when we got married, after all, and *that* was worth remembering.

Lennon led me to the reception area, where I could pay my bill and kibitz with Betty, the unbearably attractive receptionist. Betty is the kind of woman whom many men would find attractive, assuming they were heterosexual and breathing. But Sharon has always been an equal-opportunity employer, and talked her partners into hiring Betty despite her being almost unbearably hot. I recall it taking less persuasion with Lennon Dickinson than Toni Westphal. Lennon, in fact, had offered to pay Betty's salary entirely from his own pocket.

Alas, Betty wasn't in her traditional seat. "She must be in the ladies' room," Lennon said, displaying a habit for conveying too much information whenever it isn't requested. "I'll take care of it. Let me see your insurance card and a credit card."

I reached into my back pocket for my wallet and fished out the insurance card. I never use a credit card, and only carry one for identification purposes, so it took longer to find, but I managed. While Lennon was doing whatever it is one does with such items, someone to my left said, "My god, they'll let anybody in here these days, won't they?"

I didn't have to look. "Hi, Grace," I said. "Still carrying a torch for me, eh?"

"Only to burn down your house." Grace, the head nurse for the practice—about fifty, attractive, and somewhere between thin and heavy—gave me a quick kiss on the cheek by way of greeting. An older gent in the waiting area gave me a dirty look, like I was getting attention that was rightfully his. "How are you, Elliot?"

"That's what I'm here to find out," I told her. "Ask Lennon."

"He's fine," Lennon said, rapier wit at the ready. He handed me back my ID and my credit card.

I saw Betty come out of the restroom and knock on an exam room door. Betty is studying to become an RN, and sometimes observes or helps out on simple exams. Sharon let her into the exam room. My luck, I'd have to keep looking at Lennon.

I turned to Grace, but she had an odd look on her face, and I didn't say anything. I wondered whether I'd forgotten to zip up after the exam, but couldn't think of a discreet way to check.

Grace looked around me at Lennon. Her voice dropped a number of decibels. "Have you asked him yet?" she hissed at the doctor through the glass partition.

"I was just about to," Lennon hissed back, and then set his gaze on me. It didn't have the effect on me that it would have had on, say, women.

"Ask me what?" I wondered aloud.

Too loud, apparently. "Shh!" Grace said, drawing more attention from the crowd in the waiting room than my innocuous outburst had. "Keep your voice down!"

Okay, I could play that game. "Ask me what?" I whispered.

They didn't have time to answer, because Toni Westphal had walked over, apparently having completed the exam she was performing on a patient. Toni, who's around forty and exudes a maternal warmth despite having no children, threw one hand over my shoulder and the other over Grace's, as if we were in a football huddle.

"What's going on?" she whispered. "Are we planning a surprise party?"

"We were just about to ask Elliot," Grace said.

Toni looked confused. "Ask Elliot if we're planning a surprise party?"

Lennon gave her his most serious look, which is just a little more serious than that of a funeral director on a busy day. I'm only his patient because Sharon won't treat me and she thinks I should have a male doctor, but Lennon's bedside manner would be enough to cause most patients to burst into tears. I guess the women he treats just look at him and don't worry about medicine too much. "We were going to *ask Elliot*," he echoed.

Toni's eyes narrowed. "Oh. Yeah."

I looked from face to face, and found no answers. "Okay," I said, "Let's pretend that I just got out of an ESL class, and speak slowly and clearly. What are you people talking about?"

Lennon gestured for me to move closer to the glass, which had a window in it for communication and commerce. "What's been bothering Sharon?" he asked.

I knit my brow. It's not hard to do, but the needles sting like crazy. "Bothering Sharon?"

Grace, leaning over to hear, pouted out her lips. "Damn," she said. "We thought it was you."

"A lot of people think it's me," I agreed. "What's me?"

"The thing that's bothering Sharon," Lennon answered, with a tone that indicated I was a fool for asking.

"Are you speaking in code?" I asked. It was worth a shot.

Toni shook her head. "Sharon's been on edge for a few days, maybe a week," she began.

"Five days," Lennon corrected. I think he has OCD.

"Okay, five days," Toni went on. "She's not exactly snapping at people, but she's distracted. And she won't talk about what the problem is."

"Distracted? Doesn't answer you quickly? Seems to be thinking about something else?" I asked, exhausting my definitions for "distracted."

They all nodded.

I smiled. "It's something to do with a patient," I said. "When she's deep in thought about a problem that's puzzling her, she goes to another planet mentally. I'm surprised you guys didn't know that already. Is there a patient whose case has been bothering her?"

They exchanged a knowing glance, but Grace said, "You know we can't tell you that, Elliot." And of course, she was right. Doctor/patient confidentiality, you know.

"Well, I'm guessing . . ."

I was stunned into silence by a sound from down the hall. Far down the hall. And I could hear it clearly.

Sharon, shouting in anger.

"Good lord, Betty, do it right or get out of the room! NOW!"

The door to the examination room opened, and Betty walked out with an absolutely astonished expression on her face. Toni looked at Betty and said, "What was *that* all about?"

Betty, her lovely face streaked with tears, just shook her head. She pushed open the door to the restroom and walked in. I heard the lock click behind her.

There was a long silence at the desk where I was standing.

"Okay, so something's bothering Sharon," I said.

2

"SHARON is missing," Gregory repeated.

His oval face was drawn and sallow, even for him. "I mean, nobody's seen her since yesterday afternoon," Gregory said. "She didn't come home last night. She's not answering her cell phone or the phone at the house."

"If she has caller ID, that could just be a sign that she doesn't want to talk to *you*," I suggested. "You want me to call her for you?" I picked up the desk phone. The office at Comedy Tonight isn't exactly what you'd call state-of-the-art, but we do have a telephone.

"I don't need you to call her; she's missing," Gregory lamented. So I put the phone down. That had just been a ploy to annoy him, anyway. "We have to call the police."

I avoided the "what's this *we* stuff, Kemo Sabe" line and said instead, "She hasn't been missing twenty-four hours yet, and she's a grown woman. We don't know that she's even *missing* at all. The police won't get involved. Go put people to sleep for a while and see if you hear from Sharon tonight." Gregory is an anesthesiologist.

"You don't understand," he sniffed. "I should have expected this from you."

I went back to my game, trying to knock off virtual bricks with a virtual ball and paddle. "It's truly amazing that you didn't," I said as Gregory slunk out of the office.

Once he was out of sight, I reached for the phone and pressed Sharon's button on speed dial. The phone rang a number of times, and I got transferred to her voice mail. That wasn't unusual, if she was working, but my guess was that Gregory would have checked with Betty at the practice first.

"This is Dr. Sharon Simon-Freed." I took some pleasure, I admit, in the fact that Sharon had added my name, and not Gregory's, to her own. She kept it that way, even after we divorced, and even when she was married to Gregory. Not that I'm petty. "I'm not available right now. Please leave a message, and I'll get back to you."

I waited for the beep, and said, "Hi, it's me." The stupidest statement a person can make. Does anyone ever leave a message that says, "Hi, it's someone else"? "Gregory thinks you're missing. Give me a call and let me know you're not." I hung up.

It was an hour and a half before we'd open the theatre for the evening. My staff was just starting to trickle in. Anthony Pagliarulo, the projectionist, was already upstairs in the booth, doing whatever magic it is that he does to keep our ancient projection equipment running. I don't question Anthony's mechanical brilliance—I just quiver at the very thought that one day he'll graduate from college and leave me alone with the man-eating monster in my projection booth.

No need to worry about that now, however. Anthony was still an undergraduate at Rutgers, majoring in film. He'd actually made a movie of his own, a remarkably gory Western called *Killin' Time*, which had come dangerously close to being distributed by a real company only a few months earlier. Luckily, someone at the studio had actually watched the movie first, and had therefore passed on it, and now Anthony was back in my projection booth, tending to the dinosaur.

I had a favor to ask of him, though, so I went upstairs to the refurbished balcony (which was much sturdier than when it had been originally furbished) and knocked on the projection booth door. I own the place, but one time I had entered without knocking and had almost put a permanent dent in the back of Anthony's head with the door. It's not a large projection room.

"Come in," he said, so I did.

Anthony was threading up the first feature for the night, a personal favorite of mine. (We run the classic first and the contemporary comedy second.) Preston Sturges's *Sullivan's Travels* is a masterpiece about a director who discovers that making people laugh is at least as important as making a Statement. It's only after he goes through hell that Joel McCrae (playing John L. "Sully" Sullivan) realizes comedy is the thing that can get us through our most difficult moments. The title of his intended "important" project, *O Brother, Where Art Thou?* became the title of a Coen Brothers film starring . . . But, I digress.

"Can you do me a favor?" I asked Anthony. I handed him a VHS videocassette I had brought up from the office. "Take this back to your editing suite at school and transfer it to DVD for me, would you?"

He took the cassette from my hand and examined it as if it were a relic from King Tut's tomb, which is silly. Everybody knows the Boy King was into Beta. "Can't you do it at home?" Anthony wasn't trying to shirk the job; he was curious about why I'd asked.

"I could, but the picture quality would suffer on my cheap home machine," I told him. "You can get a better transfer."

Anthony nodded, and put the cassette in his backpack, which was lying on the floor. "What is it?" he asked as an afterthought.

"The video from my wedding," I told him.

His head swiveled. You'd have thought I'd told him it was a film of my recent sex-change surgery. "Really?"

"Yeah. Our wedding anniversary is coming up next week, and I thought I'd give it to Sharon as a gift. So, on second thought, make two copies, okay?"

Anthony was staring at the spot directly between my eyes, seemingly trying to decipher the strange dialect I was speaking. "You know you're divorced, right?" he asked.

"Yes."

"But you still give your ex-wife a present on your anniversary?" Anthony and his girlfriend Carla were so far from thinking about marriage that considering life after divorce was beyond his comprehension. He thinks every divorce is like the ones in movies like *War of the Roses*, ending in acrimony and, usually, violence.

"Yes, Anthony, I do," I told him. "Sharon and I try to keep up a civil relationship, and one of the things we do is continue to celebrate our wedding anniversary. Besides, I know the only copy she has is on VHS, and I'm willing to bet she'd like something that won't deteriorate over time." Symbolic, no?

Okay, so maybe sentimental anniversary gifts that feature our wedding vows go past the concept of "civil," but we still have feelings for each other. And besides, a woman who pays you alimony every month deserves at least a token, doesn't she?

He didn't answer, but shook his head and went back to threading the projector with a grin on his face that spoke volumes about his crazy boss.

I was that boss, so I exercised my authority and went back to playing MacBrickout. It's a dangerous little game, seemingly simple, that will grab you in its tentacles and steal your time away. And it always gives you just enough hope to make you think it's worth trying to win again. In many ways, MacBrickout is like my ex-wife Sharon.

Whiling away my remaining life force with the game took another twenty minutes or so, until Sophie Beringer, the snack bar attendant/ticket taker, and Jonathan Goodwin, the usher/

swing man, entered the theatre, mooning at each other, as had become their habit. They were high school students, they were dating, and it was close to unbearable how happy they were.

I left them alone. Unbridled joy is something I have a hard time with: I always want to bridle it with a dose of reality. Sophie actually mussed Jonathan's hair as they walked by the door to my office, which led me to wonder if she'd been replaced with an android that only *looked* like Sophie. Before they started dating, Sophie was about as bubbly as Coca-Cola that's been left open. For a week.

Jonathan, for his part, had undergone something of a metamorphosis once Sophie smiled upon him. He started actually looking me in the eye when I spoke to him, began wearing shoes that covered his toes (he had previously favored sandals that gave a view of his feet that I believe helped keep Comedy Tonight's crowds smaller than they should have been), and although he continued to wear T-shirts with images from great comedies (today's was a simple moustache-and-eyebrows caricature bearing the phrase "Just tell 'em Groucho sent you"), they were now clean, frequently changed, and mostly the right size for Jonathan's tall, skinny body.

I ignored this flagrant happiness and turned back to the task at hand. Before I realized the time had gone by, another thirty minutes of my life had been eaten up by MacBrickout. I looked up at the clock and frowned. Okay, now it *was* strange that Sharon hadn't called back yet, if only to mock Gregory for worrying that she hadn't called back.

The scene from the day before was starting to seem ominous. It wasn't like Sharon to yell at anyone (she never even raised her voice at me during our divorce), particularly Betty, for whom she has a great deal of affection. Whomever the patient was whose case was worrying her must have been very special.

I was suddenly glad Sharon was not my doctor, or I'd have to include myself on the list of possible doomed people.

Maybe I should walk over to her office. Sharon's medical

practice was only four blocks away, and I had a little time before we really had to be ready to open the theatre. I stood up and walked out the office door, but didn't make it any farther than the edge of the lobby.

Sophie's parents, Ilsa and Ron Beringer, burst—there is no other word for it—through the front doors of Comedy Tonight, both with the wild-eyed demeanor of Moe Howard after Curly hit him over the head with a bowling ball. Ilsa clutched in her hand what appeared to be an e-mail printout.

"Sophie!" she screamed. "Where are you, Sophie?" Sophie was perhaps fifteen feet away, at the snack bar, in direct view of her mother. Jonathan should have had the good sense to look alarmed, but the fact is, he doesn't really live on the same planet as the rest of us, and he simply kept studying Sophie with a serene grin on his face. Jonathan was still amazed that she ever went out on a date with him in the first place.

Sophie's face took on the expression of every teenage girl who hears her mother's voice: she immediately looked annoyed, and turned toward Ilsa as if her mother were an especially persistent type of mosquito.

"What are you doing here?" she asked. No, demanded.

"They *came*!" Ilsa cried, thrusting the paper toward her daughter with a vehemence normally reserved for reprieves from the governor.

"*What* came?" Sophie intoned.

"Your SAT scores," Ron said. Ilsa pivoted and stared at him. Her husband appeared amazed that he had gotten a word in edgewise. But his pride in himself was matched by Ilsa's expression of fury. "You got . . ."

He stopped once he saw Ilsa's expression. Clearly, he was not supposed to be the one to tell his daughter about her test scores. This was reserved for her mother. But Sophie took perhaps a quarter of a second to go from completely impassive to laser-focused. She snatched the e-mail printout from her mother's hand before Ilsa could get so much as a number out of her mouth.

"What were you doing reading my e-mail?" Sophie growled.

"They sent it to us, too . . ." Ron answered, but his voice trailed off, and he went back to being a paper cut-out of a man, his usual role.

I felt like I was intruding on what for a normal family would be a private moment, but I was too far from the door to go back into the office again without drawing attention to myself. Besides, I wanted to find out about Sophie's SAT scores, too. She'd never even mentioned the test before she took it, so I had (as usual, mistakenly) assumed she wasn't especially concerned.

"Twenty-two sixty!" Sophie crowed. "I got a twenty-two sixty!" I was immediately confused, because when I took the SATs, the best you could do was sixteen hundred. Sophie must be *really* smart. She showed the page to Jonathan, who earnestly tried to interpret the numbers, but Sophie yanked the paper out of his hand again before he had a chance. She reached over and kissed him on the cheek, and Jonathan, as usual, smiled a dopey smile and hugged her. If I hadn't actually heard him speak on occasion, I'd have believed he was a tall, gangly puppy dog that had learned to stand on its back legs.

"Isn't that *amazing*?" Her mother beamed. "I always knew you were a *genius*."

"A genius," Ron Beringer echoed. But nobody seemed to hear him or the sound he appeared to make. The fool on the hill.

"Do you realize what this *means*?" Sophie asked Jonathan, completely ignoring her parents. "I actually have a chance at the Ivies. I could take a shot at Harvard. Yale. Brown."

Jonathan's brow furrowed. "Does this mean you're moving away?" he asked.

"Oh, Jonathan." Sophie's hand went to her boyfriend's cheek. "You knew I was going away to school next year."

"Well, yeah," he admitted. "But I figured you'd go to Rutgers. *Everybody* goes to Rutgers."

Rutgers University is not quite walking distance from Midland Heights, New Jersey, and many of its students rent apartments here and especially in Highland Park, which is just to the south. Anthony, for example, goes to Rutgers, and lives in New Brunswick, like I do.

"Well, I have a chance to do better," Sophie said, her voice a little sad. "I should go for that, shouldn't I?"

"Of *course* you should." Ilsa, not to be denied, butted in. She insinuated herself between Sophie and Jonathan, effectively turning her back on the poor kid. "Come along home now, Sophie, and we'll start planning. You have a lot of work to do." She tried to take Sophie's elbow, but her daughter simply shook her arm free and glared at Ilsa.

"What do you mean, 'come along home'?" Sophie asked. "I have work tonight."

"You're not going to keep working *here*," Ilsa scoffed, looking around the lobby the way she might at a not-very-high-class house of prostitution (I guessed). "We'll pay you for your time so you'll have spending money, but from now on you have to concentrate on getting into the best college you can."

Ron, perhaps reeling from the "we'll pay for your time" part of that speech, stood with his jaw dropped. Jonathan, horrified, took a step back and almost squashed the box of Milk Duds that Sophie had placed on the stool behind him. I winced. I have a soft spot for Milk Duds; they saved my life once. It's a long story.

Sophie's eyebrows dropped about a foot, and her head drooped a little, like a bull about to charge. I involuntarily moved closer to my office door. "I'm not quitting work, *Mother*," she said audibly, but not loudly.

"Of course you are," Ilsa breezed on, oblivious to the storm clouds gathering overhead. "I don't know why you stayed here this long. But now you have much more important work to do."

"We've had this discussion," Sophie countered. "I'm staying here at least until I leave for college. I like the work, and I like the people." She glanced at Jonathan, who seemed to take some solace from that. "I have a responsibility here, and I'm going to live up to it."

Ilsa looked at her the way you would at a four-year-old who has just spelled the word "inadvertently" correctly—in indelible ink on the kitchen wall. "Don't be silly, dear," she said. "You don't need a part-time job anymore. Someone else can sell your little candies."

I was spared the coming explosion because the phone in my office started to ring. This gave me the excuse I needed to go inside and close the door behind me, never happier to be interrupted.

But the caller didn't sound happy. "Elliot, this is Chief Dutton at the police department," he said, as if I knew a Chief Dutton who worked at the Exxon station.

"Hi, Chief." We hadn't talked in a while, as Comedy Tonight was going through an unusual crime-free period. The chief and I have a professional relationship.

"Elliot, do you know where your ex-wife might be?"

That was a strange question, but I wasn't going to show that it had thrown me. "Not right this minute," I told Dutton. "Why do you ask?" My throat was suddenly dry.

"Well, she appears to be missing. No one at her office has seen her since yesterday afternoon."

"I'll be right there," I said.

3

CHIEF Barry Dutton's office is one of the least attractive rooms in Midland Heights, and he knows it. He tries to dress up the municipal uniformity of the chipped cinder block and peeling wood veneer with plants, an area rug, and a window curtain, but it's like putting an Armani gown on a hippopotamus—it really doesn't make the hippo any lovelier, and you're not fooling anybody.

I wasn't worried about aesthetics at the moment, anyway. It was one thing when Gregory thought Sharon was missing after less than a day, but if Dutton was concerned enough to call, it clearly justified having a knot in your stomach, so I did. It's never fun to hear from the police about a loved one, even an ex-loved-one.

"I thought you guys didn't get involved in missing persons cases until at least twenty-four hours had gone by," I said. Dutton was sitting behind his desk, and I was pacing where the area rug wasn't helping the room much. So I could notice the aesthetics and worry at the same time; I'm a multitasker.

"We don't," Dutton answered, his basso even more bass than usual. Without leaving me any time to ask about that statement, he added, "Do you have any idea where she might be right now?"

I thought of answering as Bob Hoskins did in the underrated *Who Framed Roger Rabbit?*, and saying "Cucamonga? Walla Walla? I hear Kokomo is nice this time of year." But given the gravity of the situation, I stuck with, "No. I saw her yesterday, and she didn't say anything about going anywhere."

"Is that typical?"

I shrugged. "It's not atypical. We have lunch together once a week, and then sometimes we talk on the phone a few days later, and sometimes we don't. This time was a 'don't.' "

Dutton's lips pursed out, then in, which I did not take to be a good sign. There was something he wasn't telling me, and I'm never crazy about that, especially when it comes from the cops. "What's going on, Chief?" I asked.

He didn't answer me. "Who would have typically heard from her, besides her husband, Dr. Sandoval?"

"Soon-to-be ex-husband," I noted, then thought about his question. "Best guess: the other doctors at her practice, Toni Westphal and Lennon Dickinson."

Dutton's eyebrows rose. "Lennon?" he asked.

"He was born in the seventies to parents who came of age in the sixties," I explained. "How come Dylan is all right for a first name, but Lennon isn't?"

"Sorry. Who else?"

"There is the nurse, Grace—I don't remember her last name—and the receptionist, Betty. And whatever patients she saw yesterday. Gregory says he hasn't seen her, and they still share that house."

"A typical New Jersey divorce. Everybody's afraid to leave the house because they think that means they'll lose it." Dutton sat back in his chair and closed his eyes, thinking.

"What's going on, Chief?" I repeated. "Sharon's a grown woman who's been gone for less than a day, and you're already investigating." The knot in my stomach turned into a noose. "Is there something you're not telling me?"

"Yes, but it's not what you think," Dutton answered. He opened his eyes, and looked kindly at me. "I don't think your ex is in danger, but what's bothering me is that she was last seen—"

"Don't say 'last,'" I warned.

"—at her office a little after seven last evening, and never went home. Her car is not in the driveway at her house or in the parking lot at her office. She hasn't called in to her practice. She hasn't been home, at least not according to the man living in her house. She isn't answering her cell phone or responding to e-mail. Does that sound like Dr. Simon-Freed to you?"

My lips were pressed tightly together, but I managed to squeeze out, "No."

"So you see my dilemma."

I stopped pacing and considered Dutton. I hadn't known him long, but had discovered, on a number of occasions now, that he was an honest man in a difficult job, and he cared. He could be a little manipulative when the situation called for it, but he always had a solid reason, and his judgment usually turned out to be sound. So I couldn't understand why he was being so cagey about Sharon's predicament.

"No, I can't see your dilemma," I said. "It doesn't make sense that you're even bothering with this until there's some imminent danger or a crime has been committed. Has anyone contacted Gregory with ransom demands? Have you found some evidence that Sharon's been hurt, or . . ." I didn't want to say it, so I didn't. Sharon couldn't be hurt, or . . . *anything*. Sharon was too important to my sanity.

"No, Elliot. I told you," Dutton said. "I don't believe the doctor is in any danger right now."

"Then I don't get it. If you don't think she's the victim of a crime, what do you think she is?"

Chief Dutton let out a good deal of air. "A suspect in one," he said softly.

4

"IT seems there's a man named Russell Chapman, a patient of your ex's." Dutton was driving and I was looking out the window.

I don't own a car; I'm probably the last New Jerseyan left who doesn't express his personality through a choice of automotive transportation. I try not to contribute to the global environmental crisis and the stranglehold of the big oil companies on the American consumer. So I ride a bicycle most of the time, and I get other people to drive me around, or borrow a car when necessary. We all make compromises.

"Okay, so he's a patient of Sharon's," I said. "What's wrong with him?"

"Mostly, what's wrong with him is that he's dead," Dutton answered. "He died last night."

Suddenly, the view of Edison Avenue approaching Comedy Tonight wasn't all that fascinating; I swiveled my head toward Dutton and looked for some clue to his thoughts. He was watching the road.

"Doctors have patients die all the time," I told him. "It's a hazard of the profession."

"This one didn't die of natural causes," Dutton said.

That took a second to sink in. "You think Sharon killed this guy Chapman?" I asked, and my voice was unusually high, just on the south side of screechy.

"No, and stop doing a Julie Andrews impression." Dutton has a *Sound of Music* fetish. "Chapman killed himself last night. Took a bottle of Valium."

"He must have been *really* tense," I said. When I'm nervous, my natural sarcasm comes closer to the surface. Forgive me.

"Yeah." Dutton wasn't so forgiving.

We pulled up in front of Comedy Tonight and Dutton, although in an unmarked car, stopped illegally at the curb. I sat there and looked at him. "I don't get it. If this guy OD'ed in his own home, why are you concerned where Sharon is? Come clean, Chief."

Dutton put the car in park and didn't so much sigh as simply exhaled. When I'd first met him, Dutton had reminded me of Yaphet Kotto, but today he was much more in a Ving Rhames mode.

"The thing is, Elliot, that Chapman's daughter says Dr. Simon-Freed had given her father a diagnosis yesterday. Inoperable, incurable brain cancer. No chance, virtually no treatment, very little time. And she prescribed the Valium to take the edge off."

People walked by on Edison Avenue, walking a little faster because the early December chill was being accompanied by a nice strong northeasterly wind. Riding home tonight on the bicycle after midnight would be a real treat.

I saw a sinister picture forming, but I couldn't quite make it out yet. "That happens," I told Dutton. "I lived with Sharon for years. Doctors have to give people bad news. And then they try to help with something that will help the patient calm down and deal with it more rationally. There's nothing criminal about it."

Dutton nodded. "That's true. But here's the thing: the diagnosis was wrong."

"What do you mean, wrong?" I asked.

"Wrong, as in, there wasn't anything growing in Russell Chapman's brain. The records at Dr. Simon-Freed's office confirmed it. Chapman was clean as a whistle. Something got screwed up. He wasn't dying, but Sharon told him he was, according to Chapman's daughter. And then he went home and killed himself. You might see the problem."

"Problem, yes. Crime, no. At worst—and I'm willing to bet this isn't the case—that might constitute malpractice. But it sure as hell isn't murder, and there would be no reason for Sharon to skip out. It's not her nature. I think you're fishing here, and you're looking in the wrong pond. A guy swallowed some pills because he had a wrong diagnosis. Maybe it's Sharon's fault and maybe it isn't, but it's not a crime. My guess is that she heard about the suicide and went someplace overnight to decompress. It would be more her style to do that. She'll be back to see patients by tomorrow."

"Tomorrow's Saturday," Dutton said.

"She's got hours on Saturday, Chief. People still get sick on the weekend."

I got out of Dutton's town-issued Crown Victoria (his personal car is a Honda) and closed the door. He lowered the passenger window from his side so I could hear him.

"It's not that simple, Elliot. The receptionist at Sharon's office said Sharon hadn't heard the news of Chapman's suicide before she left. And when they called, her cell phone was already turned off. So she's not somewhere trying to get past the consequences of her diagnosis, unless she knew what effect it would have before she gave it to him."

I leaned into the car, giving the people on the sidewalk the best possible view of my butt, but also giving me a chance to warm my already freezing ears. "Okay, riddle me this, Batman. What possible reason could Sharon have had to want to get Chapman to kill himself? You're saying she knew before she told him he was dying that he would be suicidal. Why would she do that?"

"Chapman had a lot of money," Dutton said. "Made himself a pile when he invented a new kind of tortilla."

"A new kind of . . ."

"It's better not to think about it. Anyway, he was pretty loaded, in the many millions, and there's talk that he had promised some of it to Dr. Simon-Freed in his will. Going to build her a children's clinic, or something."

The voice that came out of my mouth sounded like a rusty oboe played by a man with an upper respiratory infection. "Are you serious?" I asked. "You think Sharon manipulated this guy into killing himself so she could have some of his money? Because she's not doing well enough on her own yet?" Sharon had a house about sixteen times fancier than the mostly empty town house in which I "lived," and was in fact paying me alimony. I'd never heard her complain or worry out loud about money.

"As a matter of fact, I don't believe that," Dutton told me. "But there are people who do, and I have to investigate. It's very suspicious that your ex-wife isn't answering her phone right now, Elliot."

I tried to look nonchalant. I'm not very good at that when I don't mean it, so I suppose I appeared as chalant as the next guy. "It's not a mystery, Chief," I said. "I told you: Sharon's upset about what happened, and she's off somewhere regrouping. If you don't hear from her by tomorrow, *then* I'd be worried. But you will. Thanks for the ride, though, and thanks for easing my fears. For a while there, I thought this really was going to be a bad day."

I turned and walked to the theatre. I didn't look back, but I could hear the window on Dutton's Crown Vic going back up, and I could picture the look on his face as he undoubtedly shook his head at my naivete. But he didn't know Sharon like I knew Sharon. And I was glad of that.

In truth, it was a little weird that she hadn't called back yet, but maybe there would be a message waiting when I got inside. Sharon really does need some time to rebound after bad news, especially about a patient, but I had exaggerated the extent to which she normally went to get it. Usually, just going home and not answering the phone would be enough. But she couldn't do that this time. Gregory was there. So I'd hear from her tomorrow, for sure.

Certain that I'd already passed the worst part of my day, I set foot inside my nice, warm theatre, where the "crowd" was already starting to gather for tonight's showing. Leo Munson, our one-and-only regular customer, was in his accustomed seat, absolutely dead center in the auditorium, ready to see *Sullivan's Travels*, a film he'd probably committed to memory.

Comedy Tonight, in concept, should bring in fans of classic comedy movies and fans of brand-new comedy, because we show both every night. But I've found that the classic crowd tends to watch their favorites at home on DVD, and the contemporary crowd, for reasons I can't fathom, prefers an impersonal multiplex in which each theatre looks very much like a proctologist's waiting room with a huge TV and bad lighting.

Sophie noticed me walking in and waved at me as she finished selling some popcorn to a little boy who immediately dropped large portions of it on the carpet as he walked back to the auditorium. "Elliot!" she shouted, and beckoned me over. I walked to the snack bar.

"What's up?"

"I got my SAT scores, and guess what I got!" Sophie grinned.

"Let me think." I made a show of looking serious, and put my hand to my forehead. "Twenty-two sixty."

Her face fell, and I immediately felt bad about it. "You heard," Sophie said.

"I'm sorry. Yes, I heard when your parents were here. That's really great, Sophie. I'm proud of you."

She let slip from one side of her mouth, "So am I."

"Congratulations, Sophie. I mean it. I hope you get into every college in the world, and pick the one you want most."

I patted her on the shoulder—Sophie and I haven't reached the kiss-on-the-cheek level of familiarity yet, but we're ahead of a handshake, for sure—and turned to head back to my office, the converted broom closet I was considering giving back to the brooms for all the good it was doing me.

"Are you kidding?" Sophie said. Her tone made me turn back around and face her. "Do you know what I have left to *do*? I haven't even started applying to schools yet, and I have to write an essay, and get letters of recommendation . . ."

"I'll be happy to write you one, Sophie," I said, smiling.

"No, I mean from, like, people who'll *impress* them," she said.

I nodded and turned away. I knew what she meant. She wasn't trying to insult me. Not really. I hoped she hadn't seen the tiny hurt on my face.

"Elliot!" Sophie called again. Maybe she had seen it.

"Sophie, don't worry about—" I turned back to face her and made a point of smiling warmly.

"Your mother's here," she said, pointing at the office door.

And I'd thought the day couldn't get worse.

5

"WHERE *is* she?" my mother wailed. "Where's my Sharon?"

"*Your* Sharon?" I asked. "What am I, chopped liver?" A classic.

My father gave me a stern look from the farthest reaches of my office, which weren't at all far. "Don't sass your mother," he said.

"Sharon," my mother emphasized, trying to remind us of her anguish. "Where is she?"

Seeing as how my mother was occupying the desk chair, and that between the chair and the desk, virtually all of the space in the room was filled, I could barely move. While the theatre was undergoing what we refer to as "renovation," I'd actually paid a carpenter to reverse the hinges on the office door and make it swing out instead of in, just to save space— that's how small the room is. I stood in the doorway, trying to keep the volume level low enough that entering customers wouldn't be treated to a revival of vaudeville on their way in to the movie.

"Mom," I said, "how did you find out that Sharon is . . . late in getting back to me?"

"Gregory called," my father interjected.

"*Gregory* called you? Since when does Gregory have your number?"

My mother looked wearily at me. "You think we'd let Sharon marry just anybody and not make sure he could get in touch if something . . . happened?" She sniffed.

"The man plays a hell of a game of pinochle," my father added, once again unprompted. Arthur Freed is nothing if not charitable in his assessment of pretty much everybody. Apparently including the man who broke up my marriage.

"You play *cards* with him?" My head was swimming, and I couldn't even sit down.

"Once every couple weeks," my father said. "It's nothing."

"*Sharon,*" my mother reminded us, and put her head in her hands.

"She's fine," I said. "She'll call by tomorrow. Stop worrying."

Gloria Sperber Freed is not a woman to be denied under any circumstances. When Sharon and I married, my mother had mentally adopted Sharon. I believe she sincerely thinks of my ex as her own daughter. Which I tried to ignore during our marriage, because it would have taken a lot of fun out of it for me.

In the best of times, navigating my mother is tricky, but worthwhile. She is a great source of common sense, whereas my father will plunge in and worry about it later. But Mom also has an unparalleled talent for passive aggression. By seeming to be completely pliant, my mother could convince Osama bin Laden to drive her to a Passover seder, and probably to come in and have a cup of wine instead of waiting in the car.

Now, strong in her belief that "her" Sharon was in grave danger, my mother was in no mood for reassurance.

"Why didn't you tell us?" she shot at me.

"Because I didn't know. I just got back from the police station myself." Oops. Maybe she'd overlook . . .

"*The police station!*" A man walking into the theatre stopped, adjusted his jacket, and turned around to exit.

"Mom, I've got customers. Do you mind?" Closing the office door was out of the question. I hadn't sat in my mother's lap since I was six. "Why are you guys here, anyway? Why didn't you just call me?"

"It's a crisis," my mother said, her tone indicating that I was an idiot to have asked. "In a crisis, family has to be there for each other."

"Couldn't you have been there for me from home?"

Luckily, the debate didn't get a chance to progress, as Jonathan appeared behind me. "Mr. Freed?" I'll never get him to call me Elliot.

I turned to face him. "Some of the customers are complaining," Jonathan said.

I sucked in some air. "I'll keep the shouting down in here," I said.

"Okay," Jonathan said, looking confused. He started to turn away, then thought better of it. "Um, that's not why they're complaining."

The three Freeds stared at him for a while, until I asked, "Okay, then, what is it?"

"Some of the customers said there's water all over the men's room floor."

I resisted the impulse to roll my eyes. "So go get the mop and take care of it."

"Okay." He did the turn-away-and-turn-back thing again. "They said it's, like, a *lot* of water."

Before I could react, my father stood up. "I'll take a look," he said. He was out the door in a blink.

My mother and I spent a long moment staring at each other. It's not that I don't love her, or even that I don't like her, but my mother and I have always had a less relaxed relationship than I have with Dad. When I was growing up, she was the tough parent.

Gloria Freed is something of a contradiction: she'll never publicly admit that anything I do is less than perfect, because that would reflect on her skills as a parent. So when someone asks, I am a successful businessman, a responsible son, and, no doubt, a joy to behold.

But she's also a devoted realist, without the romantic streak my father and I share, and she—without so much as a word spoken aloud—maintained that my purchase of the Rialto to create Comedy Tonight would eventually lead to financial ruin, heartbreak, and possibly the end of civilization as we know it (assuming you think that would be a bad thing).

I'd bought the Rialto with money from three sources: The first was the sale of my first—and let's be clear, only—novel, *Woman at Risk,* to a production company in Hollywood that turned it into a movie called *Split Personality*, only because calling it *A Bastardization of Elliot Freed's Novel That Doesn't Make Any Sense* probably would have been bad at the box office. Probably.

Because I didn't want to have a mortgage on the theatre, I'd used all the cash from the movie sale, and had also sold my childhood home, which I'd been living in at the time, having inherited it from my parents when they moved to an "active adult community" in Monmouth County. I wasn't aware that they were active, but the community board hadn't blocked their entry, so I guess they passed the test.

That money, plus the book money, plus the alimony I get from Sharon—about which she never complains, most of the time—paid for the Rialto, which I now call Comedy Tonight. But the purchase had left a razor-thin margin of error in my profit margin, which is a euphemism for the amount of money I lose each week by showing classic comedies to audiences in the Judd Apatow era.

But I was talking about my mother, wasn't I? The thing you really need to know about Gloria Freed is that she was never happier than the day I married Sharon. If your son can't *be* a doctor, what could be better than being married to one! When Sharon and I (mostly Sharon, although I filed the papers) decided to divorce so she could be with Gregory, I was less concerned about my own emotional well-being than that of my mother.

Now, there were real tears in her eyes, and I started to see her as something more than my mother: she was a woman who was scared to death.

"Close the door," she suggested, but I shook my head.

"It gets too tight in here. With just two of us, we're already re-creating the stateroom scene from *A Night at the Opera*."

Mom stared at me, not understanding. I got the classic comedy gene from my father.

"It's the Marx Brothers. Groucho is on this ocean liner, and he gets a really tiny stateroom. Then Chico and Harpo and Allan Jones emerge from his trunk, and more and more people come in, crowding the room beyond anything that seems physically possible, until Margaret Dumont opens the door and everyone falls out."

She stared at me some more. "That's funny?"

"Let's leave the door open. Maybe Sharon will come in, and we'll see her."

"Sharon!" my mother cried. On his best day, William Shatner couldn't overact this blatantly.

I took her hands in mine. "Mom," I said. "She's fine. I promise."

"You really think so?"

"I'm sure of it." As I put my arms around her, I glanced over her shoulder and made a quick check of the answering machine on the desk. The light wasn't blinking.

We stayed that way for a few seconds, until I felt my mother look up in the direction of the door. I turned to see Dad standing in the doorway, his pants rolled up to the knees and his shoes soaked through with water. For a guy who could wear a white suit and manage to paint an entire room without getting a drop of color on his clothes, this was the equivalent of showing up naked on the pitcher's mound in Yankee Stadium.

"Dad . . ." I began.

But he didn't let me get too far. "I think you have a burst

pipe," he said. "You could film an Esther Williams movie in your men's room."

This was turning out to be a swell day. "What can we do?" I asked. "Can you fix it?"

"Fix it? Merlin the Magician couldn't fix it. It needs to be replaced, and it's possible there are more rusted-out pipes in there. This is an old building."

"I noticed," I grumbled. "So . . ."

"I turned off the water, so you won't get any more flooding, but I couldn't trace the pipe back—those things go into the floor, set in cement. So I had to turn off the main supply to the whole building."

I winced. "Which means I have no water in either bathroom," I said.

"Worse than that," Dad piled on. "There's no water to the snack bar and no hot water going into the heating system."

That one took a moment to sink in. "Am I going to have to shut down?" I asked Dad.

"I think you already have," he said.

I held out for as long as I could, but the lack of heat, more than anything else, made it obvious that Comedy Tonight would be on hiatus until I could guarantee working toilets and dry floors. After Joel McCrae's John Sullivan was finished learning that comedy is necessary during bad times (and getting Veronica Lake—whose character is called "the Girl"—to fall in love with him), I made an announcement to the audience and sent everyone home. Seventeen people asked for their money back, and got it.

This really wasn't what I needed just at the moment. I reassured Mom seven or eight more times, each time crossing my fingers just a little tighter behind my back, and sent my parents to thaw out in the car on their way home. I called the emergency line for a plumbing contractor I found in the Yellow Pages, and outlined the problem to the answering service, which promised to get back to me in the morning. Then I sent the staff home, rewound the film, and closed up shop.

The ride home was, as I'd feared, cold and unforgiving,

with a wind that would have caused a normal man to ponder why he'd taken up this whole bicycle idea to begin with. But then, a normal man probably would have been in a car, thus rendering the entire exercise moot. It did, however, lead one to question whether the whole "saving the planet" thing was really pressing. Tonight, global warming was a more difficult concept to believe in than it was on most evenings.

I was looking at an indefinite period with a closed theatre and I still hadn't heard from my ex-wife. That didn't help me feel any warmer, either.

At the door to my town house (which the real estate people, I was told, were now calling a town *home*), I got off the bike and exhaled. They say physical exercise helps clear the brain, but I was not finding that to be the case. Endorphins be damned, I was in just as much of a funk now as I had been when I mounted up, and my lips were chapped on top of it.

The bike seemed heavier in the cold weather. I can't explain why, but it did. I picked it up and carried it up the four steps to the brightly painted green door to the town *home*, and unlocked the door.

Walking into my front hall, warmth enveloped me, and that did everything those miserable endorphins couldn't accomplish. My mood immediately lightened, and my natural optimism (stop laughing!) returned. Sharon was just off licking her wounds, and I would certainly hear from her in the morning.

My buoyant mood lasted the entire length of the walk from the front door to the living room entrance, which was roughly five steps. Once I got a look at the living room, even a blazing fire in my nonexistent fireplace wouldn't have been able to warm my heart.

The floor-to-ceiling bookshelves, which I'd had installed to accommodate my admittedly enormous collection of comedy films on DVD and videotape, were empty. But that was only because every single one of the 2,394 films I had so carefully catalogued, categorized, and cross-referenced was on the floor of the living room, scattered to the four corners.

The discs had been taken out of the boxes and strewn around, so that repairing and replacing them would take at least twice as long, assuming they hadn't been damaged beyond repair. And some of those titles were irreplaceable.

The miserable little futon I was pretending was a sofa had been slashed with a very sharp blade, perhaps a box cutter or a razor. Stuffing was everywhere. If there had been other furniture in the room, I was sure it would have been equally ripped apart. Even the answering machine—a cassette-tape relic I'd inherited from my parents when I took over their house—was ripped from the wall and dashed to the floor.

My eyes searched frantically for Harry Lillis's guitar, which the brilliant comic had sort of left me when he died, but thankfully it was still on a guitar stand in a corner of the room. It had not been damaged.

I didn't know what someone had been looking for, but it sure seemed like they hadn't found it.

And immediately, I began to worry about Sharon.

DISCARD

Peabody Public Library
Columbia City, IN

6

THE New Brunswick police officers who arrived at my town *home* at eleven thirty at night were used to dealing with gang violence, armed robberies, the occasional murder, and at the very least, drunken college students. So a DVD collection in disarray did not especially excite them.

They did, however, ask me the same two questions ("Was this the way you found the room?" and "Can you think of anyone who might do this?") until past three in the morning, and were threatening to do so until three the next morning, when my phone rang.

I hadn't called Dutton at home, but had left a message for him at Midland Heights police headquarters. Clearly, the chief didn't have much need for sleep, or had been out late, because he returned the call just as I was calculating how many hours in a row I had been awake.

I asked the two cops to excuse me and picked up the phone. "Get me out of here," I hissed into the handset.

Dutton took a second, then said, "How did you know it was me?"

"I didn't. Get me out of here."

"I don't have any jurisdiction there, Elliot. I can't tell the officers to leave. Now, what happened?"

Much more loudly, I said, "I can't come to the station now, Chief. The New Brunswick police officers aren't done with me yet." I put my hand over the mouthpiece and looked at the two cops. "It's Barry Dutton from Midland Heights. Do you know the chief?"

They shook their heads, no.

Back into the phone, I said, "How urgent is the matter, Barry?"

"Barry?" I heard Dutton ask. "When did I give you permission . . ."

"That bad, huh?" I asked.

"All right, Elliot," Dutton sounded tired. After all, he'd probably been up five or six hours longer than I had. "Put them on."

I gestured to one of the cops. "He wants to talk to you," I said.

"Me?" the cop, who was maybe twenty-five, asked.

"Yes," I told him. "He asked for you specifically."

The cop appeared flustered, but took the phone out of my hand. He listened for a good few moments. "Yes sir, Chief," he said, and handed me the phone.

"Hello?" I said.

"You owe me big time," Dutton said. "You're lucky I was due at the office in three hours anyway. They're going to drive you over. Now, tell me why it is I want to see you."

"I think you're wrong," I told him quietly. "I think Sharon *is* in danger."

THERE aren't a lot of cars on the road at three fifteen in the morning, so the New Brunswick cops got me to Dutton's office before Dutton himself arrived. They spoke quietly to the overnight dispatcher, a Latino who looked like he'd been doing this job a long time and was still appalled at the hours. He nodded slowly, said something to them out of my earshot, and then the two cops left.

"Chief Dutton is on his way," the dispatcher said. He gestured toward one of the molded plastic chairs lining the waiting area, and I sat.

There wasn't much going on at police headquarters, which wasn't a tremendous surprise. A large-bellied man in ugly pants came in to bother the dispatcher for a while, but was ignored. As he was in (relatively) plain clothes and carrying a gun, I'm guessing he was the detective on the really late or really early shift. Other than that, it was me and the dispatcher, who did his best to avoid looking at me, for quite some time.

Finally, the door opened, and I began to stand, expecting Dutton. But the little man who walked in, bringing a freezing breeze with him, was the chief's exact opposite: small, thin, Caucasian, and unimposing.

"What's up, Doc?" The dispatcher grinned.

"Just on my way home," the little guy said. "Figured I'd drop the report by." He waved a blue file toward the dispatcher, who nodded.

A sheet of paper from the file flew out and landed at my feet. I picked it up and handed it back to "Doc," but almost snatched it back again when I saw the name Chapman printed at the top.

"Is this the autopsy report on Russell Chapman?" I asked the little man.

"Yuh," he said. "Just finished it. You the detective?"

I considered it, but the dispatcher was watching. "No," I said, "I'm not even an interested party." And I sat down again, trying to vanish into thin air. Like Sharon.

The little man slid the file through the bulletproof glass and waited until the dispatcher looked at it, signed a form, and gave the form back to "Doc." Then the little man yawned broadly and headed to the door.

He walked out just as Dutton walked in. The chief nodded at the dispatcher, then walked to me as I stood up.

"Why, exactly, am I here at this ungodly hour?" Dutton rumbled.

"Sharon's missing," I said.

Dutton looked at me. For a while. A long while.

"Why, exactly, am I here at this ungodly hour?" he repeated.

"I mean she's *really* missing," I said. "Up until now, I thought she was just off licking her wounds. Now I'm sure she's being held somewhere against her will."

Dutton's eyebrows did a quick cha-cha on his forehead, but his voice stayed steady. "Let's go talk in my office," he said.

On the way there, he poured himself a cup of coffee that looked like it had been sitting on the counter in the hallway for six or seven weeks. He did not offer me a cup, and I was grateful.

Dutton opened the door to his office, turned on the light, and blinked a few times to adjust his eyes. He sat down behind his desk and gestured me to the chair in front of it. "Now get your breathing back to normal and tell me what you're talking about," he began.

"When I got back to the town house, everything in my living room had been tossed," I told him. "The futon was slashed and the stuffing was all over the room. The DVDs were out of their boxes and scattered to the corners. The . . ."

"The DVDs?" Dutton's eyes widened. He's seen the DVD collection.

I nodded. "It was obvious someone was looking for something."

"Or, they just wanted to hit you where it would really hurt."

I hadn't considered that. "But it's too big a coincidence that this happens the same time Sharon vanishes. She didn't just go away. She must have been taken."

"Elliot, there's no evidence that Sharon has been taken anywhere against her will. No signs of forced entry at her home, her office, or her parking space."

I bit my lips. "Forced entry at a parking space?"

Dutton nodded. "No broken glass. No evidence anybody

broke into her vehicle. She got into her car and she drove away."

"Then maybe it was someone she knew," I suggested.

"Maybe. But as a police officer, I've got to tell you, there's nothing that points to a kidnapping. Nothing."

I sat there and looked at him.

"Okay," Dutton said, "what is it you expect me to do?"

"Look for her."

"I've been looking for her since yesterday afternoon," the chief countered. "I've sent out bulletins to other police departments. I've gotten photographs of her distributed to every cop in town and to the Middlesex County prosecutor's office and the state police. I've questioned everyone who saw her the day before she vanished. What else am I supposed to do?"

"Find her," I suggested.

"I know this is hard for you, Elliot. Believe me, I do. But everything that can be done is being done, and you're just going to have to be patient until such time as something resembling a lead presents itself. That's just how investigations work."

"So what am I supposed to do?" I asked. "Pretend everything is normal while the clock keeps ticking? You and I both know that the first forty-eight hours are critical in . . . these cases. And a good half of that time is already shot. Tell me what I can do."

Dutton put his right hand to his nose, which I'd noticed in the past was something he did when he didn't have a satisfactory answer. "You can go home and go to bed, Elliot. I'll drive you."

"I'll never get to sleep."

Dutton stood up and reached for his coat. "Take a sleeping pill."

"I can't. My doctor is missing."

7

SATURDAY

AS I expected, sleeping was pretty much impossible. The truth was, I did have some sleeping pills in the house, but I didn't take them in case the phone were to ring. I doubt my mind would have shut up long enough to allow for rest, anyway. I didn't toss and turn, since I have no idea how to toss anything but a baseball, but as the sun came up I sure did lie in bed and watch the ceiling fan, which was turned off and in desperate need of a cleaning.

My father called at seven. "Have you heard anything yet?"

"No, Dad. It's seven o'clock in the morning."

"Yeah, and you don't sound like I woke you up." My father has a rather eerie ability to see into my mind. He's like my own personal Amazing Kreskin.

"Okay, so I'm worried. Don't tell Mom."

"I know you're not worried." My mother must have been in the room. "Just let us know when you hear from her."

"You sure you don't want to ask your other son, Gregory?" Never let it be said I can't be as petty as the next man if I set my mind to it.

"It's just cards, for goodness sake, Elliot. You could come, if you knew how to play pinochle."

I tried to banish the image of myself, Dad, and Gregory sitting around a card table, and moved on. "I haven't heard from the plumber yet," I told him. "Care to give me a guess on how long I'll have to keep the theatre closed?"

Dad thought about that, which was good. It didn't really matter what his estimate would be, but it was a good way to get him onto a new subject, and away from Gregory, at least mentally.

"I'd guess a couple of days," he said. "It depends on how far down the rust goes in your pipes."

"The way my week is going," I told him, "I'd expect it goes down to the shopping center of Earth's molten core."

"Don't be negative, Elliot," Dad said. "Let me know when the plumber calls. I'll come up to supervise."

"You don't have to . . ."

"Yes, I do."

After we hung up, I checked the clock. Another five minutes had gone by, and nobody had found Sharon yet. I couldn't do much until nine, when offices opened. But there was someone I could call who would undoubtedly be awake and attentive this time of the morning.

"Homicide. Sergeant Vidal."

"Hi, Meg. It's Elliot Freed."

"It's only been two months since I've heard from you, Elliot," Meg said. "Are you forming an unhealthy attachment to me?"

I wasn't in the mood to banter. "Meg, Sharon's missing."

Her tone became professional and concerned. "Since when?" She was probably already taking notes.

"Night before last." I gave her all the details I knew.

Meg sighed a little, thinking. "Okay, consider carefully, Elliot. Is there any reason other than what happened to this Chapman guy that Sharon might be a target? Anybody mad at her, anybody with a strange infatuation, anything like that?"

"Nobody besides me, and I didn't take her."

"Sit tight. Let Chief Dutton do his job. He's good."

A sound came out of my throat that resembled pain and impatience. I'd never heard it before. "I know he's good, Meg. But I can't just sit here and wait. I've got to do *something*."

"I'm on my way up, Elliot."

That threw me. I hadn't actually seen Meg Vidal since I was doing research for *Woman at Risk*, which meant I hadn't been in the same room with her in a good number of years.

"You're coming up? Is there something you can do?"

"Yes. I can sit and wait with you."

"Meg . . ."

Her tone allowed for no argument. "I wasn't asking, Elliot."

"Do you even know how to get here?"

"I'm with the cops, Elliot. We have GPS now."

There could be no dissuading her. I gave Meg my address, and she promised to be in a car on her way from Camden as soon as possible, which would put her here in about an hour and a half. I had no idea how she'd clear it with her department, but she didn't sound like she cared.

I took a shower, because if . . . *when* Sharon got back, it would be best for me not to smell like unwashed socks. And as I was walking back into the bedroom, drying off (carpet be damned!), the phone rang.

After the ensuing heart attack, it took me roughly .04 seconds to pick up the receiver, but I'd had enough time to think, so I didn't yell "Sharon?" at the top of my lungs.

"Is this Mr. Freed?" For a kidnapper, the guy had a very young voice. Cagey little ploy, but I wasn't falling for it.

"Who wants to know?" I asked. I was leaning heavily on Bowery Boys movies now, trying to sound like Leo Gorcey, or at the very least, Huntz Hall. You had to respect a guy whose first name was Huntz.

"This is A-OK Plumbing," he said. "You called about a problem?"

WE agreed that I'd meet the plumber at Comedy Tonight within the hour, which would give me enough time to bike to the theatre and still be able to start harassing anyone I could think of about Sharon—mostly her colleagues at the practice—as soon as businesses opened for the day. I got dressed, layered myself with sweatshirts and long underwear (not in that order) to make the ride to Midland Heights tolerable, skipped breakfast (my stomach was in no mood to eat), and grabbed my beautifully reconstructed bicycle to head out.

I didn't even look at the DVDs in the living room. I didn't want to be reminded.

Now that I thought about it, I'd probably be at or near the theatre by the time Meg arrived. So I called the cell phone number she'd given me, and gave her directions to Comedy Tonight. She said she'd "dealt with the department," and would be on her way within minutes. I had no doubt she would.

It had been a while since I'd been out this early—movie theatres don't often require their owners to be early birds—so it was something of a surprise how cold it was, and how low the sun was in the sky. I'm told some people like the morning, and someday, I must ask one of them why.

I found myself pedaling much too fast, especially up the hill into Highland Park, and had to scale back. I wouldn't be very helpful in searching for Sharon if I had to do it from a hospital bed.

Perhaps a mile from the theatre, I became aware of a car on my left, so I hugged the curb a little more than usual. I'd had enough experience with cars getting too close to bicycles on the road. But this one honked its horn, and when I turned to look, I saw Chief Barry Dutton driving his own personal car up Route 27 and pointing toward the sidewalk, indicating I should pull over.

Heart in my mouth, I did so. Dutton pulled the car up and opened the passenger side window. "What have you heard?" I sort of screamed.

"Nothing yet," Dutton said. "But I need you to verify something for me."

For a hideous moment, I had a mental flash of me trying to identify a body at the morgue in Robert Wood Johnson University sity Hospital, and I closed my eyes tight to banish the image.

"What is it?" I asked.

"Credit card receipts with your name on them," Dutton said. "It looks like someone's been busy charging things. Do you still have a joint credit account with Sharon?"

"No," I said. "I have a credit card, but I haven't used it in years."

"What's the matter with you?" Dutton challenged. "Aren't you an American?"

"Yeah, but not a good one."

"Get in." He popped the trunk, and I took the front wheel off the bike and deposited it, then got in on the passenger side. When I sat down, he asked, "How did your ex-wife get your credit card?"

"We were still married when I got the card. We probably got two, and Sharon has one. Can we tell where Sharon is from the receipts?"

"Don't jump to conclusions," Dutton said as he pulled away from the curb. "We don't even know it's Sharon yet. Someone could have stolen your credit card when they were in your house last night."

"I carry it in my wallet," I told him.

"You keep records of the numbers? There's such a thing as identity theft." Dutton was intent on the road, so he didn't see me cringe.

"None of the receipts is from before the break-in?" I asked, trying to change the subject.

"Maybe, maybe not," Dutton told me. "We know that someone was in your town house between the time you left for the theatre yesterday and the time you got home. That gives them . . ."

I groaned. "Roughly twelve hours," I said.

"Exactly. So yes, the credit card receipts are all from yesterday, and you can tell me when you left in the morning and when you got home, so the time stamps on the receipts will tell us if they were all while you were out. But we don't know exactly when the break-in took place. Would any of your neighbors have seen anything, someone suspicious around the front door?"

I closed my eyes. "I've never met any of my neighbors, Chief."

"You really are a bad American."

He drove me all the way to police headquarters before I remembered about the plumber. Once we got to Dutton's office, I asked to use his phone, and he groused anew at my resistance to cell phone mania, but gestured that I should go ahead and dial.

I called Sophie, and thanked my guardian angel that I had *her* cell phone number, so there would be no danger of Ilsa or Ron Beringer answering the call.

"Hello?" she asked, tentatively, after a number of rings. It was a Saturday, and she was a teenager. The idea that she'd be awake at eight in the morning was just a little more ludicrous than the idea that I would be.

"Sophie," I said. "It's Elliot. Do me a favor, and go to the theatre. Let the plumber in to look at the pipes in the men's room. Use your key. You're in charge."

"Of what?" she asked, and I hung up.

Dutton pulled a file from a rack on the wall next to his desk, and sat down. He opened it to show me faxed copies of several credit card receipts. The chief put on a pair of half glasses to read them, creating an image of Godzilla in middle age, looking over his financial records.

"These are the receipts from a number of retailers and a hotel bar in Manhattan, all from yesterday," he said. He turned the records toward me so I could peruse them.

"These stores don't strike me as the kind where Sharon would shop," I told him.

"You really never use a credit card?" he asked.

"Really."

"How about an ATM card?"

I've never understood the word *sheepish*, because sheep are rarely embarrassed at their actions, but I believe that was the expression I gave Dutton at that moment.

"You don't have an ATM card, either?" he marveled. At least, I like to think of it as *marveled*.

"Do you have any idea how much the government can find out about you from your ATM records?" I asked him.

"I'm the chief of police, Elliot. I *am* the government. And I don't really think that the fact you withdrew twenty dollars from your checking account on a Friday night is really a dangerous piece of information."

I decided to change the subject, since Dutton was showing troublesome signs of having a point. "Anyway, why can't we take the addresses from these card purchases and trace Sharon, maybe back to the hotel?"

"I called the hotel already. Sharon is not listed as a guest there, and never has been. The card didn't pay for a room, only a bar bill. Still, you wouldn't want useful records like that to show up in *your* file if *you* ever disappeared, would you?" Dutton grinned and suddenly seemed very Bill Cosby–esque. I half expected him to put on a colorful sweater and eat some pudding.

Summoning my best judgment, I ignored him. "If someone's holding her against her will, the room could be in that person's name, couldn't it?"

"Yes, but since you're so interested in preserving our citizens' privacy, I assume you think it would be a bad idea for me to get the name of every single guest in the hotel, and then show it to a civilian like yourself to see if any of the names ring a bell?"

"You're not going to let it go, are you?" I asked.

"I don't see why I should."

"Well, if you want to show me the list, you can say whatever you want about my commitment to privacy or my hypocrisy."

"I didn't get the list. It wouldn't have done any good, anyway. I sincerely doubt a kidnapper would register at a hotel under his own name."

"Chief," I said, trying to banish any number of unpleasant thoughts from my mind, "what if the person who broke into my place didn't have anything to do with Sharon's disappearance?"

"Wasn't that the theory *you* were espousing?" A police chief who says "espousing." That's Midland Heights for you. The town probably requires an IQ test of potential residents.

"I'm still *espousing* it, but just in case. I'm thinking out loud. Aside from the coincidence, it doesn't really add up to much. Breaking into my house doesn't get a kidnapper, a blackmailer, or anybody else anything they could use against Sharon."

Dutton's eyes narrowed. "So?"

"So, let's guess for a moment that the person who has a grudge against Sharon is a member of Russell Chapman's family, or someone who doesn't appreciate the idea that he'd leave her some money."

"It's a stretch, but okay, let's guess that." Dutton, as he often does when thinking, put his hands together in a pyramid, index fingers and thumbs touching. He leaned back in his chair and closed his eyes.

"What does that person get from breaking into my house?"

"Nothing, apparently," Dutton said. "So, what does that tell us?"

I stood up and started to pace. "That maybe the person who broke into my house was looking for Sharon."

Dutton opened his eyes. The phone rang, and he picked it up, listened for a moment, and offered me the receiver. "It's for you," he said.

I pondered that, since no one but Dutton and I knew I was there. But I took the phone.

"Elliot?" Sophie's voice asked.

"How did you know I was here, Sophie?"

"Caller ID from when you called me, *duh*." Nobody can make you feel as terminally stupid as a teenage girl.

"What's up?"

"The guy says he needs to break the floor."

I considered the possibility that Sophie was speaking in code, and remembered she was dealing with the plumber. "What do you mean, 'break the floor'?"

"He says the pipes are set in concrete, and he needs to break the floor to get at the broken part."

"Tell him no," I said. "He can't break the floor."

"*Elliot*, I don't have time to fool around with this. I've got to start setting up college tours, and work on a comparison of myself to other candidates for the same academic slots."

"Put the guy on the phone," I said.

Now in the field, the A-OK Plumbing representative sounded even younger. His voice almost squeaked. "Mr. Freed, the pipes in your bathroom are set in concrete. If you want me to stop the leak . . ."

"I want you to exhaust every possibility before you start with something like that, you understand?" I said. "I'm in no mood to spend weeks with a closed theatre and pay thousands of dollars in repairs because it's your first week on the job."

The guy took a moment. "I'm the owner of the business, Mr. Freed," he said. "I've been doing this for twenty-two years. And the damage to your floor will be so minimal, you might not have to replace as many as two of the tiles."

"Break the floor," I said. Then I told him to put Sophie back on the phone. "From now on, just decide," I told her. "If I say you're in charge, be in charge."

"That's what your dad said," she answered.

"He's there?"

"Yeah. He got here before I did."

I hung up on her again, and looked at Dutton.

"I need to do something," I told him. "What can I do?"

"See what I'm doing?" he asked.

"You're sitting behind your desk," I observed.

"Exactly."

I wasn't going to do that.

8

I was at the front door of Sharon's practice, with my bike out of Dutton's trunk and locked securely on a rack to one side, when Betty the receptionist (and her *Playboy* magazine figure) opened up at eight forty-five. Patients, I knew, wouldn't start showing up until nine, unless there was an emergency, and the practice would close as near to noon as possible. It was, after all, the weekend.

"I'm not surprised to see you," she said when I came in (literally) out of the cold.

"You still haven't heard from her?" I asked. No sense in bothering with formalities. Betty has known me for years, since before Sharon and I divorced.

I reflexively curb my lust at the door whenever I enter the practice, and today, I wouldn't have been interested even if Betty had welcomed me wearing a black lace teddy and locked the door behind me. But she did bear a passing resemblance, I noted, to a Latina version of Thelma Todd, who played the "college widow" (don't ask me; maybe she was married to a college that died) opposite the Marx Brothers in *Horse Feathers*.

"No," she said. "Still not a word, and she's not answering the cell. I'm kind of worried."

"Tell me about Russell Chapman," I said.

"I'm not allowed to talk about a patient's medical records," she answered. "You know that, Elliot."

"I don't care about his medical condition," I told Betty. "I'm concerned about the sequence of events. What happened when?"

She walked behind the glassed-in counter and I could see her through the window, looking up records. "Mr. Chapman came in two weeks ago, and underwent some tests," she said, careful to leave out any details. "He came back Thursday afternoon to get the test results, and that was all we knew until the police called about his suicide."

"Did you answer the call about that?" I asked.

Betty nodded. "Yeah, but Dr. Westphal was the one who actually spoke to the police. You know, I just shepherd the calls. I knew it was the police, but I didn't know what it was about."

"Why Dr. Westphal?" I asked. "Why not Sharon?"

"Dr. Simon-Freed was gone by then," Betty said.

"Did she say where she was going?"

Betty puckered her lips, and not in the way Lennon Dickinson would have appreciated. "Yeah, Elliot. She said specifically where she'd be, and I just haven't told anybody until you asked."

"Well, that's sort of unusual, isn't it? Doesn't Sharon usually let you know where she'll be, in case there's an emergency?"

Betty took in a good deal of air through her nose. "She was upset," she said.

My head must have jerked up. "Upset? Like the other day? About what?"

"What am I, her mother?" Betty asked. Then she saw the look on my face, and shook her head. "Sorry. She got a set of test results back right before she left, and it really seemed to shake her."

"Additional test results for Russell Chapman?" I asked.

"I don't know. I didn't get the stuff from the lab that afternoon; it came when I was on break. I think Grace took them."

"Is she around?" I asked.

Betty nodded. "But she's in with Dr. Westphal, in conference about a patient. You'll have to wait."

"Where's Lennon?" I asked.

"Dr. Dickinson is dealing with a patient emergency," Betty answered.

I sat in one of the patient chairs in the waiting room, and pretended to read a magazine. It's not that I wasn't interested in "10 Tips That Will Drive Him Wild!" but I might have been just a little preoccupied. I didn't even try the fragrance sample included in the centerfold.

I've been lucky enough never to have a serious medical problem, and I was married to a physician, so I've never really been nervous in a doctor's waiting room. But today I wasn't able to do anything but stare at the door to the back offices and wonder when the hell it would open and let me in. Not that I actually thought the key to Sharon's whereabouts was back there, but I certainly didn't have much else to go on.

After about ten minutes of waiting, I was sure the door would never open, and to be honest, it still didn't. But the main office door did swing open, and a little man, about seventy years old by my estimation, shuffled in, wearing an overcoat that looked like it weighed a little bit more than I did. He had his coat closed over the lower part of his face, braced against the cold.

It took him a while to get to the reception desk, and when he did, he spoke so quietly that I heard Betty asking "Excuse me?" a few times before she could get a decent bearing on what the man was saying. Betty's replies became progressively louder, until I could hear every word she said, and nothing of what the man told her.

"She's still in the back, in a patient conference," Betty almost shouted. "But it'll just be a few minutes, if you wouldn't mind waiting." She gestured toward me, and the man nodded and shuffled over. He sat down next to me, in a room filled with empty seats, and let out an *oof* as he landed in his chair.

The man was small and trim, and wore thick glasses that made his eyes look like they were far away and also wore a hearing aid in each ear. Finally he opened the top button of his coat and exhaled. He had a thick black mustache and bushy eyebrows, bringing to mind Groucho's look. But I'll bet he touched them up with black dye. Groucho used grease-paint.

I tried to look preoccupied, since I was, but the little man bumped me on the arm and said, "That's some receptionist, huh?" I nodded inconclusively, not wanting to insult Betty by intimating that she wasn't gorgeous, but also not wanting to reduce her to a sex object, at least not today. The man was undaunted. "They named the room right, huh? Waiting room. Doctors." He waved a hand to indicate disgust. If he'd had a Yiddish accent, he could have been my late grandfather. But his voice was weaker; he was barely audible in normal conversation.

"Well, they don't want to rush people through like a factory," I said. I felt it necessary to defend Sharon's practice, with words she'd used on me many times.

"Sure, sure." The man wasn't going to disagree. "But it's not efficient."

"I guess not." I went back to looking preoccupied, but the little guy wasn't buying. He stuck out a hand. "Martin Tovarich," he said. "I'm with East Coast Insurance."

I shook his hand. "Elliot Freed," I said. "I own Comedy Tonight. It's a movie theatre—"

He cut me off. "It shows only comedies; I know," Tovarich said. "I haven't been yet, but I've been meaning to go. I love the classics, but mostly the serious stuff: Bergman, Fellini, von Stroheim. People like that."

I was amazed. It's rare that I don't have to defend my business upon meeting someone new ("You do *what*?"), and I almost always have to at least explain it. "Nice to meet you, Mr. Tovarich. You live around here?"

"East Brunswick," he said. "Close enough that I see your ads, but not so close that I can just walk in without thinking about it first. Sorry about that."

"You should try it," I said. "You seem like you could appreciate a classic comedy."

"Perhaps I will," Tovarich said.

"I'm flattered you even know about the theatre. Which doctor do you see here, Mr. Tovarich?" If he was waiting for Sharon, I figured to tell him he had a long stretch in front of him.

"Oh, I'm not a patient," he said, shaking his head. "I'm here on business."

"Insurance business?"

"Yeah. One of their patients . . . passed away a couple of days ago. I'm looking into it from an insurance point of view."

Oops.

"Really?" I said. So it wasn't original. Maybe he didn't mean Chapman. Did insurance companies investigate medical practices for suicides? Maybe they did, if malpractice was considered a cause. I must have looked worried.

"Are you a patient here, Mr. Freed?" he asked.

Well, that left me with a dilemma. I *was* a patient here, but I was also the ex-husband of the doctor he was presumably investigating. On the one hand, I'd just as soon not incriminate Sharon, but then, I'd rather not withhold information, either.

"I have been," I said.

Tovarich looked me up and down, assessing. "Of course. Freed. You're the doctor's ex-husband."

My dilemma was no longer relevant.

I realized that the insurance company would have had my name, and so admitted to my identity, but I kept stealing glances at the door in the hope that Toni Westphal and Grace would finish their conference and let me in. No such luck.

Then, Tovarich said the absolute last thing I would have expected. "Your ex-wife is a fine doctor, Mr. Freed."

My eyebrows probably circled my head a couple of times: Everybody seemed to think Sharon was somehow at fault in the Chapman situation, and yet, the deceased's insurance company, which would seem to be the party that would most want to hang the blame on her, was singing her praises.

So the hesitation on my part was understandable, if unfortunate. Before I could respond, Tovarich said, "Is that the men's room?" and got up to excuse himself faster than I would have thought he could move. I guess when you're seventy, you don't argue with your digestive system.

I was not alone long, though, because the front door had already opened to admit a woman in her early forties, wearing all black, into the waiting room.

She and Betty spoke in tones I couldn't pick up for a minute or so, and then I heard Betty tell the woman that she could speak to Dr. Westphal as soon as the doctor emerged from the private office in the back. The Woman in Black protested for a moment, in a slightly more aggravated voice, but eventually sat down two chairs from where I was seated.

I smiled my best conspiratorial smile at her and said, "I think we should make *them* wait once in a while. Go in there and read a magazine when they come in, and then tell them to hang on until we finish the crossword puzzle."

The woman gave me a less-than-enthralled look.

Undaunted—even though I should have been—I went on. "Maybe there should be a waiting room for doctors," I tried. "We could make them wear a paper gown with their butts hanging out and then call them in for an examination."

There are sculpture exhibits that react more dramatically. Tovarich had gotten me into a conversation with less material than this.

I reverted to my junior high school personality, and sat back in the uncomfortable metal frame chair. "Didn't mean to bother you," I mumbled.

The Woman in Black smiled, tolerantly, which I hadn't

expected. "I'm sorry," she said, in a low, almost musical tone. "I have a lot on my mind. My father died the other night."

That sort of thing had never happened in junior high school; it took me a long moment to regain the power of speech. "I'm sorry to hear that," I told her. "Was he a patient here? Not a great advertisement for the place."

"He certainly was," the woman said. "And make no mistake." Then her voice dropped to a whisper. *"One of the doctors here killed him,"* she said.

9

LILLIAN Chapman Mayer introduced herself, and I think I might have tried to do the same, but she wasn't listening. She was not reticent in her judgment of Sharon, Sharon's practice, the medical profession in general, the American Medical Association, and anyone wearing a white coat, especially after Labor Day. But mostly Sharon.

This time, the dilemma about identifying myself did not present itself, since I never managed to get a word in edgewise. Lillian began with the serious breach of ethics involved in "a business arrangement with a patient," and then moved on to the crass disregard for a patient's emotional state, the lack of communication among doctors working on the same patient, the high cost of medical insurance in America, Michael Moore's *Sicko*, something about avian flu, and after that I sort of lost consciousness with my eyes open for a while.

I did notice Tovarich shuffling out of the restroom and into the hallway, where he appeared to be having a professional conversation with Betty. She nodded a lot. He watched her face, which, even for an elderly gentleman, is an effort when talking to Betty. One's eyes tend to wander.

When I came to, Lillian was working up a head of steam over Dr. Simon-Freed's obvious use of "feminine wiles" to coerce her father into leaving her money, and that was when I spoke over her long enough to be heard.

"Hold on a second. You're suggesting that Sharon seduced your father so he would include her in his will?" I think my tone more than my words betrayed me.

Lillian, eyes wide, sat still for a moment. *"Sharon?"* she asked. "Do you know the doctor personally?"

"You could say that. We used to be married." What the hell.

Her mouth opened and closed a few times before she managed, "Well! You might have said so sooner!"

"I didn't have enough duct tape to keep you from talking that long," I said. This wasn't a good day to get on my bad side.

"Well, you should feel lucky you got out when you could. Your ex-wife was clearly seeing my father, and I don't mean as a patient."

I stared at her. "Excuse me?"

"You heard me. He used to make sure he was here at least one evening a week, always when the office was closing. And I know he didn't make it home for hours after, sometimes not at all." Lillian grinned at me with the smug satisfaction of someone who enjoys the discomfort of others.

"And you think he was . . . seeing Sharon?" I would have known. There was no way I wouldn't have known. Sharon would have told me. And even then, there wasn't any way. I didn't believe it.

"I know it." She stabbed her finger at me. "I had them followed."

I came close to swallowing my lips. "I beg your pardon?"

Lillian nodded. "I hired a private detective, a guy named Konigsberg. When there's that much money on the line, someone like me needs to be on the lookout for every little slut like your ex-wife."

I considered going for her throat, but there were witnesses.

And besides, Lillian didn't give me the time before she started talking again.

"Thank god my husband's out of town," she said. "If Wally knew everything I know about this, you'd be dealing with your ex-wife's murder, not my father's."

It was all I could do not to grab her by the shoulders and shake her. I gritted my teeth. "Where *exactly* is your husband now?" I considered asking if she could verify his whereabouts, as well, but I didn't want to tip my hand.

"Trying to get a flight home," she answered. "He was in Japan when we had to call him last night."

"Japan?" I asked. It's not that I'm not familiar with the name, but it seemed incongruous in this conversation.

"He had business there. Wally's in importing. I'm going to be picking him up at the airport. And he loved my father as if he were his own. This is hitting him even harder than me, I think."

I didn't care who it was hitting, or how hard. "He's flying in from Japan tonight? How long has he been there?"

"Only since Wednesday," Lillian said, surprised that I was asking. "He was supposed to stay for a week, but now, of course, he's coming home. Why do you ask?"

Luckily, at that moment the office door opened and Betty approached, smiling sympathetically, effectively saving Lillian's life. "Ms. Mayer?" she said. I understood that even though I had gotten there first, she was the family of a deceased patient, and therefore outranked me. "Dr. Dickinson will see you now." Good move. Get the handsome serious guy to talk to the dead man's daughter.

Lillian got up and walked toward the conference room. Tovarich turned away to let her by, and Betty used the excuse to walk back out toward the reception area. She appeared at the door, and crooked a finger at me, a gesture very few men would be able to resist. I walked over.

"Dr. Westphal may be a while, talking to this insurance man," she said. "Do you want to talk to Grace?"

"Yes, I do."

"I'll get her. You come right through, Elliot." She held the door open. I nodded at Tovarich and walked inside.

Betty walked back to her desk as Grace, the nurse who had been working the night Chapman got his test results, walked out from one of the examination rooms and met me in the hallway. "Elliot," she said. "What have you heard?"

"Nothing. And it's driving me crazy."

"I'm so sorry," she said. Grace was not avoiding eye contact. She'd dealt with people before who were in difficult—sometimes impossible—situations. She was there to help.

"When's the last . . . *most recent* time you saw Sharon?" I asked.

"Well, I dropped off some patient records at her house Thursday morning because she was coming in late, and then I saw her at the office until closing. Nothing since then." Grace bit her lip; she wanted to be more help than this.

"What can you tell me about that evening? Were you in the room when Sharon gave Chapman his test results?"

"No. She called him into the conference room alone."

The conference room is a separate space outside the examination rooms where doctors and patients confer. But it's rarely used for good news—you get that on the phone. Believe me, you don't want to be in the conference room with your doctor.

"Isn't that unusual?" I asked. "Doesn't Sharon usually want someone in the room with her when she calls a patient in?"

"Yeah. I thought it was a little odd, but she said she'd do it herself, and I do what the doctors tell me to do," Grace said.

"How did you find out the test results were incorrect?"

"As far as I know, we never had incorrect test results for Mr. Chapman," Grace said. "We only got one set of films for him from the radiology lab. Those films were the ones Sharon brought in to the conference room with her."

"But Betty said Sharon had gotten some new results back right before she left that night, and that whatever she saw there had really shaken her up," I reminded her. "Weren't those new results or updates of Chapman's films?"

Grace shook her head. "No," she said. "Those records weren't for Chapman."

"Another patient?" Was there another case involved in this business?

This time, Grace did avoid eye contact. "I don't know," she said.

My head snapped around in a blink. "What do you mean?" I asked.

Grace took a deep breath. "That was the weird part," she said. "Sharon wouldn't tell me."

I didn't get a chance to ask what that meant, because Toni Westphal appeared, shaking Tovarich's hand at the exam room door. He actually bowed a little to her, but he didn't leave. He just went back into the waiting room and, well, waited.

"I'm sorry, Elliot," Toni said, pulling me aside. "He has a lot of questions that I can only answer by pulling the medical records, and I couldn't tell him to go away."

"It's okay," I assured her. "But why is he investigating a suicide? Does he really believe that Sharon did something wrong?"

"From an insurance standpoint alone, it's extremely irregular for her to have kept medical records back," she said. "It's not like Sharon, and it worries me."

"I don't understand any of this," I said.

"Neither do I," Toni said. "I've known Sharon since she was a resident, and I've never seen her act like this. To just leave and not tell us where she is? Not tell *you*? It doesn't make sense."

I took a deep breath. "You're assuming she left of her own accord," I said.

Toni looked like I'd punched her in the gut. Her eyes got wide and she inhaled sharply. "Wow," she said. "Is that what you think?"

"I don't know what I think."

"Elliot," she said, sitting down on the spare desk chair. "I forget how much you still care about Sharon."

"What does that mean?"

"It means that your feelings might be getting the best of you. You can't abide Sharon leaving, so you decide she's been taken against her will."

I blinked. More than once. "Toni, do you think Sharon really is covering up something about Russell Chapman's death?" I asked.

"Honestly," she answered, "I can't be sure."

10

I didn't want to talk to anyone at the practice anymore, so I said a polite good-bye to Toni Westphal and headed for the door. Tovarich, still in the waiting room, shook my hand and took a Comedy Tonight business card, promising to attend a showing as soon as the theatre reopened. I smiled at him, hopefully convincingly, and left.

It wasn't even ten in the morning yet, and already I was having a lousy day. When I arrived at Comedy Tonight after the walk from Family Medical Practice, the A-OK Plumbing van was parked outside, my father's truck was a few spaces down, and Sophie's Toyota Prius, loaded with books on choosing the right college, was around the corner. I chained my bike to the steam pipe on the side of the building and brought the front wheel inside with me. The forecast was for cold temperatures, but no snow, so I figured I could leave the bike outside. It was a tight enough fit in my office, and a bicycle in the lobby didn't look very movie-theatre-like.

Once inside, I remembered that the plumbing problem meant that the heat was turned off, so I encountered an arctic Comedy Tonight. I found the expected chaos: my office door was closed and locked, a habit I'd picked up recently, but there was activity elsewhere. Off to the left, by the stairway to the balcony, the men's room door was wide open, and there was a large red hose running out of the bathroom and across the lobby to the open doorway leading to the basement. The hose then went, I assumed, all the way downstairs. It was better not to think about what the plumber might have found down there.

Dad, in a snappy overcoat and leather gloves, stood in the doorway to the men's room, pointing at something inside. "I think that's it there," he said to the unseen plumber. "Try the third one."

I decided I didn't want to know, and was unlocking the office door when I was frontally attacked by two irate females.

Sophie was pointing an angry finger at me and advancing like a third-grade teacher who has discovered a mischievous student writing in his social studies textbook with a crayon, but her down-filled aqua-colored parka somehow made her look less menacing. "Do you have any idea how much time I've missed?" she shouted. "I could have been taking an online seminar on college application essays!"

"So go," I said. "Get into Yale. I'll call you when we're ready to open." And she was gone before I could blink.

The other woman would be less easy to placate. Detective Sergeant Margaret Vidal is an imposing person, tall, muscular, and very attractive, in an intimidating way. She'd put on maybe five pounds since I'd seen her last six years before, and had exactly three gray hairs mingling with the black ones. She was also wearing an expression I associate mostly with my mother: disapproval.

"A girl drives for an hour and a half to help a friend through a difficult time, she expects at the very least that the friend will be there when she arrives, Elliot," she said.

"Nice to see you too, Meg. It's been way too long."

She stopped advancing just as I got the office door open. I turned to her, and we fell into a hug. I held on to her beyond when I should have let go, but Meg is nothing if not a stabilizing presence, and at that moment, I needed some stability.

"I'm sorry, Elliot. Here I promised to come up to make you feel better, and I start by yelling at you. Let me start again: Where have you been?"

I filled her in on the information, however confusing, I'd gotten at Sharon's practice. Meg listened, frowning, which I knew was her natural expression when trying to solve a puzzle. When I was researching *Woman at Risk,* I'd spent months observing her on a case, and we'd started every morning with me waiting for her to finish the *New York Times* crossword puzzle at her desk before beginning the day's work.

"You know you should let Chief Dutton handle this, right?" Meg asked. We walked out of the office after I'd checked my e-mail, noted the lack of phone messages, and stashed the bicycle wheel. There wasn't enough room in there for us both to sit, and besides, I had a nagging feeling there was something else to which I should be attending. But I couldn't remember what it might be.

"Yeah, I know, and it's not that I don't think Dutton is good, or that he's not working hard enough. I just can't sit still and wait for the phone call. I don't want to feel like there was something I could have done if . . ." Usually, I finish my sentences, but I was having an unusual amount of difficulty doing that today.

Meg nodded as we headed toward the balcony steps to sit down. I got close to the stairs, and suddenly, Dad registered in the corner of my eye. Oh yeah!

"Dad," I said.

He didn't turn his head; he was busy watching the plumber. "I don't think it's the one pipe, Elliot," he said. "He's made the right repair, and the water isn't stopping."

I decided to plow on as if he hadn't told me something I didn't want to hear. "Meg, you've met my father?"

Meg shook her head. "He seemed so busy, I didn't want to bother him."

So I turned to my father. "Dad, this is Sergeant Vidal."

Arthur Freed turned to look, and smiled. "So you're Meg," he said. "Elliot told me about you, but he forgot to mention what a looker you are."

I'd never seen Meg Vidal blush, but there it was. "You're too kind. Arthur, isn't it?" Meg and I had gotten to know a lot about each other in our time working together on *Woman at Risk*. She remembered more than I did; what was her ex-husband's name, again?

Dad took her hand in both of his. "You're here with news?"

"No, Arthur. I'm here to be with Elliot until the police find something."

My father looked sad and sentimental. "You're a good friend," he said.

"So is Elliot. You did nice work."

I decided to end this part of the conversation before we were arrested for public maudlin-ing. "What do you mean, we've still got water, Dad?" I asked.

His attention turned immediately back in toward the men's room. "Not as much, but the leak is still there. And I don't think his current plan is the right one."

I considered walking inside to deal with the plumber, but my head wasn't operating the way it's supposed to, and I knew it. "Do me a favor, Dad," I said. "If you could supervise this one, just make whatever decision you think is right, and tell me how much to pay for it, okay?"

Dad frowned. "I'm not going to let you spend all kinds of money if you don't have to, Elliot."

"That's exactly why I trust you with this. Please."

He smiled a little, and nodded. "But you tell me the minute you hear something."

"No. I'm going to keep it to myself. Of course I'll tell you." I came close to hugging him, but was afraid that if I did, I wouldn't be able to stop. Dad turned back, and walked into the men's room with more determination than most men show when doing so.

I opened the door to the auditorium, and Meg and I took

seats in the last row. If we'd been dating, and there had actually been a movie playing, it would have been perfect. Instead, it felt weird.

"It doesn't make sense that Sharon wouldn't tell her own nurse about the medical records," I said when we'd picked up the conversation again. "That's basic. It's part of the process. Why wouldn't she put them in the patient's file?"

"You're obsessing," Meg said. "It's natural, but you have to try not to do it."

"If you've got something better to do, I'm listening," I said. I hadn't realized before how uncomfortable the seats in my theatre could be. No wonder I wasn't drawing crowds. Wait. No. I wasn't drawing crowds because nobody wanted to watch old comedies in a dilapidated old theatre; that was it. The seats weren't the problem. Were they? Or was I obsessing again?

"Where was your head just now?" Meg asked gently.

"Business school," I said.

"I wasn't aware you'd gone to business school."

"I didn't."

We sat for a while longer. "If it's a kidnapping," I said out of the blue, "why hasn't there been a ransom demand?"

"A good question. Maybe it's not a kidnapping. Maybe your first instinct was correct, and Sharon is just off recovering from Chapman's suicide. You might know your ex-wife better than the police do. Ever think of that?" Meg's smile looked satisfied.

I shook my head. "She's been gone a day and a half already. She knows the practice is open today. I would have heard from her by now, if everything was okay."

A light flashes at the back of the auditorium, very faintly, when the phone in the office is ringing, so it doesn't interrupt the showing, but so I can see there's a call if I'm in the auditorium. When it started to flash, I made it from the back of the auditorium to the office in the amount of time it takes Harpo Marx to pull a hot cup of coffee from inside his trench coat. That means really fast.

I grabbed the receiver before I'd really stopped running, which in my office can be a serious health hazard. I came close to strangling myself with the phone cord and slamming headfirst into a file cabinet at the same time. It's a wonder I'm insured at all.

Toni Westphal was on the line. "I went over what I said to you, and it seemed cruel," she said. "I didn't want you to think I believe Sharon did anything wrong. Not Sharon."

After letting out my breath for what seemed like an hour, I told Toni it was all right, and we were still friends.

"I hope so," she said. "And I thought of one more thing: That second file, the one Sharon wouldn't show anyone. It wasn't any kind of X-ray or film. It was a blood test; I know because I remember the orange sticker on the file, and that's the one that comes from our blood lab."

That didn't help much, but I promised to let Toni know if I heard anything, and she promised the same. I was thinking of getting "I'll let you know when I hear something about Sharon" printed on a T-shirt just to save time, but that wouldn't help much on the phone. And it was too cold to just wear a T-shirt, anyway.

I had barely hung up when the phone rang again, and the caller ID indicated that the Midland Heights Police Department was on the line. I was getting used to having my heart in my mouth, and the taste was disgusting.

"I don't know anything yet," Dutton said as soon as I picked up. "But your ex-wife's current husband called. "

"Soon-to-be second ex-husband," I corrected him.

"Yes. Because that's so much easier to say."

"What did Gregory want?" I asked. "Is that pesky kid next door walking across his lawn and trampling the petunias again?"

"He says someone broke into their house and tossed the place," Dutton said.

"I'm on my way."

I heard Dutton say, "Elliot . . . ," but I ignored him and

hung up. Then I walked into the lobby and told Meg where I was going.

"Do you want me to come with you?" she asked.

"No. I don't want Dutton to think I'm bringing in my own cops," I answered.

"Barry wouldn't mind," Meg told me. I'd forgotten she and Dutton knew each other professionally.

"Okay, let's go," I said.

Meg drove to Sharon's house, mostly because riding on the handlebars of my bicycle didn't seem dignified. To her. We didn't talk much, but then, it wasn't a very long drive.

The house Sharon was unwillingly sharing with Gregory is, actually, not unlike the one I'd grown up in: it was a Victorian with a wraparound porch, but where my old house had been lovingly restored by my father over thirty years, this one had been profitably restored by contractors at Sharon's behest. It was still very attractive, but not as idiosyncratic, and therefore not as lovable. It was a very nice house, whereas mine had been a lovely home.

Dutton's Crown Vic was already outside when we got there, but he was still sitting in the driver's seat. He got out when he saw me, and buttoned his woolen topcoat against the wind. He is a very dapper police chief.

"I don't suppose there's any way I can dissuade you from going inside," he started. A lot of people would have opened with "hello," but Dutton was his own man; I admired that.

"You called me," I said, passing him on my way to the door.

"Teach me to share information," I heard Dutton say behind me. Then he noticed Meg, who was walking up the drive, and smiled. "Margaret Vidal," Dutton said. "How did he talk you into coming up here? He think I can't solve this one myself?"

Meg gave Dutton a peck on the cheek, and then shook her head. "Elliot tried to talk me out of coming," she said. "I'm just here for moral support."

They caught up before I rang the bell. Gregory opened the door, looking surprised to see me there, as if it *didn't* make sense that calling the police would naturally summon his soon-to-be ex-wife's previous ex-husband (try saying *that* five times fast!). "Elliot," he said. "Have you heard something?"

"Yes," I said, "but not about Sharon." I can't ever give Gregory a straight answer; it's against the code. A man steals your wife, you have to sass him forever. It's a very specific code, one designed especially for me. All right, so I designed it myself.

"May we come in?" Chief Dutton asked, apparently feeling that my tormenting the man who broke up my marriage wasn't as important as the investigation of a burglary and possible clues into Sharon's disappearance. Some people don't get the code.

Introductions were made, and Gregory let us in. I could see that Meg was sizing up Gregory, and finding him wanting. Dutton, trained investigator that he is, looked around the room and said, "Where did the break-in occur, Dr. Sandoval?"

The question seemed to puzzle Gregory, who swept his arm dramatically around the extremely tidy and well-furnished living room—two things you could never say about mine—and said, "Right here."

Now, that *was* pretty puzzling: There wasn't so much as a throw pillow out of place. The hardwood floor was buffed to within an inch of its life; the sofa, armchairs, love seat, and ottoman were all perfectly placed and dust free; even the Persian rug appeared to have been recently vacuumed. I flashed on a mental image of my own living room, with the state's largest comedy collection strewn about it, and came very close to tears.

"Well, nothing appears to be out of place," Dutton observed, quite accurately.

"Of course not," Gregory said, his tone clearly wondering how this man ever graduated from the police academy. "I *cleaned up.*"

THERE wasn't much point in Dutton filing a report, he said. Gregory had noticed nothing missing, and there was no obvious sign of forced entry, although Gregory told Dutton that a back window had been open when he'd arrived home. It was, of course, closed and locked now. Dusting for fingerprints would have created, you know, *dust*, and it wasn't clear whether Gregory was as interested in finding out who had burglarized his home (he said there had been photographs, videos, books, and CDs strewn about the living room, all neatly replaced on shelves now) as he was in keeping the place spotless.

"I don't want Sharon coming home to a mess," he said.

I saw Meg Vidal stifle a laugh.

There was also no point in talking to Gregory—there never is—so Meg asked Dutton whether he'd gotten the report on my burglary yet.

Gregory, now officially superfluous in the conversation, looked like he wanted us all to leave.

"Yes, they faxed it over," Dutton told her. "There wasn't anything in it that Elliot hadn't already told me."

I asked Dutton if anything had come of the credit card receipts. Gregory's ears perked up at the mention of credit cards, and Dutton filled him in on the apparent purchases in Manhattan, informing me along the way that there was no further news on new purchases.

"The purchases were all made after seven in the evening, but since we don't know what time your house was burglarized, Elliot, that doesn't help us much," Dutton reported.

"Have you asked the NYPD about the businesses where stuff was bought?" I asked. "Have they sent anybody in with a picture of Sharon?"

"Believe it or not, Elliot, I did call the New York police," Dutton said, his tone a bit irritated. It wasn't that I didn't respect the man. It was that Sharon was still missing. "They'll get someone out there within a day."

"A day!" Gregory moaned. "Anything can happen in a day."

"He's right," I said, not believing I'd used those words in connection with Gregory. "If you give me a list of those businesses, I'm taking the train into the city right now with a picture of Sharon."

"I'll go with you," Gregory said, already reaching for his very expensive Burberry trench coat.

"In that case," I said, "you drive."

Dutton held up a hand. "I can't send a couple of civilians in without badges to . . ."

"Do you want to deputize us?" I asked.

"Hell, no."

"Then you don't have a choice. You're not sending us. We're going. All you're doing is providing a list of businesses."

"I don't see any reason to provide sensitive police data to . . ."

Gregory gave Dutton his best condescending look, which I've seen directed at me many times, and I can tell you it's effective. "Then all Elliot needs to do is call his credit card company and ask for the charges from the past forty-eight hours," he said.

"Fine," Dutton sighed. "I'll give you the list. But . . ." Then his cell phone rang, and he took the call.

I used that opportunity to ask to borrow Meg's cell phone. "What's wrong with yours?" she asked.

"Aside from the fact that I don't own one, nothing."

She didn't say what she was thinking, and handed me her phone. I called the theatre. Dad answered. "We've got it narrowed down," he said of the mysterious leak. "Everything works but the urinals."

"Isn't that a problem?" I asked.

"Yeah, but not one that closes the theatre. Men can use the stalls too, you know."

"This isn't the time to relive my potty training, Dad. Thanks for the help. I'll call Sophie."

"I can call her. What do you need?" Dad asked.

"Tell her we'll open tonight. I didn't have time to cancel the ads, so at least Leo Munson will be there. Leo comes every night, and he gets mad when I close and don't let him know.

Tell Sophie I'm going into the city to check on something, and she's in charge."

He was clearly writing all this down. "Of what?" Dad asked.

I didn't hang up on him, but I ended the call as soon as I could.

I turned back toward Meg. "Can I borrow this"—I indicated the phone—"for the rest of the day?" I asked.

"Maybe I should come with you two," Meg suggested.

"Do you really want to be around when two civilians start conducting an investigation?" I asked her.

"Good point. Maybe you should stay home, and let me go."

Dutton was putting his phone away. "Meg, how do you think your captain would react if I asked to borrow you for a day or two?" he asked.

"I'm a homicide detective," she said.

"Yeah," Dutton said. "We don't have a detective dedicated to that."

My blood pressure spiked. "Why do you need a homicide detective?" I asked, my voice only slightly higher than Frankie Valli's.

"Calm down; it's not Sharon," Dutton answered. "That was the ME." He looked at Sergeant Vidal. "Meg?"

"Since I basically told my captain I was leaving for a few days and he'd have to deal with it, I don't think it would be a problem," she said. "What did the medical examiner want?"

"They have a slight problem in the Russell Chapman case."

Meg raised an eyebrow. "Oh?"

"Russell Chapman's body is missing."

Meg looked at me "I think I'll be needing that phone, Elliot," she said.

11

"**WHAT** do you suppose it means?" Gregory asked. He was driving his almost-new Lexus (a car with which I was uncomfortably familiar—he had once tried to run me over with it) up the New Jersey Turnpike, heading toward the exit for the Lincoln Tunnel, which I estimated was now about ten minutes away. "Does that mean Chapman *didn't* kill himself?"

"Who am I, Carnac the Magnificent? How the hell am I supposed to know what it means?"

"Jesus, Elliot, calm down a little. You're not the only one who's worried, you know. I mean, what did I ever do to . . ." Then he realized he had stolen my wife, and the car was quiet (luxury vehicles excel at quiet) for a while.

"It's entirely possible they just misplaced Chapman's body," I said, mostly to myself. "Dutton said Chapman's body was there Thursday night; his daughter identified him. Maybe they mixed him up with someone else. Things happen at hospitals, right? I mean, when you're not knocking people out, you're a doctor, right?"

Gregory, still smarting from my tone a moment ago, drove on without saying anything.

Maybe I was being too hard on him. After all, Sharon had obviously seen something in the guy that I was lacking, or she wouldn't have left me for him. Well, she still might have left me, but not for him. I figured I should try to find out what that something might be.

"You and Sharon met at the hospital, right?" I asked. She was, after all, the only topic we had in common. I didn't even know what kind of movies Gregory liked. He probably only watched documentaries on PBS, and went to see foreign films and independent, gritty dramas released by ministudios about New Yorkers who dress in black and use heroin. That would be my guess.

He smiled, probably despite himself. "Yes," he said. "She needed an anesthesiologist for a patient whose face had been cut by some broken glass, and I was on call that night."

"You crazy romantic," I said.

Gregory's face closed up again. "I didn't expect you to understand," he said.

"But I do," I told him. "I met Sharon when she was a med student and I was writing for a trade magazine for teachers. A feature on teaching hospitals. I first saw her when she was on rounds, tending to a patient with phlebitis."

"You crazy romantic," Gregory said. I might have seen the tiniest hint of a grin on his face. Then it clouded over. "So, have you seen a lot of Sharon lately?"

"Why, is there more of her than there used to be?" You watch enough Groucho and it becomes a reflex.

"I've just gotten the feeling that she was . . . involved with someone since we . . . separated. Thought maybe it was you. Sharon would be one to fall back on a familiar face."

I didn't even try to respond to that. For one thing, Sharon and I *had* been out a few times (and *in* one time, if you know what I mean), but not recently. If there was another man, I didn't know about it, and wasn't sure I wanted to. No, I was sure: I didn't want to know.

"Not me," I told Gregory, and then I shut up.

He maneuvered us into the E-ZPass lane for the tunnel,

and the traffic was unusually light. I guess either going into Manhattan on a Saturday after the matinees have already begun isn't as popular as it used to be, or E-ZPass has really speeded up the toll process.

We were through the Lincoln Tunnel in fifteen minutes, and looking for a parking lot within twenty-five.

"Are we splitting the parking?" Gregory asked.

"Don't be cheap. You own a Lexus."

He scowled, probably wishing he could use that Lexus to run me down again, but said nothing else. We found a lot on Forty-sixth Street near Broadway, and left the car there. A quick reading of the rates indicated parking there for two or three hours wouldn't cost Gregory more than forty dollars, the skinflint.

There were four stores and the hotel bar on the list Dutton had provided, showing purchases on the credit card with my name on it. The first was a jewelry store on Forty-fourth Street, between Eighth and Ninth avenues. We walked there, and I noted as ever that Manhattan creates a wind tunnel effect unparalleled in my experience. I felt like I was at the top of Mount Everest, but for the Sherpa guides and oxygen tanks.

The "jewelry store," when we got there, turned out to be one of those cheap souvenir places in Midtown that specialize in Broadway-themed items made in Bangladesh, pictures of Marilyn Monroe standing on a sewer grate (did you know her first movie was *Love Happy*, with the Marx Brothers?) and "gift items" from New York's most bizarre tourist attraction, Ground Zero. If I'd stopped to think about it, that would probably have led me to wonder if there was now a gift shop outside the Auschwitz concentration camp area, selling T-shirts showing the crematorium with the phrase "We Must Never Forget" written in German over it (tastefully, of course).

Luckily, I didn't stop to think about it.

"Sharon would never shop here," Gregory said as we approached.

"No," I agreed, rubbing my hands together, "but I'll bet it's heated."

He nodded. "That isn't a bad thing."

We went inside. The man behind the counter was working diligently to sell a woman in her forties a souvenir T-shirt. Judging by his accent, he must have been born somewhere outside the tristate area. *Far* outside the tristate area.

"Sure it'll fit you," he said (I'm pretty sure) to the woman. "It's one size fits all. It fits everybody."

"You sure? Can I bring it back if it doesn't fit?" Her husband, who looked profoundly embarrassed, was wearing horn-rimmed glasses, a down-filled parka, and one of those headbands that covers your ears but doesn't cover your head. Sort of an almost-a-hat.

"Back? No, you can't bring it back. But it'll fit." The salesman looked disgusted at the very prospect.

"I dunno. I'll think about it." The woman walked to her husband, who now looked profoundly relieved, but never took his hand off his inside jacket pocket, and they left.

"She's gonna think about it. Six ninety-nine, and she's gonna think about it." The guy rolled his eyes a little, and then looked at us. "So what can I do for you?"

I had found a photograph of Sharon on my computer and printed it out seven times, for reasons I could not possibly explain. I took it out of my jacket pocket and showed it to the guy.

"Have you seen this woman?"

His lips pursed and one eye squinted. "You guys cops? This is a legit business here."

"We're not cops," I said. "We're her husbands."

"Mormons?"

I shook my head. "You haven't even heard of our religion yet. Have you seen her?"

"How do I know you're not cops?"

"Because I would have shot you by now. Look at the picture. *Have. You. Seen. This. Woman.*"

He took what could charitably be called a glance. "No."

"What do you mean, 'no'?" I shouted. "You barely even looked at the picture!"

"Elliot," Gregory said.

"No! We're trying to save a woman's life, and this guy thinks he's a day player on *Law & Order SVU*!" A couple of heads turned at the back of the store.

I heard one guy near a rack of 9/11 ties say, "Are they filming here?"

"What do you want me to tell you?" the salesman asked. "I don't memorize every face that comes in here."

"We have some credit card records," Gregory said before I could jump down the salesman's throat a few inches deeper. "Would they help you trace the purchase? At least tell us what was bought?"

"I don't know. Maybe. I've got customers; I can't stop everything to look up some receipts." He motioned over to a frightened-looking man wearing an FDNY baseball cap that had probably been purchased the same day.

"Sir." Gregory's eyes took on a liquid, pleading quality. Either he was truly distraught, or Dr. Sandoval could have taught at the Actors Studio. "Please. This is a very important matter, and you could help enormously. Isn't there some way?"

"Sure, there's a way," I muttered. "We could beat him to a pulp until he agrees to do it."

But I don't think the salesman heard me, because he took a long moment to search Gregory's eyes. Without turning his head, he screamed, "Mahmoud!" A young man seemed to appear in an instant. "Sell things. I'll be right back."

He walked behind the counter and through a door with a bead curtain, and without being invited, Gregory and I followed him into the back room.

If the front of the store was dingy, this area was downright disturbing. An unidentifiable odor permeated, and pretty much everything was covered with a substance that lived in the netherworld between dust and grime.

The salesman settled on a metal stool behind the screen of a computer that hearkened back to a simpler, less technological time. He typed in a few lines and green text appeared on the screen. I felt like I was visiting the Hewlett-Packard Museum.

"Give me the numbers," he said.

Gregory took Dutton's list out of his jacket pocket and read off the transaction numbers for this store. The salesman typed them in slowly, and then pushed a button. Things whirred. Things clicked. I half expected to see a hamster running on a wheel powering the computer. If Fred Flintstone had built himself a computer, it would be newer than this one.

"It was Thursday night," the guy said after his screen spit out more incomprehensible data. "She bought a history of Broadway musicals and a pewter ring in the shape of the World Trade Center."

"A ring in the shape of . . ." I marveled.

"You'd be amazed," the guy said.

I looked at Gregory. "That's not Sharon," I said.

He shook his head. "No. It's not." He turned to the salesman. "Sorry for wasting your time."

The guy looked up. "Well, if you want to make it up to me . . ."

"I don't want a 9/11 tea cozy," I said. But I gave him a Comedy Tonight business card and told him to call if he thought of anything. The guy probably used it to pick his teeth and threw it away the minute I walked out the door. Some people just don't pick up on my innate charm.

Gregory handed the guy a twenty-dollar bill. "Thanks for the help," he said.

We left the store, and stood out on Forty-sixth Street. People went by on their way to see *Wicked* and *Mamma Mia!*, and we just stood there.

"Now what?" Gregory asked.

I had no idea.

12

WE couldn't think of anything else to do, so we went to visit the other retailers on Dutton's list. The first three were variations on the theme established at the "jewelry" store: an electronics outlet, a clothing store that specialized in "adult lingerie" where some rubber garments had been bought (Gregory came close to passing out a couple of times), and a high-end cookware outlet that didn't seem to fit the list. None of the salespeople or managers at the stores remembered seeing Sharon, and none of the purchases were anything Gregory or I could imagine her buying, although I confess I did try to imagine the lingerie.

At the bar in the Affinia Manhattan hotel, across the street from Madison Square Garden, we struck pay dirt. Sort of.

"Yeah, I remember her," the bartender said. My head broke the land speed record for swiveling in his direction. "Just a couple of days ago. Came in for about an hour. It was the busy time of the night, so I didn't talk to her much." The guy was maybe thirty, with the chiseled face of an actor who makes his living serving drinks to the well-off.

Gregory and I, stunned at our sudden success, must have

had eyes the size of silver-dollar pancakes. I regained the power of speech first. "How do you remember her?" I asked.

"Well, she was pretty, but we get a lot of nice-looking women in here," he answered. "I remember her because of what she was drinking."

We waited, and he eventually came to the conclusion that we would like to know what that was. The bartender smiled. "Milk and seltzer," he said. "Can you imagine?"

Gregory and I stared at each other. "Milk and seltzer?" Gregory asked, after a moment. "You're sure?"

"I don't get much call for it," the bartender answered. "Believe me, I remember."

"But you're sure it was the woman in the picture," I emphasized. "It couldn't have been someone else."

The bartender shook his head. "No, that's her, all right. First thing when I saw her picture, I said, 'Milk and seltzer.' Does she drink that all the time?"

"No," Gregory answered. "I've never seen her with that one." He turned to me. "You?"

I shook my head. "Never," I said. "You should have added some chocolate syrup and made her an egg cream."

"I offered," the bartender said.

Gregory remembered something then. "We have her credit card receipt from that night," he told the bartender. "The total was over thirty-two dollars. That's a lot of milk and seltzer to drink in an hour."

"Well, the guy she was with was drinking Dewar's," the guy answered. "That's most of the bill. I don't even think I charged her for the milk."

I jumped in before Gregory could inhale. "The *guy she was with*?" I asked. "She was with a guy?"

"Yeah, for a while. He left after a couple of drinks, and she stuck around maybe twenty minutes."

"What did he look like?" Gregory asked breathlessly.

The bartender shrugged. "Nothing special; nothing I can remember," he said. "I'd say thirties, dark hair, ladies would probably find him handsome. I don't remember the guys as well as the women." He smiled his devilish smile. It didn't have much effect.

"And he left before her?" I said. "They didn't leave together?"

"No. I mean, I was busy at the bar, but I don't remember seeing him again."

I had to ask. "When he left, how did she say good-bye?"

The bartender's brow wrinkled. "I didn't hear her say good-bye," he said. "I don't listen in on customers' conversations."

Gregory's lips had flattened out to a straight horizontal line. "He means, did she kiss him good-bye," he said.

"I think so, but just on the cheek, like a friend," the guy said.

"Did she have any luggage with her?" I asked. If Sharon knew she was going away for a while, she'd bring changes of clothes, cosmetics, and enough other stuff to fill a U-Haul van.

"I didn't see any," the bartender answered. "Hang on, I have somebody at the other end of the bar." And he went down to take an order from a guy who was trying to impress a woman of maybe twenty-five in a silver dress you could clean with Windex.

"I thought *you* were the guy," Gregory said. "I guess I was wrong."

"I guess so."

"What do you think it means?" Gregory asked.

"I think it means she was here," I said. "It doesn't sound like she was being held against her will. It doesn't sound like she was especially distraught. I can't imagine what she was doing here in the city after the whole business with Chapman, but she hadn't heard about his suicide yet—if he committed suicide. And it doesn't help us at all to figure out where she is."

The bartender wandered back from his post, shaking his head. "Guy's trying to get laid," he said, "and he orders a chocolate martini. For *himself*. Maybe it's me."

"Is there anything else you can tell us about the night

our . . . friend was here?" I asked him. "Anything about the other guy, anything about where she might have been going when she left?"

He made a show of thinking, so the tip Gregory would give him could be larger. "I wasn't looking, so I don't know if she got into a cab or took the subway."

"Cab," Gregory and I answered in unison.

"I do remember, though, that her hands were shaking," the bartender added. "When the guy was there, you couldn't tell. He said he could stay if she wanted him to, and she said no, she'd be fine if she could just get away fast enough. After he left, I think there were a couple of times she started to cry, but then she pulled herself together."

"It's a good thing you don't eavesdrop on customers," I said.

I gave him a Comedy Tonight card. Gregory gave him a fifty.

ON the way back in the car, I called Dutton on Gregory's cell phone and filled him in on what we'd discovered, which really hadn't been much beyond a mystery man in the bar whom we couldn't identify. I'd handed a Comedy Tonight business card to virtually every cheap retailer in Manhattan and the bartender at the hotel, and Gregory was down about a hundred and fifty bucks, which didn't bother me in the least. Dutton refused to elaborate on the strange report from the medical examiner, which I found rude, but grudgingly understandable. Then I called the theatre and got Sophie on the phone.

"We're just about up and running," she said. "Jonathan is taking tickets so I can run the snack bar, and I called Anthony to get here early because you aren't threading up the projector. He's upstairs getting the movie on now."

"You're my hero, Sophie," I told her.

"I have to go," she said. "Brown University recommends the SAT *and* the ACT. I have studying to do."

"Anything else I need to know?"

"Yeah. Some guy came in from an insurance company. Said he met you at the doctor's today. Are you sick?"

"Just heartsick," I said. "Was this guy's name Tovarich?"

"Yeah," she said. "He's here now. The movie starts in fifteen minutes."

"I'll be back before intermission," I said. "Hold down the fort."

"What fort?" Sophie asked.

I should have hung up. In retrospect, it would have been so much better. "There's a woman here, too, looking for your ex-wife," Sophie continued.

Okay, *that* was odd. "Looking for Sharon? At the theatre?"

"Ye-ah." A tone indicating that I was even stupider than usual.

"What's her name?"

"Elliot, I sell snacks. I'm not supposed to be your secretary."

That was true, but didn't seem relevant. "Is the woman still there, Sophie?"

"Didn't I just say that?"

"Don't impersonate my mother. You're too young, and I'll have strange dreams. Look. Don't let the woman leave before I get there, understand?"

"What am I supposed to do, physically block her at the exit?" I was starting to get nostalgic for the old monosyllabic Goth Sophie. This new one had way too much equity in the Bank of Sarcasm.

"If she tries to leave, tell her I'm on my way. I'll be there as soon as I can." And this time, I did hang up.

I told Gregory what Sophie had said, and he increased his speed from a limit-obeying fifty-five miles an hour to a downright death-defying sixty. The man was an animal.

While we were hurtling toward Midland Heights in an attempt to set a new land-slowness record, I called Meg Vidal on Gregory's phone, which I'd decided would be my phone until he grabbed it out of my hand.

"Well, it's about time," she said, after I assured her it was not Gregory reaching out to her.

"We've been busy."

"Did you find out anything?" Meg asked.

"A few things. I'll tell you when I see you. Where are you now?"

"On my way to your house," she answered. "You dad gave me his key. I assume it's okay if I stay the night."

"Stay as long as you want, but if you expect hanky-panky, I'll have you know I'm not that kind of boy," I answered. "Dammit."

"Thank goodness for small favors," Meg said. "Listen. The hospital is a zoo; every cop in the county is tearing the place apart looking for Chapman's body. There wasn't much point in sticking around there, so I spent the afternoon working with Barry and making a few phone calls. I've found out a few things, but nothing astonishing."

"I'll be the judge of what's astonishing," I told her. "What'd you find out?"

"I'll tell you when I see you. Are you on your way to the theatre?"

I assured her I was. "We're racing there to meet a mysterious woman who might be the key to the entire mystery," I told her, to make it sound important. "It's possible Gregory is actually exceeding the speed limit by a mile or two." Gregory scowled at me. It's the simple pleasures that make life worthwhile.

"I'll wait up," Meg said. "Call if you need me."

We got back to Comedy Tonight in a record (for Gregory) hour and fifteen minutes from door to door. It would have taken a normal person forty-five minutes, but one must make allowances for the adrenaline-deficient. I was out of the car and at the door of the theatre pretty much before he declared his vehicle parked.

It was warmer inside, but not that much. The heating system had probably been built while Hope and Crosby were filming *Road to Morocco*, and had not responded well to being dormant for the better part of a day. I touched the radiator in the lobby on the way in, just to make sure it was hot. Well, warm.

Not cold, anyway.

Sophie was behind the snack bar, sitting on her stool and reading *The Real ACT Prep Guide*. Jonathan, without any tickets to tear in half, stood by her, adoringly and silently. He was the perfect lapdog.

I unlocked the office and put my parka inside. Then I wasted no time getting to Sophie. "Where is she?"

Sophie looked up. "Who?" Twenty-two sixty. I'm asking you.

"The woman who was asking for Sharon. Where is she?"

"Oh. Near the back, I think." She pointed vaguely in the direction of the auditorium, and went back to her book, putting a pencil in her mouth.

"Sophie," I said, as Gregory walked up beside me. "What does the woman look like?"

"Oh, she's old," Jonathan volunteered, doing his best to keep us from disturbing Sophie. "She's got to be at least forty."

Gregory, who is forty-one, coughed. "You saw her?" I asked Jonathan. "Can you show me where she is?"

Jonathan whispered, gesturing to the ever-concentrating Sophie. "Sure. Come on."

He practically tiptoed away from Sophie, who was highlighting passages in the book with an expression of seriousness I had only seen on her once before, when she was deciding whether her new ringtone should be Marilyn Manson or vintage Megadeth. Manson had won, but it had been close.

Jonathan led us to the auditorium door, which he opened slightly. On the screen, John L. "Sully" Sullivan was at his low point, confined to a chain gang for a murder he didn't commit, and the guards were allowing the inmates their one and only pleasure: Pluto cartoons shown in a church. It is Sullivan's epiphany: the moment he realizes that making silly comedies might just be a high calling after all. That one always gets to me, and for a moment, I was caught up in the film. Jonathan tapped me on the shoulder.

"There she is," he said, pointing.

I followed his finger and saw the woman he was indicating: She was in her late thirties, by my estimate, and overdressed for a night at Comedy Tonight, as anyone not in jeans and a flannel shirt (and tonight, a parka) would be. This woman was wearing an actual dress and a hat, of all things, and was watching the screen with no facial expression.

People were starting to look around to see why there was light in the auditorium, so I crept in and closed the door after Gregory followed me inside. I walked slowly to the woman, and since there was no one else seated nearby, I spoke quietly to her (I would *never* talk during the movie if it would disturb another patron, and would appreciate it if you would follow the same code the next time you're seated near me).

"Were you looking for Dr. Simon-Freed?" I asked.

She looked up, sharply. It wasn't so much that she had been intent on the film as that she simply wasn't expecting to hear that question at that moment. But she recovered quickly. "Yes," she said quietly. "Are you him?" I decided not to correct her grammar.

Gregory and I exchanged a glance. "No," I said. "Dr. Simon-Freed is a woman. I'm her ex-husband."

"Simon is a woman's name?" she demanded, apparently intending to prove to me that I *was* Dr. Simon-Freed.

I motioned toward the door. "Let's talk out there," I suggested. The woman nodded, and we all went back into the lobby.

Once we could speak at a normal volume again, I explained to her who I was and why Sharon's name sounded like a man's. Then I asked the woman for her name, and she gave it to me.

"Gwen Chapman," she said. "My father died Thursday night, and your ex-wife was his doctor."

"Nice to meet you," I said.

13

"DON'T get me wrong," Gwen Chapman said. "I don't think Dr. Simon-Freed was involved in my father's death."

That was a relief—a member of the Chapman family who wasn't accusing Sharon of murder. I was starting to like Gwen.

"That's refreshing," I told her. "I met your sister, and . . ."

Gwen made a face. "Lillian," she said. "I imagine you got an earful."

I smiled. "Both ears."

She laughed. "Lil's always been like that," she said. "Everybody's out to do her wrong, even people she's never met. I imagine it's a hard way to live."

"Harder for the people who live with her, I'll bet," I offered.

Gwen shrugged. "My father loved her," she said.

"How do you know your father's dead?" I said to Gwen. "The last I heard, they couldn't find a body." It hadn't sounded so unfeeling in my head.

"He would have gotten in touch by now," she said with a catch in her voice. "It's been two days." That struck to my heart, because it was the same period of time since anyone had heard from Sharon. Just about forty-eight hours.

"Besides," Gwen Chapman continued, "my father left a suicide note."

It took a moment for that to sink in, but Gwen went on. "It said that he couldn't live with the idea of deteriorating before our eyes, of the excruciating pain he would be experiencing. He didn't want to end up in a bed waiting for someone to turn off the machine."

Behind her, I saw the auditorium doors open, and a few people wandered out. Sullivan must have concluded his travels. Among the stragglers was Martin Tovarich, who grinned as he caught my eye and then veered right and headed for the men's room. The urge hits fast when you're over seventy.

"Ms. Chapman, believe me, I'm very sorry your father was so upset, and I understand why he would be under the circumstances." I would have bet the farm I was saying those words, but the voice was actually coming from a little to my left, and belonged to Gregory. Doctors know what to say when somebody dies; it's like when your mechanic tells you that the transmission on your fifteen-year-old Buick has gone belly-up, and offers you the phone number of his brother's junkyard. "But I don't think we know exactly what happened yet."

Gwen Chapman did what might be described as a classic double take, and then settled her gaze on Gregory. "I'm sorry; who are you?" she asked.

"I'm Dr. Gregory Sandoval." He probably had monogrammed boxer shorts that said "Dr. Gregory Sandoval" on them, but it was better not to think about that. "I'm Sharon's husband."

"Soon-to-be ex-husband," I answered, as a reflex.

Gwen looked like she was getting a headache. "I thought *you* were her ex-husband," she said to me.

"Who says you have to be limited to one?"

Gwen, wisely, let that go. I asked her why she'd come to Comedy Tonight.

"I called Dr. Simon-Freed's practice, to see if there were anything I could find out about my father's diagnosis, and whether it would have affected his brain—you know, suicide might have been the outcome of a drug-induced depression, or something of that nature—and I was told the doctor wasn't in. The woman on the phone suggested I check with you." I mentally cursed Betty for sending a distraught, if pleasant, woman to me when I was at least as distraught, if not as pleasant. I guess Betty hadn't known what else to do.

"Ms. Chapman," Gregory said. "There's something you should know." That threw me off, because I *knew* Gregory wasn't stupid enough to tell Gwen that Sharon was missing, so I had no idea what he was going to say. Medical information, maybe? "Dr. Simon-Freed has been missing since Thursday night. If there's anything you can tell us that would help us find her . . ."

Well, what do you know? He *was* stupid enough, after all!

"Gregory . . ." I growled. Never give away information to the opposition, even when they're charming (and sort of cute).

"Oh, my goodness," Gwen Chapman said. "The doctor disappeared just about the time my father . . . ?"

"I'm afraid so," I told her, immediately in damage-control mode.

Gregory was more in damage-creation mode. "We're afraid she might have been taken against her will," he said.

"Good lord, really?" Gwen said. "I hope that's not the case. That would be terrible."

I don't know why, but I guess I felt that Gwen was really concerned, and that she had some insight into her family that could help. "You identified your father?" I asked. "How did you find out what had happened?"

Gwen's eyes narrowed, but only because she was trying to follow my train of thought. "Come out and ask it, Mr. Freed," she said. "You want to know where I was Thursday night."

"I didn't mean to make any insinuations."

"My sister called me," she went on. "I guess the police

had called her. The maid in Dad's house had discovered his body." She closed her eyes for a moment, then opened them again.

"Why didn't your sister go to the hospital, then?" I wondered aloud.

"Lillian doesn't handle . . . situations well. She usually leaves that to her husband, Wally."

"And he was in Japan that day, right?" I said.

Gwen nodded. "How did you know that?"

"Your sister mentioned it. On business, she said. Were your father and your brother-in-law involved in any business together?" So sue me; I was looking for a scapegoat. I'm a bad person.

Gwen saw where I was going immediately. She blanched. "Wally?" she asked.

I nodded. Gregory was looking at me as if I'd sprouted a third leg, growing out of my nose.

Gwen Chapman's demeanor underwent an instantaneous overhaul. Her soft, concerned brown eyes darkened and her expression went from concern to something more worried— some would say panicky. "I . . . I don't want to talk about Wally. He scares me," she said. And before I could answer, she turned on a dime and walked out of the theatre.

I was about to tear down Gregory and put up a convenience store on his site, just for being idiot enough to tell Gwen about Sharon's disappearance, but I was called off by a voice to my right.

"Who was that?" asked Martin Tovarich. "She was talking to you for so long; she must have loved *Sullivan's Travels*."

I introduced Tovarich to Gregory (although I considered not doing so, just to piss Gregory off), and then told him the woman he'd seen was Russell Chapman's daughter. Tovarich reached into his coat for a reporter's notebook and a pencil, which he licked. Really.

"It was?" Tovarich asked. "Which one?"

"Gwen," I got out through clenched teeth, still staring at Gregory with death-ray eyes.

"The younger one," he said, probably remembering from his files. "What was she doing here?"

"She has . . . issues," I answered. I turned to look at Tovarich, and saw the same broad grin he'd had when he left the auditorium. "But you look like *you* enjoyed the movie."

"I *loved* it!" he erupted. "The idea of this man, this artist, who doesn't realize what an important thing he's doing with his life . . . What a joy!"

I beamed. Another convert; I only had three billion to go. "And funny, too," I said.

"Yes, of course," Tovarich answered. "Mr. Freed, what you're doing here, this theatre . . . this is a mission! Just like Sully, you, too, are performing a good work which can better the human condition!"

"Well, yeah, but there's no point in making a big deal out of it." You've got to stay humble.

"I suppose Mr. Chapman's daughter is too sad to find the uplifting message in such a film," Tovarich said, doing his best to look concerned.

"I guess so," I answered. "At least she seemed upset about her father. When I met his other daughter at Sharon's practice, she didn't seem to care about anything but the inheritance that she thinks she's owed."

The adjuster's eyebrows shot up, but he caught them in time to say, "Really!" He shook his head sadly. "It's not good when families are like that," he said. "A father, no matter how stern he might have been, deserves respect, if nothing else."

"Lillian seems to respect his money," I said. "I couldn't tell you about Gwen."

"It's not right," Tovarich reiterated.

I figured he might have some information Dutton wouldn't have shared. "Have you heard Chapman's body is missing?" I asked.

The insurance man's head snapped up, and his eyes looked like they were trying to see into my skull. "Of course," he lied.

"What do you make of it?" I asked.

"It happens in hospitals," Gregory volunteered, as if someone had asked him. "I've seen things that would make your hair fall out."

I considered his bald pate. "So that's what happened," I said. Sometimes, he makes it too easy.

Chapman wrote something in his notebook. "So his daughters weren't showing much in the way of grief," he said, effectively changing the subject before Gregory could make our hair fall out with his hospital stories. Baldness loves company.

"Like I say, Gwen seemed sad, but not what I'd call devastated," I told him. "Lillian suggested he wasn't a candidate for Father of the Year, and wondered aloud about financial statements."

He didn't seem to hear me. Tovarich looked toward the doors to the street. "That's a shame," he said, and his mustache twitched.

"She's entitled to her opinion," I ventured. "Maybe he spent so much time in the tortilla factory that he didn't have time for his children."

Gregory looked at me. "The tortilla factory? Is that a new Mexican restaurant?"

Neither Tovarich nor I answered him. Tovarich, his mood seemingly punctured by the thought of Chapman's family, said good night and shuffled, head down, out of the theatre.

"Man takes his work seriously," I said to myself.

"He's an insurance adjuster," Gregory said. "He doesn't like complications."

I decided to walk away from him, but Gregory apparently believed we were now friends, and he followed me. "It doesn't tell us anything about where Sharon is," he said. I kept heading to the office. "But if Chapman's not dead, that could mean she's off the hook in terms of liability."

"It's nice you're concerned about her legal position," I snapped at him, "but I'm still worried about whether she's breathing or not." It wasn't a kind thing to say, but my emotions weren't kind today. And if Gregory never forgave me, it probably wouldn't keep me up nights, pacing the floor of my bedroom with regret.

Before I got to the office, though, I spotted another familiar face from the corner of my eye.

"Lennon Dickinson," I said. "How have you been?"

"I'm fine," Lennon said. Of course. He was always fine. When you looked like he did and you worked all day next to Betty the receptionist, what was not to be fine? Besides, Lennon was the kind of guy who could have his leg sawn off and would continue to say he's fine. He's like John Cleese as the Black Knight in *Monty Python and the Holy Grail.* "'Tis but a scratch."

"What are you doing here?" I asked him. Lennon is allergic to comedy. It's possible he had his sense of humor surgically removed. A lack of humor is the one flaw in his personality that keeps me from committing suicide. "Is it something with Sharon?"

"I don't know where Sharon is," Lennon said. "But something occurred to me that might be significant." Talking to Lennon is like talking to Mr. Spock, but with rounder ears.

Gregory, in the meantime, was doing everything but dance the tarantella in front of me to get Lennon's attention. Gregory likes to remind everyone he's in the doctor club, when in fact he should be beaten with a doctor club.

"Oh, hello, Gregory," Lennon said, when he couldn't logically ignore the man anymore.

"Lennon," Gregory said, as if just noticing he was there.

"What did you remember, Lennon?" I asked. I understand parents sometimes have problems keeping four-year-olds on topic, as well.

"All I know is that there had been some suspicion that Mr. Chapman had brain cancer, but Thursday afternoon, Sharon told me she'd gotten the results that the lesion in his head was benign."

"So Sharon knew Chapman wasn't cancerous before she left Thursday evening," Gregory said, in a desperate attempt to restate the obvious.

"That's right," Lennon answered. "It was my understanding that she told him so during his appointment."

"Why have the appointment? Why not tell him on the phone?" Gregory asked.

Lennon shrugged. "No idea."

"Did you see Chapman when he left? Did he look like a man with a weight lifted from his shoulders?" I asked him.

"Sorry, Elliot. I was in with a patient and I didn't see him when he left."

"Any idea why Sharon wouldn't have a nurse in the room with her when she had the conference with Chapman?" I asked.

Lennon's face took on a "deep thought" expression, and then he shook his head. "I can't think of why, but it's not an absolute necessity. Some patients don't like to be given test results with anyone but their doctor in the room. In case it gets . . . emotional." Vulcan that he is, Gregory said the word "emotional" with obvious distaste.

"Did you know Chapman? Was he like that?"

Again, Lennon shook his head. "I didn't really know him," he said. "Sharon had pointed him out once or twice, you know, 'that's the guy who invented a new tortilla,' but that was about it."

"A new tortilla?" Gregory asked. We ignored him again. I was starting to enjoy it.

"Thanks, Lennon," I said. "You want to stay for the next movie?" I just said that to see how he'd react. It's a minor compulsion. I can deal with it if I want to.

Lennon Dickinson shook his head. "No, thank you. I'm a little busy tonight." Liar. He was probably going home to read Dostoyevsky and ponder the meaninglessness of life. I'll stick with Preston Sturges, myself.

I offered my hand. "Well, the invitation stands for whenever you'd like. Let me know if you hear anything."

"I will. You do the same." He turned and started for the door before he called over his shoulder, "Good night, Gregory."

Gregory beamed. He said his good nights and went in search of the perfect apple to polish and bring to Lennon's office in the morning. I managed to hold down my lunch, but only because I hadn't eaten any.

I opened the door to the office, but never made it inside. From behind me, I heard Jonathan call, "Mr. Freed," and I turned to see what the current problem might be.

"What's leaking now, Jonathan?" I asked.

He assessed my face, trying to determine if this was some kind of new code he was being expected to decipher. "Um, nothing, I think," he said.

He was a nice kid; I shouldn't do stuff like that to him. "What is it, Jonathan?"

The house lights in the auditorium never go completely on during the break between movies, but Anthony does bring them up just a bit when the first feature ends, and then lowers them again after showing some trailers and a few vintage drive-in-movie promos for the snack bar. Now, the lights went back down. Anthony was starting this week's contemporary comedy, *Train Trippin'*, a road movie about two guys who get stoned and fall asleep on a train to Juneau, Alaska. Don't ask me.

"I was walking through the theatre, you know, during intermission," Jonathan began. "There's something strange."

"You're going to have to be way more specific than that, Jonathan. Pretty much everything about this theatre is strange."

"Well, it's Leo," he said.

I tensed. Leo Munson, our one-and-only steady customer, had been to Comedy Tonight for every showing since I'd opened the place almost a year before. Leo was a veteran of the merchant marine, and could be Popeye the Sailor's tougher, older brother. I had no idea how old Leo might be, aside from the fact that he probably had seen Abraham Lincoln live at Gettysburg. I didn't want to think about what could be wrong with Leo.

"What's wrong with Leo?" I asked.

"That's just it," Jonathan answered. "He's not here."

14

We cherish our friends not for their ability to amuse us, but for ours to amuse them. —EVELYN WAUGH

He deserves Paradise who makes his companions laugh.
—THE KORAN

THERE was no possible explanation for Leo Munson missing a showing at Comedy Tonight short of his being dead. Leo had once broken his foot kicking a rock in his backyard (it's a long story) and still made it to the theatre that night, on crutches, to see a showing of *A Guide for the Married Man* (1967), a movie he had seen the night before (and the night before that) and didn't especially like.

I called Leo's home (I have his number in my Rolodex in case we have to close the theatre on short notice, which seems to happen more often than you might think), and it simply rang. Leo doesn't have an answering machine; his philosophy is that "if I'm not home, I can't talk to you." The lack of an answer *really* freaked me out, so I called Chief Dutton, but he said that a man not going to the movies on a Saturday night wasn't an incident the police necessarily had to investigate.

"Lots of people aren't in your theatre tonight, Elliot," he said. "If I look for all of them, I won't have time for the odd cat up a tree."

"I thought the fire department handled those."

"We cooperate with our fellow public servants," Dutton

answered. Then his voice deepened a bit, as he indicated concern. "Believe me, if there's any reason to think Mr. Munson is at all in trouble, we'll look into it. I'll have someone go by his house in the morning if you haven't heard from him."

"In the morning! Chief, by then he could be . . ."

"If you're so concerned, why don't you go over there?" Jonathan asked over my shoulder.

"I already know he's not there, or at least not answering his phone," I said. "If I can't get into the apartment, it won't do me any good. He's a customer, not my ex-wife. Besides, I don't have a key." It felt like everyone I knew was missing. Sharon, now Leo. I'd never met Russell Chapman, and his body was missing. I made a mental note to call my parents and make sure they were still in Manalapan, New Jersey.

"Please call me if you hear anything," I asked, and Dutton agreed he would.

The screening of *Train Trippin'* went as you'd expect: Though I kept a vigilant watch, there was nevertheless a distinctly pungent odor—attributable to the audience *en masse*—in the auditorium by the time our two "heroes" arrived in Alaska and discovered, to their dismay, that the local drug of choice was bourbon, and besides, there were no munchies to be had. But the upside was that, within an hour and a half the movie was over. And Sophie had sold out of every item in the snack bar. Coincidence? I think not.

Riding home on the bicycle gave me time to assess (as well as to freeze my assess off), which was exactly what I didn't need: Another full day had gone by without word from Sharon or any sign that she was alive and well. That most certainly wasn't good, but it also wasn't all. I had met both of Russell Chapman's daughters, and couldn't understand either one of them.

I kept to the sidewalk on the Albany Street Bridge into New Brunswick. I liked having a concrete barrier between my bike and the few cars on the bridge at one in the morning. Getting closer to the town house reminded me of the break-in, and the one at Gregory's house. Who besides Sharon could have managed to get into both our homes without leaving a sign of forced entry, and what could they possibly have been looking for? I barely owned anything aside from the comedy collection, and that had obviously been a target of some contempt from the burglar. Sharon would never have done that, not even during our divorce proceedings. And she liked me better now.

It didn't make me feel better to think of the job I had ahead of me, restoring the collection to its previously well-catalogued, categorized and displayed state. I only hoped none of the irreplaceable discs were damaged beyond repair.

Add to all that Leo's disappearance coming on top of Sharon's, and I was approaching my "home" with more trepidation than I'd had when I left. That wasn't the sign of a good day.

They could have the comedy collection; they could have Chapman (if they could find him) and his estate; Leo forgive me, but they could have Leo; if only Sharon were returned safe and sound.

Climbing up the steps to the outrageously green door of my town house (don't blame me—I rent), I was ashamed of myself for thinking so little of everything else, but it didn't dampen my dread that something truly awful might have befallen my ex-wife.

Did she know I still loved her?

I reached for my keys, my left hand holding the bicycle. When I managed to drag my keys out of my right-hand pocket, I fumbled for a few seconds to find the front-door key, which is sad, since I don't have a large collection of keys to confuse me. The only others on my ring are the front door keys to my parents' house, the theatre, and Sharon's. I reached out with the key and touched the door.

It swung open.

I almost dropped the bike. I knew for a fact that I'd locked the door when I left this morning, and here it was, swinging open with barely a touch. That did not seem like a good omen at all.

My options, as I saw them, were limited. Gregory had reappropriated his cell phone, so calling the police would be a problem. I could ask one of the neighbors if I could use their phone, but it was one in the morning, and I don't actually know any of my neighbors. This didn't seem like the time to make friends. I could close the door and ride away, but that wouldn't help me find out who was inside my house—plus, that someone might have information on Sharon's where-abouts. No, this was a time for me to go against every instinct, every personality trait, every gene in my makeup, and be brave.

Besides, it was cold, and I was sick of being cold.

I pushed the door open, doing my best not to notice when it creaked on its hinges. I'd just have to hope the intruder wasn't listening very closely.

Stepping inside, I put the bike down in the hallway as gently as I could. Yes, it made a noise too, but there wasn't much I'd be able to do to an intruder while carrying a bicycle in one hand. You make choices and you have to live with them.

The hallway is exactly twelve feet long; I had to measure it once when some shelves were being delivered. The living room was a ninety-degree turn at the end of the hallway, the stairs to the bedroom just in front of me, and the kitchen ahead and to the right. No one could see me before I reached the entrance to the living room.

That meant I couldn't see them either, of course, and as I crept down the hallway, I noticed every creaky board in a floor that couldn't be more than ten years old. They don't build 'em like they used to.

Unfortunately, the hallway is about as bare of furniture as the rest of the place, so I wasn't able to pick up the usual fire-place poker, socket wrench, or ornamental sword that always seem to be handily available in the movies. Not even a baseball bat—I've never understood the utility of having one if you're not going to play baseball, although Sharon is an advocate of the old Louisville Slugger as a defensive weapon. I could have taken off the bicycle's front wheel and used it as a discus, I sup-pose, but that would have been very noisy, and in all likelihood would have succeeded only in making me look silly.

I stopped breathing about five feet from the corner, and tried to move even more slowly. Through the heavy knit hat, I could hear voices—more than one, for sure—in the living room. Just a few more inches now, and I'd be able to see . . .

Seated on the humiliating furniture in my living room were my parents, Meg Vidal, and Leo Munson. The floor was completely free of discarded DVDs and videocassettes, and the futon cover, which had been slashed and gutted, was gone, replaced by extra pillows and blankets from my bedroom closet. The answering machine was back in its traditional place, and the red light was, in accordance with tradition, not blinking.

"For crissakes," I said, "you people almost gave me a coronary."

15

IT took a while to sort out the various stories, but after the initial shock, I wasn't averse to sitting and listening for a while. Made me glad I didn't own a baseball bat, because I most certainly would have ended up cracking the skull of someone who was just trying to do me a good turn.

What had happened was:

Meg (who had, after all, told me she'd be at my place, if only I still had a working mind) had decided, until such time as a formal agreement could be drafted to "lend" her to the Midland Heights police, to make my town *home* her base of operations, so she could use the phone, fax, and computer. She'd have done so at Comedy Tonight, but she also wanted to feel her fingers and toes again, and the current state of our heating system wouldn't allow that. But before she could leave the theatre, she'd been accosted by Leo Munson, patron saint/eternal pest of Comedy Tonight, who was there to see if we'd have a showing that evening. Leo has an eye for the ladies.

On hearing about the mess that had been made of my prized comedy collection, Leo volunteered to come by and try to sort it out, something Meg would never have been able to do on her own. She's a lovely woman and a smart cop, but she doesn't know her Wheeler and Woolsey from her Martin and Lewis. Meg was happy to have the help, and gave Leo a ride to the town house.

Dad had lent her his key to the town house. But when you engage Dad in anything, Mom finds out about it, and while she doesn't often descend upon my business or my home (preferring to pretend that Sharon and I are still married, and I'm simply between jobs), when she heard that two people were about to visit my home without me (and, I can only assume, horrified by the thought of what must surely be living in my refrigerator in place of food), she hopped—as well as Mom hops these days—into her car and headed for the town house, stopping along the way at a deli that makes sandwiches by the pound. No matter what else Meg and Leo were to find at my house, they would certainly encounter heartburn.

I was told there was a half a salami on rye in the fridge, which would otherwise be sent to Africa to feed an entire village of starving people. I decided to spare the villagers the dangers of excess cholesterol, and was eating part of the sandwich as I gathered all the previous information. This took longer than you might think, as no one in the room was at all shy about interrupting when a detail was missed or a possible punch line wasn't being properly accentuated. It was quite a group performance.

"I can't stand it," my mother said, to no one in particular. If she'd really been up to her usual form, it would have been a performance worthy of the Yiddish theatre, or at least an early Charlie Chaplin movie, with her hand to her forehead and some serious "oy vey," to go with the moan. But I understood. I was worn out, too.

I had to get up and move around to keep from falling asleep, and I didn't want to fall asleep with guests in the house. "You did a huge job here, Leo," I said, admiring the way he'd organized the comedy collection.

"I never saw so many movies in one place before, Elliot,"

he said, his voice just a little too excited, like he was trying to think of a way to come back and watch lots of those movies whenever he wanted. "You didn't have an inventory or anything, so I had to improvise."

I shook my head with some admiration. "You did a better job than I did the first time," I told him. I don't know why it had never occurred to me to organize by decade as well as by comedian.

Suddenly, I remembered: "Meg, you said you found something out."

Meg nodded. "It doesn't answer anything, but it might help. There were some new hits on Sharon's card—her debit card, this time."

"That sounds more like Sharon," I said. "She hates owing people money, even MasterCard. Where were they?"

"First, a parking receipt at the hotel where she had the drink with your mystery man," Meg answered. "Then, at a Sunoco station on the New Jersey Turnpike."

Everyone else in the room, myself included, asked, "What exit?" We Jerseyans measure everything in exits.

"It was at fifteen-W, just where the turnpike meets Route Two-Eighty," Meg said. "Then, there was a debit of seventy-eight dollars, at a supermarket in Tunkhannock, Pennsylvania, late this afternoon."

Tunkhannock! There was something about that name . . . and then I got it.

Meg Vidal's eyes narrowed. "You know why she's there, don't you?" she said.

"I don't know why, but I might know where," I admitted. "Sharon's family has a vacation house, a cottage really, near there, in a town called Lake Carey. She used to go there when we first met, especially during her residency, when things got too heavy for her to handle. So I've got to go up there."

"Why don't you tell Barry?" Meg asked.

"Because I don't want the local cops going up and asking her what she's doing. I don't want this to be about how everyone here is freaking out over her not being around. And if

Peabody Public Library
Columbia City, IN

she's up there dealing with guilt over Russell Chapman, I want her to hear from me that he might not be dead."

"What if she's not alone?" Meg wanted to know.

I'd thought of that. "If I see any evidence that she's being held against her will, I'll call the police. Can I borrow someone's cell phone? I'll make sure to case the cottage from outside before I ever consider going in."

"What if she's not alone *intentionally*?" Meg asked.

I hadn't thought of that one, and wished I didn't have to now. "Then I'll turn around and come back, without ever going inside. Either way, if you don't hear from me within four hours after I leave, call the local cops."

Mom lowered her head a little and bit her bottom lip. "You're going up there now?" she asked.

I nodded. "But I'm going to need a car," I said.

"I'll drive you," she said.

"No, you won't. I need to do this alone."

My mother gave me a look.

Did I mention she's really good at the passive-aggressive stuff?

16

SUNDAY

"IF you get a speeding ticket, will it show up on your record or mine?"

My mother was white-knuckling the passenger's door handle because I was daring to exceed the speed limit on Route 287 heading north in her 1992 Oldsmobile Toronado, a car so large you could land aircraft on its roof. I had insisted on driving for this very reason: With Mom behind the wheel, we'd get there sometime in February, instead of making the trip in, according to MapQuest, two hours and forty-three minutes. MapQuest is very specific about such things.

I had tried—believe me—to avoid this lineup. I have a friendly arrangement with Moe Baxter, the Midland Heights magician of body work and mechanics, to test drive cars whose repairs he's completed when I need a ride somewhere, and I suggested to my mother that I call Moe. But it was barely daybreak when we set out, and my arrangement with Moe isn't *that* friendly.

"Don't worry, Mom. I'll take the rap for you." You can go ninety on Route 287 if the traffic is flowing, and still make the case that you're just keeping up with the pack. I've seen state troopers go for that argument.

Meg had offered to come along, too, but I'd declined, saying I wanted her at my home base in case any other information came in while I was out, and that she could call Mom's cell phone (yes, my mother is more technologically advanced than I am) if necessary. What I didn't say was that it would be better if the law enforcement officer was not along for the ride should I have to commit breaking and entering, or any other infraction she might otherwise feel compelled to report. Meg hadn't put up much of an argument.

Dad decided to stay at the town house and try to get some sleep—he wanted to be back in the theatre supervising repairs as soon as possible. Leo made noises about going home until I told him that as payment for his hard work, he could watch as many movies as he liked on the flat-screen TV until I got back. I thought that might annoy Meg, but she grinned at the thought, and said she'd see if IHOP does take-out (turns out they do). Leo and Meg were starting to bond over my movie collection and simple carbohydrates.

By the time we were on Route 80, I asked Mom to try calling Sharon again. As had become the custom, Sharon's voice mail picked up immediately, only to say it was full and we should "try again later." It had been worth a shot.

The knot that had been growing in my stomach for three days tightened just a little bit.

What if I found Sharon with another guy? It had happened before, after all, so I had a set of behaviors I could kick back into gear. But this time, I would be the ex-husband, not the current husband, and that meant less righteous indignation, mostly because I had no right to any kind of indignation. Sharon was divorcing Gregory and, despite our plans to go to dinner on our wedding anniversary, was not planning on returning to me. She was a free agent—as was I, theoretically. What if I found out that she was off on a romantic weekend? That would make for a jolly two-hour-and-forty-three-minute drive back to Midland Heights, wouldn't it?

"Do you want to stop for breakfast?" my mother asked.

I chose to ignore the question, and pondered—very briefly—how much the gas this thing was guzzling would cost to replace.

"Breakfast?" Mom repeated.

"Mom. We're on a mission. We're trying to find Sharon. This is not an afternoon visit with Aunt Selma, okay?" She was puncturing my sense of purpose, somehow.

"Of course," Mom answered. "I was just asking."

Stopping for breakfast only added an hour to the trip. I didn't eat anything, partly because my stomach was still in motion and partly because I could give the ol' passive-aggression myself when pushed, and I wanted Mom to know I wasn't happy about the pit stop. I called Meg from the diner to let her know the clock was on pause while we were off the road, and she didn't have to call the Lake Carey police just yet.

Mom ate, I had a soda, and when the bill came, I snatched it from the table faster than Mom could reach. She protested, but possession of the check is better than nine-tenths of the law, and besides, her arms were too short to grab it out of my hand. Score one round for me.

Then I realized I had virtually no cash on me. I couldn't concede the victory to my mother (this passive-aggressive thing is really inconvenient at both ends), so I took out my "last resort" credit card and handed it to the waitress. Score round two for me.

Moments later, the waitress returned, saying my credit card had been declined, and she was required to destroy it rather than return it to me. Idiot that I am, I'd forgotten the credit card company had cancelled the card when Dutton and I called about the charges in New York. They were mailing me a new one, which I was sure would be a comfort to me in five years, when I'd want to use a credit card again.

Game, set, and match to Mom, who grinned broadly while paying, and then got in a good couple of lecture points on maintaining a healthy credit score. And I'd thought this was going to be a difficult trip.

Back in the car, Mom read from the MapQuest directions, and after a few eternities, we finally reached Tunkhannock.

I knew my way around from years before. Sharon had taken me up to this spot a number of times early on in our marriage, even when she didn't need to get over a bad day or an especially difficult diagnosis.

Lake Carey is just that: a lake, with houses ringing it. Most of them are strictly for summer vacations, but some, like the one belonging to Sharon's mother's family, were winterized and usable year-round. I approached the house slowly, and not just because I suddenly wasn't in a hurry to see what I had driven all this way to see.

There is no garage behind the house, but there is a driveway, and sort of a carport area that opens to the kitchen door in the back. I parked Mom's car in front of the house next door, so that I wouldn't be detected if someone were watching from inside the house.

"This is it?" my mother asked, ever the arbiter of what is and is not acceptable. She seemed to think that a hundred-year-old lake house should look like I. M. Pei had just gotten finished with it.

"Yeah. This is it. Now, let's not talk for a while. You stay here, and . . ."

She was already opening the car door. "I didn't ride all the way up here to sit in the car," my mother said.

I love my mother I love my mother I love my mother . . .

No vehicles were in the driveway, but the frozen ground showed tire tracks. I'm no expert, but they weren't especially large, and didn't have a very wide tread. I was guessing they weren't from an SUV, at least not one of your more absurdly macho ones. They could have been from Sharon's Volvo.

I felt foolish keeping my head down as I walked toward the rear of the house. It was so *Man from U.N.C.L.E.,* but it couldn't be helped. I didn't want to be seen through the windows before I was ready.

Luckily, Mom is small enough that she wouldn't be seen from the windows if she were walking on stilts.

"Why aren't you going to the front door?" she asked, much more loudly than I would have liked (in fact, having asked her not to talk, *any* volume was much more loudly than I would have liked).

"Mom!" I hissed. *"Keep your voice down! I'm not ringing the doorbell because if Sharon's being held here, I don't want to alert anyone that we're here!"*

"Oh, that's just silly," my mother said. But she followed me up the driveway.

The ground floor of the cottage is essentially two rooms: a front room with a fireplace and some old, beat-up furniture (no television, and therefore no movies: I always felt that spending time here was a way of showing Sharon how much I loved her); and the kitchen, with its picnic-style table and benches, a stove that Julia Child had probably watched her grandmother cook on, a refrigerator that could keep things slightly cool, and about one-tenth the necessary amount of countertop and cabinet space. Anorexics couldn't get by on the amount of food you could store here.

We crept (only one of us intentionally) up onto the carport to look through the kitchen window, which was closed (of course) and locked. There wasn't anyone in the room, and no food or cleaning products out on the counters. From this viewpoint, there was no sign anyone was here now, or had been for some time.

"Isn't spying on people illegal?" Mom asked, once again in a voice that could be heard in the third balcony. Ethel Merman herself would have been envious.

I ignored her.

I walked around to the far side of the house (thinking as I did of the Monty Python bit where an older woman shows a younger woman photos and narrates "this is your uncle behind the house; this is your uncle on the side of the house," only to have her younger relative tear up each snapshot as it is handed to her) and found two tires in the driveway next door.

Mom was content to wait on the back porch, as she said it was "ridiculous" to do anything but go through the front door. It took five minutes of tense whispering (on my part) and passive-aggressive braying (need I say?) to convince her not to go back around and knock. I told her I'd be right back.

The owner of the house next door had clearly boarded up for the winter and gone home, so I was relatively sure he wouldn't mind if I used his spare tires (on rims) to boost myself into a position where I could see through the window. And if he did, I could point out that using such old tires on any moving vehicle would probably result in a horrible crash, so I was probably saving the poor man's life.

This is how my mind works, and yes, it is sad.

With the added height from the tires, I could see through the downstairs window into the front room.

But I didn't see Sharon. Or anyone else, for that matter. From this angle, the fireplace didn't appear to have any ashes in it, and there would surely have been some temptation to light a fire for anyone staying there recently. The house was winterized, but it wasn't exactly cozy. A nice fire would help neutralize the chill.

I could tell there was no one in the room, but I couldn't see into every corner from here, and dragging the tires from window to window seemed a less-than-efficient plan. It was time to do something that would make Meg happy she hadn't come along.

In the driveway, near the tires' original resting place, was a cinder block, undoubtedly used as a jack-substitute for whatever rent-a-wreck the owner of the house had taken the tires from. I hefted it; too heavy and bulky to be of real use. There had to be something else . . . There!

It was a cliché, but an effective one. A nice handy rock, just the right size and weight. I don't know why, but I wrapped it in my pocket handkerchief.

Normally (as if there were a "normally" in this situation), I'd have gone in through the kitchen, but I knew there was an alarm system attached to that door, so entering that way would have made a racket.

Instead, I stood about ten feet from the side of the house, wound up like Sandy Koufax, and hurled the rock through the window. When no alarm sounded (apparently there had been no security upgrades since I'd last been here), I climbed up carefully on the tires and knocked in the remaining pieces of glass with my elbow. Then, gingerly, I unlocked the latch, raised the frame, and climbed through the window.

I was careful not to kill myself on the broken glass inside, but there really wasn't very much. Getting back to my feet, I scraped myself slightly on the left forefinger, but it barely bled.

The room was empty, as I'd thought it would be. For one thing, any people who had been inside would surely have come to investigate what the breaking glass was all about. I took a look around the room—mystery books; fireplace (indeed without ashes); pile of firewood, about half full; over-stuffed chairs from the Johnson Administration (not sure if it was Lyndon or Andrew); and a throw rug that, if there had been sense, would have been thrown—away—long ago. No people, nor signs of people.

Except my mother.

"Didn't I say you should wait back there?" I asked.

"I got tired of waiting. My leg hurts."

"How did you get in here?" I whispered.

Mom pointed. "Through the back door, in the kitchen."

My voice caught a time or two. "There's . . . there's an *alarm* on that door."

She shrugged. "It didn't go off." Then she looked at my hand, and at the broken glass on the floor. "Elliot! Did you break the window?"

I ignored that. I was working on my ignoring skills. Perhaps I could be the captain of the Ignoring Team at the next Olympics.

There was no one downstairs, clearly, or they would have sent a welcoming committee because of all that had been going on. I knew the house, and all that I'd find upstairs would be three bedrooms.

"This time, I'm going to insist," I told my mother. "You stay down here."

She thought about it, but after a moment said, "With my knees? Naturally. I'll be the—what do you call it?—the lookout."

Having left the Jewish Squanto in the living room, where she took a book off the shelf and leaned on the easy chair (far too dusty for her to sit on), I crept up the stairs as slowly as I could, because the stairs creaked like my grandmother's knees on a rainy day, except they didn't yell "oy." (To be fair, Grandma's knees didn't yell "oy," either, but they caused the yelling, and that was close enough.) I winced with each stair, and it felt like an hour before I made it to the landing. I'd given serious thought to giving up somewhere around stair number seven, but plodded on, trying very hard not to break into a sweat, breathe audibly, or throw up before I achieved the summit.

There were three bedroom doors, and they were all closed. I heard no moaning coming from behind any of them, of either the excited or tortured variety.

I searched all three bedrooms, and to spare you the gory details, each one was empty, although one was somewhat less dusty than the other two. It was a relief to have found no one holding my ex-wife hostage, and I had to admit, not to find her Evelyn Wood speed-reading through the *Kama Sutra* with some guy she might have just met. But I was back to square one: Sharon was still missing.

The trip downstairs took considerably less time than the one upstairs had taken. I didn't have to worry about finding anyone in the house this time.

So it was really a surprise to discover the two police officers in the front room when I hit the landing. That was bad enough, but the guns they were pointing at me were even more disturbing.

"Nice looking out, Mom," I said.

"Didn't I say you shouldn't have broken the window?" my mother answered.

17

PROBABLY the best tactic here was to treat them to a smile. They can smell fear. "Hello, officers," I said.

"Please put your hands behind your head and don't take another step, sir," the officer closer to me barked. Apparently, he was trying to take a bite out of crime.

"I just came in through the back door," my mother said.

"Can you tell me why you're pointing your weapons at me?" I asked, putting my hands exactly where he suggested.

The lead cop holstered his weapon while the other kept his trained on my head, which was an improvement, but not much of one. He found a pair of zip strips—the white plastic handcuffs that are all the rage in the cop biz these days—on his belt, and took first my right hand, and then my left, and tied them up like a Christmas present.

"Sir, what is your name?"

I told him. "Why are you arresting me?" I asked. He hadn't started to read me my rights yet, but the handcuffs were a dead giveaway. I had an urge to ask why he wasn't arresting my mother, but that seemed to be in poor taste.

"We're taking you in for questioning, sir," the cop said. He was maybe twenty-four on a good day, and still practiced in what they'd taught him at the academy.

"Questioning? About what?"

"We'll tell you at the station, sir," the cop said.

His partner, seeing my hands bound by plastic, put his gun away.

"I don't understand," I tried. "Should I be calling my attorney?"

"I think your cousin Herbie is in Acapulco on vacation," said Mom, pulling out her cell phone, "but I can call."

"Why are you here, sir?" The second cop had decided he could speak now.

"I'm looking for my ex-wife," I said. "I thought she might be up here. Her family owns the house."

They opened the front door with the apparent intention of leading me out and putting me in the police car. I was determined not to let that happen unless I had no choice, but it was starting to look that way.

"Just a second," I said. "Why are you here? Did someone call? Did you hear from Dr. Simon-Freed?"

"My Sharon," Mom moaned. Perhaps the cops would appreciate her suffering.

No luck; the cops were trying out for the Ignoring Team, too. "All I know is, we got a call from a resident across the lake that someone was breaking into this house," the second cop, slightly older and less vehement, said. "And sure enough, there's broken glass right by that open window."

I chuckled. "Yeah, I forgot my keys, can you believe it? And I was concerned about my ex, so I decided to . . . Across the lake? Somebody saw me from all the way *across the lake*?"

"The guy has a telescope, apparently."

"That's rude," Mom said.

Great. Now I was self-conscious about the times Sharon and I had spent up here alone. "I just needed to get into the house, and I didn't have a key," I reiterated.

Neither cop was buying it. "Come along now, sir, and we'll

get this all straightened out down at the station," the older one said. They started to move me toward the door again.

Not that I minded the odd trip to jail now and then, but I really didn't have time for this today. "Look, fellas, this is all very innocent," I said. "Do we really have to spend all this time and make you fill out all that paperwork? Can't we just straighten it out here?"

"Are you trying to bribe us?" the younger cop asked. He looked like he'd been waiting to say that all his life.

"*No*, I'm not trying to bribe you. I'm just saying, you'll have to fill out lots of reports. Just let me tell you what happened." I know cops hate filling out forms.

The older cop rolled his eyes a bit at his partner's behavior, but he shook his head slightly. "We have to do the paperwork whether we arrest you or not," he said. "Nice try, though."

"Look," I said to him, ignoring the younger cop entirely, "you can see I haven't stolen anything. I haven't damaged anything, except the window. And that was just because . . . Officer, please. My ex-wife is missing. I'm seriously worried about her, and I . . . I guess I wasn't using my best judgment. I had to see if she was okay." I don't like to admit it, but I think my eyes were starting to moisten.

I'm willing to bet the older cop would have cut the cuffs off at that moment, but the younger one said, "You're breakin' my heart, pal. But you divorced her for a reason, right?"

"She divorced me."

"Imagine that."

They moved me toward the door, and my secret weapon finally became useful. Mom stood up.

"You're not *really* going to arrest my son, are you?" she asked.

The cuffs were off in seconds.

The cops made sure I cleaned up the broken glass and plugged the hole in the window with some paneling I found in the crawl-space under the kitchen. Then they led Mom and me outside, and watched us get into my car. They followed us to the town limits, which was just about the time Mom's cell phone rang.

The cops were watching, and I didn't want to get fined for using a cell phone while driving, so I pulled over when Mom told me it was Meg.

"She wasn't here, but I think she might have been recently," I told her.

"Well, she hasn't shown up here, either," Meg said. "But there has been a development." And my adrenaline started its roller-coaster trip around my body again.

"What kind of development?" I asked as casually as I could.

"Mr. Chapman's lawyer called," Meg said. "She got a call from him last night. He's alive."

18

THE drive back to Midland Heights was pretty much like the drive up to Lake Carey. I wasn't thinking much about the road, and my speed was probably ten to twenty miles an hour faster than I normally would do in any borrowed car, let alone Mom's ancient Olds. But she didn't make me stop for food this time, and we were back at Comedy Tonight in about two and a half hours, just in time to watch Sophie scowling at having to set up for the matinee.

"There aren't enough hours in the day," she said when Mom and I walked in. "Do you think I have time to do my job and yours and still get through two separate practice tests in the next twenty-four hours?"

"No, I don't," I answered, and kept walking, despite her annoyed cries of "Elliot!" as I found Meg and Dad at the entrance doors to the auditorium. Mom gave me a look that indicated her disapproval of the way I treated Sophie, but I ignored it. I took a mental inventory: Anthony would be in the projection booth, and Jonathan was probably cleaning up the auditorium.

Dad hugged me, something he'd been doing more often

lately, and said, "Nothing?" I shook my head and turned toward Meg. I told her our story. Even the part about almost being arrested, which led to a cry of "I can't leave you alone for a minute," something I'm used to hearing from my mother, but not a homicide detective. My mother, to my right, just rolled her eyes and let her face speak volumes on the embarrassment and suffering she endured on my account.

"She was there," I said. "Sharon was at the lake house. Recently. Maybe yesterday."

"Sharon?" Dad said, his eyes widening. "How do you know?"

"One of the rooms wasn't covered in dust," I said. "The rest of the place looked like Vincent Price's dungeon."

Mom made a face. "That's disgusting."

I decided to ignore that, too, and talked to Meg again. "She was there. I don't know how recently, or if she was alone or not, but she was there."

"You should have told that to the cops," Meg said. "They could be on the lookout for her now."

"I couldn't risk it. Next thing you know, they'd be accusing me of chopping her up and dumping the body in the lake. I couldn't give them an excuse to hold me there."

"Elliot!" my mother said. I put an arm around her shoulder, and she looked at me like I must be in need of some strong mood-altering drugs.

"I'll call them in an hour or so," Meg said. "If there's a chance they can find Sharon up there, we should take it."

"Tell me about Chapman," I said.

Sophie had turned the "closed" sign in the front window to "open," so a few people were starting to drift in for the early show of *Sullivan's Travels*. I half expected to see Martin Tovarich come back for a second viewing, just to get his mojo back, but he didn't arrive. When customers started reaching the auditorium doors, I motioned my posse (as I was now thinking of them) back toward the office door. We couldn't all sit, or, for that matter, enter, but we could be out of the way near there.

"All I know is, the word came in to Barry Dutton either late last night or early this morning," Meg said. "Chapman's lawyer, a woman named Angie Hogencamp, called the county prosecutor to let him know Chapman had gotten in touch with her over a legal matter, so that meant he was alive. She'd spoken to Chapman himself, and there was no mistake."

I hadn't slept nor eaten in a long time (my exercise in teaching my mother a lesson had been a miscalculation, I was realizing), and my brain didn't seem to be functioning at its normal level. "Is it me, or does that not add up? Why didn't Dutton send someone out to see Chapman when he got the call?"

"It's not his jurisdiction," Meg said. "No crime was committed in Midland Heights. The East Brunswick cops have been investigating, so they might have gone, or the prosecutor may have sent an investigator, but I don't know that for sure."

"What about Sharon?" my mother insisted. "What does this do for her?"

"Not very much, Mom," I told her. "We still don't know where she is, or why."

"At least she's not a murder suspect anymore," my father offered. Dad is a walking ray of sunshine.

But there was a walking veil of darkness approaching from the left, and it had a voice. "Yes, she is," said the voice.

Lillian Chapman Mayer, resplendent in a black business suit, had slithered into the theatre when nobody was looking, and stood, hands-on-hips, surveying us with the same expression I imagined she'd give Charles Manson if he'd decided to drop by for an evening's entertainment.

"So this is where you work," she said to me, with what I perceived to be a sneer in her voice. (I don't often get to hear genuine sneers, so I might be out of practice.) "It's cozy."

"I don't care for that word," I answered. "I like *inviting*."

Meg gave me a questioning look. "This is Lillian *Chapman* Mayer," I said to the group. "We met at Sharon's practice yesterday morning."

"And you were rude, and didn't tell me who you were until it was too late," Lillian added.

"Nonsense. I merely pointed out that you don't stop talking very often. You must have been vaccinated with a phonograph needle." Groucho. If you steal, steal from the best.

"Elliot!" My mother, more offended than Lillian Chapman, would have swooned or taken the vapors if she'd been a Southern woman. Instead, she was from Eastern European stock (by way of the Bronx), and with her delicate constitution, could no doubt have pulled a plow through the lobby if that had become necessary. Luckily, it did not.

Dad, ever the diplomat (salesmen are peacemakers by nature, and Dad was an excellent salesman: never pushy, always ingratiating), shifted the conversation back into drive. "What brings you here, Mrs. Mayer?" he asked.

Meg tried to bring order where there was no order; that's *her* nature. "There's no point in looking for Dr. Simon-Freed here," she said. "We have no idea where she is."

"Yeah, she's flown the coop; my sister told me that," Lillian responded. "Just a little suspicious, don't you think? Right after the doctor gave my father a death sentence that she knew was wrong, she disappeared."

I considered pointing out that Lillian herself could disappear without making much of a dent in America, but Meg was quicker—and saner—than me. "I don't think it's relevant," she said. "We were told your father is still alive, so the doctor's whereabouts don't have anything to do with him."

Lillian actually smiled. She looked like Mr. Burns on *The Simpsons*. I think I preferred her *not* smiling.

Finally, I drew in my breath, swallowed, and said, "Miss Chapman, shouldn't you be plotting the end of civilization at your evil lair? Why aren't you visiting the father you thought you'd lost? Now that your inheritance isn't imminent, aren't you his loving daughter anymore?"

Meg and my mother shot me exactly the same look; it was eerie.

"It was important I see your face when I tell you this, Mr. Freed," Lillian said. "My father's body was discovered in his study this afternoon at one. The medical examiner is still investigating, but it appears that his throat was cut. With a scalpel."

19

"OH, yeah," Chief Barry Dutton said. "I knew there was something I'd forgotten to tell you."

I sat in his visitor's chair, a municipal mail-order beauty of chrome and vinyl, squeezing my eyes with my thumb and forefinger. Maybe if I pressed hard enough, I could push each eye into the opposite socket and see life differently. "Something you'd forgotten to tell me?" I asked. "Is that the police version of wit?"

"Let's recap a little," Dutton said, leaning back in his chair and putting his hands behind his head, lacing the fingers. "You chose not to mention that you drove up to some postage-stamp town in Pennsylvania looking for a woman whose disappearance we're investigating, that you broke into a house and damn near got yourself arrested, that you discovered something you chose *not* to tell the officers at that postage-stamp town in Pennsylvania, and now you're chiding *me* about not promptly disclosing everything I have no obligation to tell you?"

I stopped rubbing my eyes and fixed my sleep-deprived, bloodshot gaze on him. Both of him. "Chiding?" I asked.

"Don't change the subject."

I put my head down on his desk. I realized that I hadn't really slept since . . . Thursday. That seemed a very long time, now. "You're right," I said. "I should have told you all that stuff. I had reasons I didn't, and at the time, they seemed really good."

"Apology accepted. When Meg gets back from the prosecutor's office, I might even let you stay in the room."

I didn't answer. Since I wasn't looking at Dutton (or anything except the insides of my eyelids), I can't be sure, but I think he actually stood and leaned over the desk to see if I was asleep. "Elliot, I've never seen you like this," he said.

His desk tasted like furniture polish. "Due respect, Chief, you haven't known me very long. *I've* never seen me like this."

"You've got to pull yourself together," he said. "Sharon wouldn't want you to . . ."

My head popped up off his desk like it was on a spring. "Don't you do that!" I shouted. "Don't talk about her like she's dead!"

Dutton's eyes widened, for about a third of a second. He nodded slowly, then leaned forward, elbows on his desk. "You're right. I shouldn't have done that. There's absolutely no reason to think she's in any danger at all."

"That's better." I realized I was acting like a petulant eight-year-old, and I didn't care. "Don't let it happen again."

"I won't." And I believed him. Dutton inspires confidence, and I've never seen him do anything he said he wouldn't. I tried to remember if I had him on my holiday card list. His eyes were still moving around a little, as he tried to think of how to deal with this wreck of a man before him.

"What's going on with Russell Chapman?" I asked him, mumbling. "Is he dead? Is he alive? Is he a zombie?"

"He's dead, all right." Meg Vidal must have entered through Dutton's office door. I hadn't opened my eyes, so I couldn't tell you when. "The ME made a positive identification. He's dead, and he's got a big slit in his neck that's not attractive."

"You saw him?" Dutton asked.

"No, but I saw pictures."

"I don't get it," I said. "The guy's dead. Then we *think* he's dead, but he's missing. Then he's alive, because he calls his lawyer. Then he's dead again. I can't keep up."

"What do we know about the lawyer?" Meg asked Dutton. I didn't see her, but I could be sure she wasn't asking me.

"She's a perfectly legitimate estate planner working in Spotswood," Dutton said. "I've never heard a word about her that wasn't professional and efficient, and I've dealt with her before. She called because she didn't want to be involved in whatever deception there was regarding Chapman being dead when he wasn't."

"And now he is," Meg said. "Again."

"And Sharon's back on the suspect list," I said. "She probably wasn't at the lake house when Chapman died, if it was today." I raised my head. A little. "Do we know when Chapman died this time?"

"His daughter Gwen found him in the study at one this afternoon," Meg said. "ME isn't done yet, but thinks it was between six and eleven in the morning when he died."

"I'd forgotten how nice it is to have a competent detective on staff," Dutton said. "I might hire you full-time, Meg."

"You don't have enough homicides," she said.

"Nonsense. We have one wherever Elliot goes."

Dutton thought I'd laugh at that, but I wasn't in the mood to be amused. "What about Sharon?" I moaned. "This gets worse every minute."

"You sound like your mother," Meg told me.

Suddenly, it occurred to me again that sleeping wasn't the only thing I hadn't done since Thursday. "I think I need food," I told Dutton.

"Come on. I'm buying."

BELINDA McElvoy, the brilliant, beautiful waitress at Big Herbs, took one look at me as Dutton and I sat down and shook her head. "My god, Elliot, you look like you've been hit by a bus. I guess there's no news about the doc yet?"

I shook my head. "Everybody in this town knows everything about everybody else, don't they?" I asked her.

"Not everybody. Just me." Belinda could see that I was in no condition to read a menu, so she said, "How about a nice veggie burger, Elliot? If they cook it long enough and put lots of toppings on it, you can't tell it's really seaweed." Big Herbs is a vegetarian restaurant, but Belinda is a steak-and-potatoes (with a side order of steak) kind of girl.

"Sounds great," I said. "Are the fries real?"

"Potato's a vegetable, isn't it?"

Dutton asked for a Caesar salad, and Belinda was off to put through a rush order.

Meg had begged off, saying she was going back to the town house to pry Leo away from my video collection and maybe get a little Internet research done. Meg doesn't always tell you everything she's thinking, but I got the impression she'd had an idea about Sharon she needed to track down, and didn't want to get my hopes up.

"What do you think it means, Chief?" I asked. "Why would Russell Chapman pretend to be dead? Or was someone pretending to be Russell Chapman when he was already dead?"

"Slow down," Dutton said. "We don't even know if the body in the morgue *is* Chapman this time. We don't know that it wasn't the *first* time. You could fill an encyclopedia with what we don't know."

"I'll tell you the truth, Chief," I said. "I don't care who killed Russell Chapman. I never met Russell Chapman. For all I know, the guy was a heartless swine. I only care about Chapman as his case relates to Sharon's. And it has to relate, somehow."

"We don't know that until there's more evidence," Dutton said.

"Glad to make your acquaintance, Mr. Holmes," I said. "May I call you Sherlock?" Dutton made a face that said *droll*.

"Do you know the detective who took the lead in East Brunswick?" I asked him.

"Yeah. His name's Kowalski, and he's good. If there are any ties to Sharon, he'll call me."

Belinda brought the plates over. I could tell she'd given me extra fries and she placed a chocolate milk shake I hadn't ordered on the table next to my plate. I almost said something about it, but she was gone before I could open my mouth.

"Some people like you," Dutton said.

"I've never been able to figure out why," I told him.

Dutton nodded. "Don't think too hard. You'll hurt your head."

I covered the burger with as many different toppings as the table would hold, and then concentrated on eating the fries. Through a mouth full of potato, I said to Dutton, "I don't get it. A guy leaves a suicide note on Thursday and then dies Sunday morning? He didn't cut his own throat, did he? What did the note say, anyway?"

"Why should I even . . ." Dutton looked at me for a moment, and decided to skip the argument. "Basically, it said that he couldn't live with the idea of a long, protracted illness, that he didn't want to be a burden to his children, and that this was the best way."

"Did he sign the note?"

"Nope. It was on the computer screen in his study, right next to the open terrace doors. Open terrace doors, in this weather."

"I guess it didn't matter if he was cold. So, if Chapman was alive last night, that means the dead guy Gwen identified in the morgue wasn't him, right? So who was it? And how did the body get lost? It's one thing to have a clerical error with the toe tags, but to lose an entire corpse?"

"You'd be amazed," Dutton said. "The things I've seen go missing. There was this toe, once . . ."

"Chief. I'm eating."

I swallowed, and drank some of the shake. It was delicious (I'm sure Belinda made it herself), but I was going to need coffee soon if I would make it through two complete double features. "Chief," I said, "something's been bothering me."

"Just one thing?" Dutton speared a crouton.

"Suppose Sharon *isn't* just out there on her own. Suppose she's *not* just trying to get over the Chapman thing."

He frowned. The chief had already lived through one of my pre-adolescent outbursts at the suggestion that all wasn't right with my ex, and now I seemed to be setting him up for another, in a public place. He clearly had to consider how to respond honestly, without prompting a meltdown. "Okay, I'll suppose. I don't think that's the case, but I'll suppose. What are you getting at, Elliot?" Nice dodging. The man was a pro.

"If that's true, and Sharon is being held against her will, we have to concentrate on the people who are angry enough at her to do her harm."

"The Chapman family has been under a certain amount of surveillance since this began," Dutton said. "None of them has been doing anything other than what a family does when they're preparing for a funeral. The son-in-law is on his way back from Japan, and should be at Newark Airport in about four hours. And Chapman's wife, the girls' mother, died five years ago, of liver cancer. Believe me, Elliot, they're not acting like people who have a woman held hostage somewhere."

"I wasn't thinking of the Chapmans," I said.

20

IT'S amazing how few Konigsbergs there were in the Yellow Pages under "Investigators." But once I got past the voice mail and the answering service and the phone rang, Allen Konigsberg sounded friendly enough. A little oily, and I found myself wiping off the earpiece of the phone every now and again, but with private investigators, this sort of thing is to be expected.

"Mr. Freed," he said. "Tell me how I can help."

"First of all, sorry to bother you on a Sunday, but this couldn't wait."

"I understand completely," Konigsberg, ever the businessman, had a concerned tone. "Please, tell me what I can do."

"I understand you did some work for Lillian Mayer recently," I began.

He sounded pleased. "Yes, I did. Did Ms. Mayer recommend me?"

"Sort of. I need to know what you found out about her father possibly having an affair with my ex-wife."

The smile in his voice faded, as he realized that no new business was coming his way today, and on a Sunday to boot.

"That's confidential," Konigsberg said. "I can't tell you anything about that."

"Dr. Simon-Freed is missing," I said.

"Would you like me to find her for you?"

"I trust the police, and they're looking," I said. "But I need to know why Lillian Mayer thinks Sharon was fooling around with her father."

"Sorry."

Jonathan ambled by my office door, inadvertently reminding me to keep my voice down. "Listen," I said, breathing just a little too heavily. "A woman I care about a great deal hasn't been heard from since Thursday, and you have information that might help clear that up. You're going to tell me what you found, or I'm going to become unreasonable."

Konigsberg laughed. "Are you threatening me?"

"You don't know me, Mr. Konigsberg. These might be the only circumstances in my life to this point for which the answer to that question would be yes. And believe me, I'm in a state where I don't care anymore. You can sue me, you can threaten to have me arrested. But before the cops come and haul me away, I'm going to find out what you have on my ex-wife."

He considered. "I'll tell you what," he said. "I've done a lot of divorce work. I've testified at a lot of divorce hearings. But you are the first ex-husband I've ever heard of who cares that much about the woman who took him for half of what he owns." I didn't feel the need to tell him that it had been the other way around; it felt like things were starting to go my way in this conversation. "I shouldn't do this . . ." Konigsberg hesitated.

"Here's what I know. Every week for three months, Russell Chapman drove from his house in East Brunswick to your ex's practice in Midland Heights. He got there at six thirty, exactly, because that was when the office closed. I didn't follow him in, because the office is small, and he'd have seen me. But I parked across the street every week, and took some pictures.

"He came out with a woman, every time, and they took Chapman's car. They were, let's say, tastefully affectionate. Nothing overly physical. He drove her, every week, to the Hyatt Hotel in New Brunswick, where they would have dinner and then go up to a room Chapman booked in his own name.

"Sometimes they'd come down a couple of hours later, and once or twice they spent the night. Chambermaid said they ordered the odd bottle of champagne from room service, and the bed was always well worn when they left. They were not up there discussing real estate deals or playing gin rummy."

"Are you sure the woman was Sharon?" I asked.

"She was the only doctor at the office a few of the nights I saw them," he said. "I have pictures, which you're *not* going to see, but even from a distance, it's clear that the woman sure as hell isn't the hot-as-a-pistol receptionist."

"There are other women who work there."

"Yes, there are," Konigsberg answered. "But the fact is, last Thursday morning when they got out of the hotel and Chapman drove her back to the office, I followed her instead of him, like I usually did. And she drove to this address." He read the address, and it was Sharon's house.

"I don't believe it," I said.

"I get that a lot," Konigsberg said.

THE phone call with Konigsberg had not been as helpful as I'd hoped, and I tried to clear my head by stepping out into the lobby. This turned out to be the wrong strategy: I could hear the beginnings of *Train Trippin'* from behind the screen, but there was another sound I didn't recognize—and it didn't sound good.

It was something like a gorilla being strangled by a boa constrictor underwater, although I doubted that could be the case in the theatre. I wasn't ruling it out entirely, however—at Comedy Tonight, anything can happen. Get your tickets early.

The gorilla sound was coming from the ladies' room, and the large red hose was extended from inside the restroom to

the basement stairs. Dad was standing in the doorway looking less confident than when I'd last seen him. I stopped in my
tracks.

Jonathan was behind the snack bar, reading from a ragged
piece of paper on the top of the candy counter. He had the top
of the corn popper open—we use the real thing, with actual
corn oil and real butter—and had the very same look on his
face that would be there if someone asked him to build a
space shuttle out of a cantaloupe and three mustard seeds.

There was no sign of Meg or Mom, but Gregory was standing at the door to the auditorium, looking at his watch and
tapping his foot. I wondered who'd invited him.

Since the popcorn machine was not an inexpensive item,
and the plumbing was already costing me money by the minute, I decided to head for Jonathan first. He did not look up
when I approached.

"Where's Sophie?" I asked.

"In the projection room," he answered, as if that explained
anything.

"Why, is Anthony away?" Maybe Sophie was needed to
make reel changes. I wasn't sure she knew how, but it was
possible.

"No." His tone indicated that my question was not only
stupid, but in a language other than the one Jonathan and I
normally spoke.

"Then what's Sophie doing in the projection room?" It was
one of those conversations where you know it's never going to
get any better, but you keep plowing through anyway, defying
all logic and every experience you've had up to that point in
your life.

"She says with all the noise going on in the bathroom,
that's the only place quiet enough to study, as long as Anthony
turns the sound monitor off." He twisted his torso around to
look for something. "Do you know where we keep the popcorn
oil?"

"Jonathan. Stop." He doesn't like to look me—or anyone
besides Sophie—in the eye, so he stopped and stared at his

sneakers. "How large is the house?" I asked, gesturing toward the auditorium doors.

"Small. Maybe thirty people." Thirty people who were trying to hear a stoner comedy through the cacophony of plumbing noises. Great. And I wondered why I got small crowds. Maybe it wasn't worth fixing the plumbing, and I should just abandon the building and let someone turn it into the world's most cavernous Carvel.

"Then don't you think maybe we have enough popcorn made already?" I asked.

"There's another show tonight," Jonathan argued.

"We can make more later. Wait for us to get close to running out before you go filling it up; go upstairs and ask Sophie to come down and see me."

He looked relieved, but then seemed to consider the fact that he had to go tell his girlfriend she was in trouble. "Are you going to yell at her?"

"No, but if you don't go right now, I'm going to yell at you."

Jonathan left in a hurry.

There wasn't time even to breathe before Gregory was upon me. "I'm told you went to Sharon's lake house. Why wasn't I informed?"

"Sorry. From now on, I'll post my travel plans on the theatre's website." I strode as purposefully as a man who hasn't slept in three days can stride to the entrance to my ladies' room. It's hard to look authoritative when you're a man entering a women's bathroom, but I did what I could.

Dad turned and assessed me. "You look terrible," he began, and if that was his opener, I couldn't say I was looking forward to the rest of the conversation. "Have you eaten anything?" He knew he'd have to report back to my mother at some point.

"That's all I have done. What happened here?"

I heard a voice from deep inside the ladies' room. It was not a ladylike voice. "Water started shooting out of the toilets and into the air," said the voice, which I took to be that of the plumber. "It was like you'd put in bidets on steroids."

"And I'm willing to bet this had nothing to do with the work you did in the men's room yesterday," I said.

"'Course not."

I turned toward Dad and gestured in the plumber's direction. "You're overseeing?"

"When did I not?"

"Thanks." I kissed him on the forehead. "Let me know if I have to close the theatre again. It's starting to look like an attractive option."

"Now, if you don't mind . . ." Gregory began.

"Just a second," I said, noticing Sophie and Jonathan walking downstairs from the balcony, Sophie carrying a large book in her left hand. I walked over to the landing and waited for Sophie, so I wouldn't have to raise my voice.

"What are you doing leaving Jonathan in charge of the popcorn machine?" I asked her. "He's never done that job before."

I didn't realize my tone would be that harsh when I set out to talk to Sophie, but fatigue was eating into my brain, and worry, its constant companion, wasn't doing me a great deal of good, either. She looked at me as if I'd slapped her.

"When did you become such a *boss*?" Sophie asked. She barreled past me and stood behind the snack bar. "I can see the problem; the line is all the way out the door!" She slammed the book down on the counter and pouted.

"You said you weren't going to yell at her," Jonathan whined. Now he'd be blamed. Oh well, it would be good practice for his dealings with women for decades to come.

"Get on the phone to my house," I told him. "Tell whoever answers that I said Leo Munson can't watch any more movies. I can't afford to have my only regular customer sitting at my house watching DVDs."

"But, Sophie . . ." Jonathan usually had a rather flat affect, but now he looked like he was going to cry. I couldn't feel anything but tired. I waved him away, and started toward my office. Gregory followed me there.

We got to the door of my office, and I was reaching for the

key when Chief Barry Dutton appeared at the theatre doors. He looked over at the office, and saw us standing there.

I wasn't at all crazy about the look on Dutton's face as he approached me.

"Gentlemen," he said. "I'm glad you're both here."

I *really* hated the way that sounded.

"It doesn't mean anything yet," Dutton went on. "But there's a woman's body the medical examiner has that they can't identify."

My world no longer functioned.

21

THE corridor outside the morgue at Robert Wood Johnson University Hospital in New Brunswick was as depressing a place as I had ever been in my life. It was institutional and bland, with absolutely nothing to distinguish it. The walls were painted green and tan, because they had to be painted something. The floor was old linoleum tile, off-white with no pattern. The dropped ceiling showed signs of water damage.

Gregory had wanted to use his hospital ID and the fact that he was Sharon's husband (at the moment) to get into the room, but when she had filed for divorce from him, Sharon had been clear about changing her medical and insurance forms back to indicate me as her next of kin. I remembered her telling me so at the time and explaining, particularly about the insurance, "If I die, you'll need the money more than Gregory would. Besides, you'll be able to handle . . . everything . . . better."

I'd probably made some joke about how I'd blow it all on DVDs and a new popcorn machine, but now, standing in the corridor that would have been cold even if it had been the Fourth of July and not less than two weeks before Christmas, I wasn't thinking about the money.

I was thinking about how much better it would have been if Gregory could have been the one to do this.

Dutton, as a courtesy from the Middlesex County Prosecutor's office and the New Brunswick Police Department, stood to my left. He watched me study the floor, waiting for the door to open when we'd have to go in.

"They found the body in a burning car on Ryders Lane in Milltown, the same model and year as Sharon's," he said. "Apparently the fuel line had ruptured and the driver hit a tree. Car burst into flames." The two cops who had met us at the hospital entrance and escorted us here had told me virtually the same thing, but Dutton had seen the look on my face, and wasn't sure I'd absorbed the information.

"Are they sure it was an accident?" I asked. My voice didn't seem to be emanating from my own body, and it sounded shaky.

"Nobody's sure of anything yet," he said.

Before I could respond, the door opened, and a man in blue scrubs walked out, picked up Dutton first in his line of sight, and then looked at me. He was short, curlyhaired, and wore thick glasses; if you were casting the part of "Nerd" in a Hollywood comedy of 1986, he'd be your guy.

"We're ready" was all he said.

I might have stayed rooted to the spot if Dutton and the cops hadn't started walking. I followed them into the room, which appeared to be an average operating room, except that the form lying on the table was covered entirely by a sheet.

They had asked if I'd prefer to "view the remains" on a video monitor from the next room, but I didn't want distorted color or lighting to get in my way; if I had to see Sharon this way for the last time, I wanted to see Sharon, not a TV image of her.

"Okay," said Nerd Guy. "Are you ready?" He looked me in the eye.

I bit my lips, and nodded.

"Keep in mind the body is pretty badly burned." It was nice he was softening the blow. "But the face isn't too bad."

He walked to the table and gently reached over to the top of the form lying prone on the operating table. He looked at me again, to be sure I was watching, and he lifted the sheet just enough to see the face. I looked.

And then the tears began to flow.

I put my head in my hands, covered my eyes, and felt the sobs emanate from my chest. I hadn't cried this hard before in my life. My body shook as if I were convulsing.

Dutton walked toward me, and held out his arms. "My god," he said. "I'm sorry, Elliot." I opened my eyes and saw him, and thought he was going to lead me out of this awful room, but he spread his arms and reached out to embrace me. I appreciated the gesture, unexpected as it was, but I stepped back and shook my head. Dutton froze in his tracks.

I couldn't do anything but shake my head back and forth: no, no, no.

Gently, Dutton leaned down (the man is very tall) and said, "Let's get out of here. You don't want to see this anymore." Again, he reached out to put a hand on my shoulder, and I backed off. I did everything I could to regulate my breathing. I bore down. I had to stop crying.

"You . . . don't . . . understand," I managed.

Dutton nodded. "I know. I've never had to face it, but I can—"

"No!" It came out more forcefully than I'd intended. "You don't understand!"

Dutton looked like he might pick me up and carry me out of the room. "I don't understand what?" he asked.

"That's . . . not . . . her!"

22

IT took me a while to get my emotions under control: the lack of sleep, the constant worry on the edge of panic, the combination of enormous relief and continued panic had all hit me at the same moment when the medical technician had raised that sheet. I wasn't sure how to get back to what passes for normal with me.

But after a few moments my eyes felt puffy and my breath was coming naturally. I stopped shaking. Dutton led me out of the morgue and, after a few questions from the uniformed cops, out of the hospital.

"It doesn't answer anything," I said when we were getting back into his car. "This might just postpone the inevitable."

Dutton started the car up and began driving back to Comedy Tonight. "It's true that we don't know anything more than we did before," he admitted. "Except that wasn't Sharon."

"I should call Gregory," I said.

"I already have," Dutton told me. "When you were talking to the officers. He's relieved, and still at the theatre."

"Swell. I can't wait to see his cheery face."

We drove in silence for a while. I had to adjust my level of fear, since it had reached epic proportions a short while before, and now had to lower back down to that constant nagging in the stomach and the hint in the back of your mind that you can't ever relax, because the next time the phone rings, they might not be wrong.

"Maybe the way to approach this is to concentrate on Chapman," I said, more to myself than to Dutton. "Maybe by talking to Chapman's family and following the trail through him, I can figure out what happened to Sharon."

"You are not a police officer, a private investigator, an investigative reporter, or even a skip tracer," Dutton said, just to remind me of everything I'm not. "You have no authority to approach those people and ask them for anything more than directions to the bus station."

"Who needs to approach them?" I asked. "They keep coming to my theatre. If I stand still long enough, one of them will show up."

"I'm telling you, Elliot," Dutton said in his best chief-of-police voice. "You can't investigate Chapman's death. The East Brunswick police are doing that, and they're good. They'll get the county involved if they have to, but even I'm not doing a thing about Chapman right now. I'll keep you informed on anything about the case that's not sensitive, but you can't go blundering in there and hope to find a clue to Sharon's whereabouts. It doesn't work that way, and you could easily be cited for interfering in a criminal investigation."

I hate it when he's right.

We didn't speak for the rest of the ride, which admittedly was only about six minutes. But it gave me time to wonder if most ex-husbands would have been that frantic about the lives of their ex-wives. Maybe I just couldn't let go. Maybe I was afraid of moving ahead with my life.

Maybe Sharon really was dead. Would I be able to deal with that if it hit me in the face? This most recent episode had suggested that I might not. And that was, by any normal standard, weird. Most ex-husbands would greet the news of their former spouse's demise with a shrug, a wince, or barely disguised glee. But there weren't many whose lives would be devastated. What was wrong with me?

When we pulled up to Comedy Tonight, I was already onto my next plan, which involved going door-to-door and asking people if they'd seen Sharon recently, starting on the block around the theatre, and continuously widening the search until, theoretically, an ocean voyage could be necessary. I admit, it wasn't much, but it was all I had.

We arrived after the matinees were finished, but before it would be time to reopen for the evening showings. Meg had returned, with a message from Leo that he would be back in time for "Sully's Travels." Apparently my steadiest customer and the fictional hero of Preston Sturges's comedy were on a nickname basis.

The nozzle of the red hose leading out of the ladies' room was rolling across the lobby toward the restroom as I entered, leading me to hope against hope (what does that expression mean?) that Mr. A-OK Plumbing had succeeded in his task and was packing up. I could hear Dad's voice emanating from the ladies' room, giving him instructions I couldn't make out, presumably on how to best roll the hose for efficient transport back to his truck.

Mom and Gregory were sitting on the balcony steps, chatting. Clearly Gregory had spread the word about my trip to the morgue. I was, at least, grateful that I didn't have to repeat that one; perhaps Gregory was useful for something after all. Other than playing pinochle.

At the snack bar, Sophie was cleaning off the glass case with one hand while using the other to type on a laptop computer perched atop a carton of popping corn. Perhaps she really was a genius.

Anthony, with nothing to do, was stretched out on the balcony steps, asleep. College students aren't like the rest of us.

And to one side of the lobby, standing completely by herself, was Gwen Chapman, looking a little dour. I couldn't imagine why Gwen would be here.

Meg noticed Dutton and me first. "Elliot, I'm so glad," she

said, and gave me an industrial-strength hug. "You must have been terrified."

I nodded. That was all I could do, as the emotion was starting to overwhelm my reason again. I didn't want to break down in front of virtually everyone I knew, and I certainly didn't want to appear weak in front of Gregory. Yes, it was adolescent and petty, but it kept me going; what was your question?

Before Meg could say anything else, Mom spotted me, and she and Gregory were up and on their way to the office door, which I had not yet managed to unlock. Gregory, of all people, stuck out his hand and took mine.

"Thank you, Elliot," he said. "I'm not sure I could have handled it."

"You should be proud of Elliot," Dutton told Mom after I introduced them. "He was very brave." I never knew the chief could lie so convincingly.

"I am," Mom answered. "But Gregory was brave, too." I considered ordering DNA tests to see which one of us was her son.

"I'm sure," Dutton said.

Gwen Chapman sort of wandered onto the scene, as if she'd somehow gotten lost and found herself in Comedy Tonight's lobby entirely by accident. She stood a little outside the group that had encircled me, and looked very much like a little girl who'd gotten invited to a birthday party where she didn't know any of the other kids.

"I was glad to hear about Dr. Simon-Freed," she said to me.

"Thank you, Gwen," I said. "What brings you here?"

Gwen seemed embarrassed; looked down toward my knees. "I'm here to apologize for my sister," she said.

"There's no need for that," I said.

"Yes, there is. You're still worried about the doctor, and Lillian was here practically reveling in your pain. She told me about it, and I'm ashamed for my family. My father raised us to take responsibility for our actions, not to blame everyone else."

I couldn't think of anything to do but take her hands and make her look me in the eye. "Apology accepted," I said. "And I'm very sorry about your father."

"Thank you. I'm sorry; I have a funeral to plan. But I might come back in a few days." She turned to walk toward the door. "I think a comedy might be just the thing by then." And with that, she left.

Meg, diplomat that she is, stood back and took a look at the shell of a man where I used to stand. "You look terrible," she said. "Go home and get some sleep."

It wasn't a bad idea; maybe if I were functioning normally, I'd start getting better ideas. I nodded. "Yeah, maybe I will," I said.

But from the snack bar, I heard a scream. "Oh, no, you don't!" Sophie shouted. "You're not leaving me to supervise another double feature when I have *real* work to do!" She stormed out from behind her station—which was just as well, since there would be no customers to serve for another two hours—and advanced on me like a rhino on a first-time safari hunter armed with nothing but a camera. The hunter, not the rhino.

"Sophie," I said. "I haven't slept since . . ."

"I don't care! You've been blowing me off for days now! It doesn't matter to you if I get into a good school—you just care about your theatre! Well, if that's the way you're going to be about it, I *quit*!"

Don't ask me to explain it, but that was the death blow. I sat down on the floor of the lobby right where I'd been standing, as if she'd knocked me out with a vicious left hook. I looked up at the crowd gathered around me—Mom, Gregory, Dutton, Meg, Sophie—all staring at me like they would a harmless but pathetic mental patient. Except Sophie probably wouldn't have used the word "harmless."

"You can't," I croaked.

Jonathan came running over from . . . somewhere . . . and stared pleadingly at Sophie. "You're not serious," he said. "You're not leaving."

"Sure I am! If you can't even take my suffering seriously . . ." That was directed at me.

"Your suffering?" Anger took on despair inside my head, and it wasn't a fair fight. I got shakily to my feet. "*Your* suffering? You're a teenage girl with every advantage, a first-class brain and good sense, who's going to get into every single college she applies to without all the courses and strategy, because she's brilliant! Do you have any idea what *we've* been going through for the past few days?" I asked Sophie, gesturing at the gathered group, which now somehow included my father.

Sophie blinked. "You think I'm brilliant?"

"I always have. But you're not the one who's suffering. We are!"

Sophie blinked twice. "Why?" she asked.

It wasn't possible. It couldn't be that she hadn't known, that she'd missed every conversation. Could Sophie have buried her nose so deep into her books that she didn't know what was going on?

My voice calmed, and descended in volume. "Sophie, please pay attention. For the past few days, I haven't been acting like myself; I know you've noticed that."

"Sure," she said. "You were mad because I was studying during the movie."

"No," I said. "I'm very emotional right now—and so is everyone else here—because Sharon has been missing since Thursday night."

Sophie's eyes doubled in size. "Really?"

"Yes," I said. "And there's a really good chance that none of us might ever see her again."

"Don't you think you'd better check with me on that?" asked a voice to my left, and my head turned ninety degrees in one frame of film (that's one twenty-fourth of a second).

Sharon, hand on her hip, was standing at the front door to the theatre, with a look on her face that can only be described as bemused.

"Did I miss something?" she asked.

23

THE avalanche of humanity that launched itself toward the front doors of Comedy Tonight would probably have frightened most people. Sharon, not being most people, seemed to find it amusing and, in a way I couldn't figure, gratifying.

All eight of us (minus the plumber, and Anthony, who remained blissfully asleep on the balcony stairs) began launching questions at the same time. Okay: Jonathan didn't say anything, only because he deferred to Sophie. I arrived first (not that I'm at all competitive) and kissed my ex-wife with a passion I would leave to a more private audience on virtually any other occasion.

"Well, it's good to see you, too," she said when we finally came up for air. Out of the corner of my eye, I saw Gregory looking peevish. I felt better than I had in days.

"Where have you been?" Mom shouted at Sharon. "We've been frantic."

"Why didn't you answer your cell phone?" Gregory asked. "I tried you every hour until the voice mail was filled." The needy wimp. I'd only called every two hours. I kept my arm around Sharon's shoulders. That would show him.

Gwen Chapman walked back into the theatre, but stood to the side, just watching the group. I was thinking only about Sharon.

"The practice has been looking for you," I told her. "Nobody's known where you were since Thursday night."

"Why didn't you . . . ?"

"When did you . . . ?"

"Who was with you . . . ?"

"Have you eaten anything?" My father. A man of basic concerns.

Dutton raised an arm and whistled loudly. "If everyone would please give the doctor some breathing room, I have some concerns that I want to address privately with her before anyone else has a chance to influence her answers," he said. "Elliot, can we use your office?"

"Sure," I answered, and the crowd did its best Red Sea imitation to let me lead Sharon through toward the door. I reached into my pocket with my right hand for the office key, but kept the left on Sharon's arm. I was formulating a plan that included never actually losing physical contact with her again.

The door opened, and I ushered Dutton inside. Sharon followed him, a quizzical look on her face. I started into the office behind Sharon, and Dutton raised a hand, telling me to stop.

"Just the doctor and me," he said.

"But, I . . ." The plan about physical contact, like most of my plans, had not lasted long.

"It's okay, Elliot," Sharon said. My face fell. I picked it up and left the office, closing the door behind me.

The gathered assemblage was facing me when I turned around. "All right, people," I said, motioning like a traffic cop. "Show's over. Nothing to see here."

We moved, in a pack, toward the snack bar. Sophie took up her usual post, on the barstool I've installed there for her, and Jonathan took up his, perched on an inflatable chair he installed there himself so he could look at Sophie as much as possible. Jonathan's approach to women was taking on an ee-rily familiar look; I shuddered, thinking of high school.

Dad shrugged and went back to instructing the plumber, who surely must have finished reeling in his hose by now. I got Mom a folding chair from behind the snack bar and set it out to one side, so she could sit and memorize how everyone there was in some way failing her at that moment. She liked to savor such memories at a later date.

That left Meg, Gregory, Gwen, and me. We all stood around, watching the office door, trying to look inconspicu-ous. And failing miserably.

I walked over to Gwen. "Something I can help you with?" I asked. It was the first chance I had to find out why she'd re-turned.

"No, no," she answered. "I saw the doctor walking into the theatre when I was getting into my car, and I just wanted to see the relief on your face. Right now, that's a real treat for me, to see other people feeling better."

"You must be having a very rough time," I said. "I'm sorry if I didn't seem sympathetic enough, but . . ."

"Believe me, I understand," Gwen said. "But I would like to ask the doctor something when she comes out."

"Of course," I said.

And that pretty much exhausted our supply of conversa-tion. We all watched the office door for a while longer.

"Barry just doesn't want her answers to be practiced, or corrupted by anything one of us could tell her," Meg said after a few minutes. "It's standard procedure. It's what I'd do. It's nothing to worry about."

"That's what I thought," I answered. "Dutton already told me he didn't suspect Sharon in Chapman's death. He's just going through the motions, taking care of formalities."

"I don't think Sharon killed anyone," Gregory said, pre-sumably because he thought it was his turn. Nobody even glanced at him; we were doing our best to pretend he wasn't there.

The number of "casual" glances toward the office door

increased. I even caught Sophie stealing a look in that direction as she restocked the nonpareils, which only led me to wonder why no one ever ate pareils. My mind tends to travel in strange directions when my ex-wife is being questioned by the police. I wasn't sure if that was useful information, but I noted it and saved the analysis for later.

"So where do you think she's been for the past three days?" Sophie, the eternal fount of tact, asked.

"She'll tell us when she's done in there," Meg assured her. "I'm sure there's a very simple explanation."

"The important thing is that she's safe," said my mother, for once echoing what I would have been thinking if I weren't such a petty, self-centered . . . Damn! She could do it even without trying!

Dad wandered out of the ladies' room and approached me with a look that spelled no good for my theatre and its vital systems. He motioned me aside, and spoke quietly, to preserve confidentiality. "The guy thinks there's a good chance your sewer is backing up," he said. "It could possibly affect other systems, like air-conditioning."

"That's not a very big deal in this weather," I said.

"Eventually, the backup could reach the heating system," Dad warned.

"Eventually? I'll worry about that eventually, then."

"There's also the possibility that any water in the basement could interfere with—"

The lights in the lobby chose that very moment to go out. They flickered, went completely dark, and stayed that way.

"—the electrical system," Dad continued.

I wouldn't have been able to see my hand in front of my face if it had been there for some obscure reason I wasn't able to conjure at the moment. "Swell," I said. "The flashlight is in the office."

The plumber's voice came from somewhere in the distance. "Just a minute," he shouted.

The lights came back on.

"That's going to be a problem," Dad suggested.

"Yeah. Do you know an electrician?" I asked.

"Several."

"Call one."

"Which one?" Dad asked.

"The cheapest one."

The office door, which we'd momentarily forgotten about, swung open, and Barry Dutton walked out into the lobby. "What's the problem with the lights?" he asked.

"It's being taken care of," I told him.

Then I saw Sharon walk out of the office behind Dutton. She walked slowly, as if she were afraid she'd fall, hands behind her back. For a moment, she looked like an attractive, female version of Ed Sullivan.

In handcuffs.

Meg Vidal seemed to focus on the cuffs. Gregory's mouth dropped open. My stomach, recently returned to its normal place in my abdomen, fell, rose, and fell again. It would take an MRI machine to accurately locate it, but that wasn't my most pressing problem at the moment.

"Chief," I started, and he held up a hand. Jonathan stood up to get a better look at Sharon. Then, as fit his attention span, he looked back at Sophie.

"For the time being," Dutton said, "I'm asking for your patience. I'm taking the doctor back to headquarters to question her on suspicion of murder in the first degree."

Anthony began to snore.

24

We know what happens to people who stay in the middle of
the road. They get run over. —ANEURIN BEVAN

Anything that begins "I don't know how to tell you this" is
never good news. —RUTH GORDON

MONDAY

THE Midland Heights police station doesn't really have a jail;
there's a holding cell they use occasionally, and most of the
more serious criminals are sent to county lockup for any extended stay.

But today, Chief Barry Dutton wouldn't even let me near
the holding cell while Sharon's release was being arranged.
I'd tried to call Grace at Sharon's practice for information, but
she was out sick, and Betty said Dutton hadn't called them,
anyway. He had not informed me about her arraignment, and
I hadn't been notified as to the attorney she'd hired to defend
her.

I was starting to think Dutton didn't love me anymore.

"This isn't like you," I said to him, sitting in the same
waiting room I'd inhabited the night Sharon had vanished. I
had slept (a little), showered, and shaved for the first time in
days, and was wearing clothes that didn't make me look like I
should be carrying a cardboard sign asking for donations for
a Gulf War veteran down on his luck. "You're a cop, but most
of the time, you're human."

"This is murder," he answered, reading something on a

clipboard. His half-glasses didn't seem as charming as they once had. "This is not something where rules can be bent. I have to play it by the book."

"You told me yourself that you didn't suspect Sharon in Chapman's murder. And it took place in East Brunswick, not Midland Heights, but you're holding her here. Something's not kosher about this whole business, Dutton."

He didn't look up. "You usually call me Chief," he said.

"You usually deserve respect," I answered.

Dutton's mouth twitched; it was the only sign that I'd struck a nerve. "Don't cross the line, Elliot. Wait for things to play out."

"Are we speaking in haiku today? Say what you mean."

"That is what I mean. Show some patience. The truth will come out, and you'll see that you don't know everything you think you know." Dutton stood up and left the room. It must have been his day to be vague.

I sat there for a few more eternities, not knowing exactly how long Sharon would be held. She'd been in custody since leaving Comedy Tonight the previous afternoon, and now, at nine thirty in the morning, more than fifteen hours since she'd been back, I had answers to exactly none of my lingering questions. That was not acceptable.

Finally, the dispatcher behind the desk pushed a button and a buzzer sounded. The inside door swung open into the waiting room, and Sharon walked through it.

Escorted by Gregory.

That wasn't acceptable, either. But there was a grand total of nothing I could do about it. I stood.

"Are you okay?" I asked first.

Sharon nodded. "We need to talk," she said.

"That doesn't sound good," I answered. It was the very sentence she'd used to tell me she wanted a divorce. Come to think of it, Gregory had been involved in that one, too.

"Let's get out of here," Gregory offered. He put his hands on Sharon's shoulders to guide her out the door, but she patted his hand and stepped away from him.

"I'm okay," she said.

We walked outside and were immediately overcome by a cold wind. Gregory had parked his Lexus directly in front of the building, in a no-parking zone. There's never a cop around when you need one. He opened the door for Sharon, and then hesitated, turned to me, and said, "Do you need a ride?"

I didn't actually know where we were going, but I said, "Yes, thanks," and got in the back seat. Okay, so it was silly and juvenile. But Sharon had been out of my sight far too much in the past four days. I was determined not to let it happen again.

Gregory got in and started the car, and cold air started blasting through the heating ducts. "Jeez, Greg," I said, "I'd think a big fancy car like this one would come with heat as a standard feature."

"It *does,*" he blustered. "It's just been sitting here for . . ."

"He's teasing you, Gregory," Sharon said. "He's just teasing."

"So, kids," I said, "where shall we go?"

"Since Sharon hasn't been home in a while," Gregory said, "we thought we'd go back to our house."

I didn't care for the way he said "we" or "our house," but I kept it to myself. Nothing makes you feel more like you're back in junior high school than riding in the back seat of a luxury car.

My first impulse, of course, was to ask Sharon to explain everything that had happened since Thursday, but something inside me that was petty and small wanted that conversation to happen without Gregory present. To be fair, I didn't want anyone else present, either, but Gregory topped the list of people I didn't want around. Some things don't change no matter what the circumstances.

But I couldn't wait for everything. "Where have you been all this time?" I asked Sharon.

"Mostly, I was up at my aunt Margie's cabin at Lake Carey," she said. "You know how I go up there when I need to clear my head."

"But I was there," I told her. "I went there. I looked for you." I was going to prove to her that she hadn't been where she knew she'd been.

"Was that you who broke the window?" Sharon asked.

I stayed silent.

"You broke a window?" Gregory said. I could hear him smile, the rat.

I didn't respond, but my eyes were boring holes into the back of Gregory's head. Luckily, the lack of hair made it easy to aim.

"I understand," I said to Sharon, completely ignoring both Gregory and the fact that I'd broken a window at her aunt's house. "You needed to get up there to sort out what had happened with Russell Chapman."

Sharon turned around to face me. "Oh, no," she said. "I didn't know Mr. Chapman was dead until Chief Dutton told me yesterday afternoon. The poor man."

"Chief Dutton?" Gregory asked.

"No, Russell Chapman." Sharon shook her head. "I can't believe someone killed him."

"I'm just glad you're back," I told her. "But if you didn't go up there to get over the Chapman thing, what did you need to get away from?"

She turned back to face the windshield again, and I got the impression it was so she wouldn't have to meet my eyes. "Just doctor stress, I suppose."

"You didn't need to cut yourself off like that," I kept on. "You never get out of touch with your practice. Why didn't you at least check your voice mail?"

"I forgot to bring the charger with me, and besides, you know how I am at those times. I wanted to be completely alone to sort through . . ."

"Your doctor stress?" I asked.

"Yeah."

"You could have at least left a message," I told her. "You could have called someone before you left."

"Elliot," Sharon said with a reproach in her voice.

"What, 'Elliot'?" I asked. "It's unreasonable for me to ask why you didn't call someone to let them know you were disappearing? So we wouldn't be pulling our hair out—sorry, Gregory—and trying to remember what your last words to us were? That's unreasonable? Why didn't you call someone?"

I guess she was over the no-eye-contact phase, because Sharon looked me straight in the eyes and said, "I *did* call someone, Elliot. I called *you*."

Well, that took the wind out of my sails. At the very least, if Sharon had called me, I should have known it. And after all the excitement about her disappearance, all that had happened . . .

"When?" I managed to get from my dry throat.

"Before I left Thursday night. I called right before I left the practice."

"I was at the theatre," I said.

"That's right, so I left you a message on your machine at home."

Of course. "The machine was disconnected. I never got the message."

"Why'd you turn off your answering machine?" Sharon asked.

"I didn't. Someone else did."

"Who?"

I thought of the machine, its cord ripped from the wall, lying on the floor among the futon stuffing and the mountain of discarded videos. "We haven't found out yet," I said.

Sharon looked at me with a question in her eyes, but let it go.

Gregory coughed. "You didn't call me," he said quietly.

"Oh, don't start," Sharon said.

I squirmed in the back seat. "Mom, are you and Dad fighting?" I asked. Sharon gave me a distressed look, and I shut up.

Luckily, we had reached what I always thought of as "Sharon's house," and Gregory parked the car in the driveway. He rushed around to open Sharon's door for her before I could even unbuckle my shoulder harness.

He needn't have hurried. It never would have occurred to me to open her door. I'm a Neanderthal at heart.

Sharon seemed a little confused by the (now embarrassing) competition between Gregory and me, and shot me a look as he did everything but take her arm and escort her to the front door. I shrugged. So my shoulders weren't in an especially articulate mood. But I decided to stop competing. We were both ex-husbands; we were equal. I couldn't help it if I was more equal than Gregory.

We sat in the living room, Sharon on the couch, Gregory trying as hard as he could to sit close to her, and me on the overstuffed chair facing them. No one said anything for a very long moment.

"Tell me . . ." I began.

Sharon turned toward Gregory with the speed of a frog's tongue going after a fly. "Gregory, could you do me a favor?"

He puffed himself up until he looked like the Gregory balloon from the Macy's parade. "What can I do for you?" he asked. I sincerely believe if the answer had been "jump up and touch Pluto," he wouldn't have hesitated, other than to ask if she meant the former planet, or Mickey Mouse's dog.

"Elliot and I need . . ." Sharon saw Gregory's face harden. He glared at me with serious violence in his eyes, and I did my very best not to put a gloating grin on my face. Honestly, I tried. Sharon began again, "I need something to . . . take the edge off, you know? With all the excitement of the past few days? Do you think you could call Toni and ask her to prescribe something for me?"

Gregory's expression couldn't possibly have been more smug. "Of course, darling," he said, and stood up to walk into the kitchen. He reached for the phone.

"And could you go to the pharmacy and fill it right away?" Sharon continued.

Gregory didn't read between the lines, and nodded. "I'm on my way," he said, and within seconds, his coat was on, his cell phone was in his hand, and he was indeed on his way.

The moment the door closed, Sharon turned to me with

urgency in her eyes. "We don't have much time," she said, "and we have a lot to talk about."

I leaned forward on the chair, which wasn't easy on a microfiber overstuffed special. My pants wanted to stick to it. "Okay," I said. "Tell me. What happened with Chapman? How come he thought he was going to die? Who were you with at the bar in the city? And what's this about Chapman leaving you money in his—"

"I'm pregnant," she said.

25

I blinked. A number of times; I can't tell you how many. There was so much information in those two words that I'm not entirely sure how much time went by before I could respond.

"You're . . . wow," I said. Oh, and I suppose *you'd* be more articulate under the circumstances.

"Yeah," Sharon replied. "And before you ask, no, I have no doubt, and yes, it's your baby. There weren't any other candidates." I *knew* I was right about Sharon and Russell Chapman. Either Konigsberg was crazy, or just bad at his job.

I stood up. I think better on my feet. Normally when dealing with my ex-wife, I have found myself trying to anticipate her reaction to whatever I was saying or doing. I didn't want to make a wrong move, or be misunderstood. But now, with this in my head, my thought patterns were scrambled. I'm not sure I knew I was speaking out loud.

"This is . . . great!" I said, wandering around the room, not looking at anything in particular. "This is amazing."

"Well, I'm glad you feel that way," Sharon grinned. "I

wasn't sure exactly how you'd react. I wasn't sure exactly how *I* was reacting."

"It's just—it's so much to think about. We have to plan. Tell me when your divorce from Gregory is going to be final, and then we can get married again."

She looked like I'd hit her with a cream pie, minus the cream. "We can get . . . what?"

"Sure. Then you can sell the house, and I can sell the town house, and we'll find a place to raise the kid in, you know, like our old place. Midland Heights has a good school system, doesn't it? I mean, I went to the schools here, but that was a while ago." The room was a blur, but I wasn't really focusing on anything, so that was to be expected.

Sharon stood up and grabbed me gently but firmly by the forearms. "Elliot," she said. "Slow down. It's the adrenaline you're feeling right now."

I stood still, because I liked her hands on my arms, but I didn't really stop. "No, it's perfect," I said. "We have enough time before the baby is born to get it all done. And I guess I'll even buy a car, you know. Can't take Junior to pediatrician appointments on the handlebars of a Schwinn. Maybe a hybrid, so I can still feel like I'm conserving fuel. I'll ask Sophie about her Prius."

"Elliot," Sharon started, but I was on a roll.

"You're going to have to take some time off when the baby is born. Will you go back to the practice? I could sell the theatre and get a real job, if I have to."

"Elliot!" Sharon shouted, I think just to get my attention. "Focus. Listen to me."

"Yeah. Yeah, I'm listening. What?"

"No."

That didn't make any sense. I hadn't asked anything. "No?"

Sharon made sure we maintained eye contact. I've seen her do that with patients who weren't entirely mentally stable. "That's right. No."

"No, what?"

"No, we're not getting married again." She let go of my arms. "Not that your proposal wasn't charming, in its own completely self-absorbed way. I'm sorry, but no."

Keep in mind that at this point I hadn't really gotten a good night's sleep since roughly April. "Why not?" I asked, but my voice sounded softer than I'd expected.

"For any number of reasons, like for example that we'll still have the same problems we had when we were married, but we'll be adding a child to it. That's one thing. But mostly because I've been married or living with a man for more years than I care to think about, and I want to see what it's like on my own for a while." Sharon sat down and looked at me with a sad expression. "Not that I'll be alone, exactly. I'll have another person in the house with me."

"Who?" Sometimes, I can be monumentally dense.

She gave me a look that reiterated my previous sentence. *"The baby,"* she said.

"Oh, yeah."

"Look, Elliot, I know I'm dropping a lot on you all at once, but Gregory will be back in a few minutes, and I wanted you to know before anyone else. The test reports that came back Thursday night weren't Russell Chapman's; they were mine. I already knew—I'd done the home test, and those are almost always accurate—but seeing it on paper made it real for me. So I spent a few days up at the cottage to think, and believe me, I thought about all the options. But I know I want this baby. And I'd like you to be involved with it, but if you don't feel like you can . . ."

I stared at her, and my expression must have been enough to silence her. "Don't you even think that," I said. "That's my baby, and you're my . . . ex-wife. I love both of you. Of course, I'm involved. Whether you want it or not, I'm the father." The thought made me sit down. "Jesus, Shar—I'm the father!"

Naturally, that's when Gregory walked in.

Sharon, being something approaching a genius, and having had more time to absorb the situation, shifted gears like a Ferrari on the Autobahn. "There never really was an arraignment," she said. "Gregory knows, because he thought he'd have to put up the money for bail. Right, Gregory?"

What? Bail? Arraignment? Who were these people, and what were they talking about? I felt like I'd wandered onto the set of an Ingmar Bergman film, and nobody was translating from the Swedish.

"That's right, honey." Gregory still thought we were still playing the "Who Wants to Be the Best Ex-Husband" game, and sat down next to Sharon. He handed her a small pharmacy bag. "Here you go."

"Thank you." Sharon put the bag on the coffee table and ignored it. Gregory's eyes narrowed, but Sharon plowed on, talking just to me. "You see, Chief Dutton saw Gwen Chapman at the theatre when I arrived, and he considered it an opportunity. If he arrested me as a suspect in her father's murder, she and the rest of the family would hear about it and figure they weren't under suspicion. The chief thinks that will lead them to make a mistake. He thinks one or more of them is involved in Russell's death."

"Of course." I nodded. Sure. Death playing chess with a guy on the beach. Nobody notices. Whatever.

"That's why he never transferred me to East Brunswick, or the county," Sharon continued, pretending I was absorbing what she said. "The fact is, I came home last night and had a really good sleep."

"Wish I could say the same," I managed. I don't know what I was complaining about; with my worrying, I'd gotten in a healthy ten or twelve minutes of sleep the night before.

"Me, too," Gregory said. "She came in so quietly, and left so early, I never even knew she was here." Gregory hadn't gotten over sleeping in the guest room yet. He wasn't a professional ex-husband, like me. He hadn't even moved out yet. The poor kid. Someone ought to take him aside and show him the ropes. Someone other than me, since I'd be likely to wrap the ropes around his neck.

"So now the East Brunswick detective and Chief Dutton can watch the Chapmans without them knowing they're under surveillance." Sharon was determined to get the whole story out. "I don't know if it's a good plan, but it's the best one they had, I guess."

"I'm going to owe Dutton an apology," I told her. "But that is a pretty nutty plan."

"Gregory," Sharon said, managing not to bat her eyelashes, "would you mind getting me a cup of tea? I think it would help me relax."

And god bless him, the poor sap fell for it again.

Once he was out of the room, Sharon said, "Look. Go home. Rest. Take a day or two and think about this. It's a huge decision and it's not something you should commit to when you've been going through hell all this time. We'll have a chance to talk later."

"Lunch at C'est Moi! tomorrow?" I asked.

Sharon smiled. "Sure."

"But let's be clear, Shar," I said. "I don't need the time to think. I need time to get used to the idea, but I'm not going to change my mind. I'm this baby's father, and I'm going to be part of its life." I stood up, and so did she.

Sharon walked over and kissed me lightly. "I never really doubted it," she said. "No matter what I was thinking, as I went over it again and again, that part was never in question. You're going to be a great dad."

I put my hands on her shoulders. "And you're going to be a great . . ."

Gregory pushed open the kitchen door. "Regular or herbal?" he asked.

"OKAY, so I owe you an apology," I said.

I'd had to walk back to police headquarters to get the bicycle anyway, so making amends with Dutton immediately was probably the best way to go. I'd said things that, in retrospect (it had been close to two hours ago, after all, so now I had time to think more objectively) were a little harsh.

"Yeah, you do," the chief said. "But I can understand that you were pretty emotional at the time."

"And by all appearances, you were railroading my ex-wife," I said. "What kind of crazy, twisted, bizarre logic led to . . ."

"You're not very good at apologizing," Dutton pointed out.

"I'm sorry," I said. "It's been a rough week."

"For everyone," he answered. Dutton can sometimes come across as Superman's older brother and other times like your aunt Mildred. It can be difficult to keep track.

"Are you convinced one of the Chapmans is responsible for Russell's death?" I asked him.

"I'm not *convinced* of anything, but it's the best theory for the time being," he responded. There was a file on his desk labeled *Chapman*, which was blue, as opposed to all the other files, which were green. He opened the blue one and leafed through it idly. "None of them seemed to like him much. He had a lot of money that he won't be needing now. There were rumors that he was leaving a chunk of it to the medical practice that seemed—and you'll pardon me, but I want to emphasize that *seemed*—to have bungled his case. Yeah, there were a few angry people in that family, and that's always a good breeding ground for violence."

"What about the son-in-law, Wally?" I asked. "Did he ever get back from Japan?"

Dutton's eyelids fluttered a bit, but he said, "Wally showed up last night, jet-lagged and cranky. At least, he said it was the jet lag that made him so cranky. I get the feeling Wally is cranky most of the time, jet lag or no."

"You questioned him?"

He shook his head. "No, East Brunswick is doing the investigation. But I was sitting in. Kowalski let me watch from behind one-way glass. He did a good job."

"Wally, or Kowalski?"

"Actually, both. Kowalski asked all the questions I would have asked, and Wally dodged most of them without looking like he was dodging anything. It was an interesting interrogation to watch."

I watched him closely. "So you think our pal Wally knows more than he's saying."

"I don't think anything. I just watch."

"I think you know more than *you're* saying," I tried.

Dutton looked as coy as an eighth-grade girl when you ask if she, you know, *likes* you likes you. "Maybe," he said.

"Come on, spill."

"Meg Vidal checked the airline records. The only reason Wally took so long to get back from Tokyo was that he had to fly out there yesterday."

He got the response he'd been seeking: *"Huh?"* I asked.

"Yeah. Wally was somewhere else when he was supposedly doing business with the Kyoto Blue Fin consortium. Russell's death caught him off guard, and he hightailed it to Tokyo yesterday, to make it look good, never left the airport, and flew right back."

"Lucky for him he doesn't have deep vein thrombosis," I said. "So, where was he?"

"Meg's working on that."

He started to close the blue file, and I caught a glimpse of something that flashed by, and did a double take. "Wait a second," I said.

Dutton looked up. "What?"

"Let me see that."

"Elliot, this is a file I got from another police department. *I'm* not even supposed to have it. If you think for one second I'm going to let a civilian see it . . ."

"The picture, Chief. The picture from the autopsy. Just let me see the picture, okay?" It would nag at me for days if I didn't get to figure it out.

Dutton considered, but saw the look on my freshly shaved face. He was very careful about extracting the photo without showing me anything else in the file. He took it out gingerly and held it up for me to see without handing it to me. I leaned over to take a close look. My throat suddenly felt dry.

"If you're not used to seeing autopsy photos, it can be . . ."

"It's not that, Chief. I mean, it's probably not the best picture he ever took, but that's not what's bothering me."

"What *is* bothering you?" Dutton knew how to deliver a straight line when it would further his own agenda.

"That's not Russell Chapman," I said.

Dutton withdrew the picture and put his head down on his desk blotter. "Not again," he said.

26

BEFORE this trip to the morgue at Robert Wood Johnson University Hospital, I stopped at home to pick up an item I thought I'd need and give an update to Meg, who was staying in my guest room for the duration. Homicide detective that she is, Meg couldn't give up on the Chapman case until she was at least satisfied that she'd done everything possible, and that hadn't happened yet.

She was also working out of my house half the time because someone needed to guard the door against Leo Munson, who had abused the privilege of watching DVDs. Leo came by every three hours, and Meg would block the door. I wasn't sure if Leo was really deluded enough to think I'd given him a lifetime pass to my home, or if he just liked seeing Meg.

In any event, I told her everything I knew, and Meg went to work on the phone while Dutton and I drove to the hospital for another corpse viewing.

It still wasn't a comfortable place to be, but I didn't feel like all my internal organs were melding into one, as I had the last time I was here. Yes, I was going to view a dead body, but there was absolutely no possibility it was that of a woman I had loved at any time in my life. There's a feeling of security that goes with that knowledge.

The procedure, however, was very similar: Dutton and I stood outside the room with Detective Eugene Kowalski of the East Brunswick Police Department until the same little curly-haired guy came out and told us the corpse was ready for his close-up. But this time we stayed in the waiting room, at the ME's insistence, since none of us was the next of kin, and viewed the body on the video monitor.

Of course, the body was covered with a sheet, presumably to allow the morgue attendant his moment of high drama as the sheet was lifted to reveal the face of the victim. The face itself was largely undamaged, but there was the equivalent of a scar on his throat. I tried to focus on the facial features.

The man was not tall, although it was hard to tell on a video screen, even if he'd been in HD. He was almost bald, in his late sixties or early seventies, and clean-shaven. His face was lean, and he reminded me of photographs I'd seen of the Marx Brothers when they were "off duty" and not wearing the familiar makeup.

"That's not Russell Chapman," I said.

Kowalski, who at first glance seemed a trifle peeved at all the people in the room who weren't from the East Brunswick Police Department, sighed. "Yes, it is," he said.

"No, it's not," I insisted.

"It is."

"I'm telling you, it's not."

"Boys," Dutton said.

"We have Russell Chapman's fingerprints on file," Kowalski said, looking straight at me. "He was in the Army, during peacetime. The fingerprints match. That's him."

"You thought it was him the first time," I pointed out.

Kowalski eyed the morgue attendant with a certain disdain. "That's what we were *told*," he said, shooting words like bullets in the attendant's direction. Even through the closed door, he could hear that.

The attendant reddened, as he was being challenged. "The daughter came in and identified him," he said over the monitor. "You're lucky we did the fingerprints on him at all; normally we wouldn't with a positive ID. Besides, Doc said it was Chapman. How am I supposed to know it's some drunk fell on the tracks at the railroad station? It wasn't until I checked the toxicology that I saw he'd had alcohol in his blood, and not Valium."

Doc! I'd seen him hand in the autopsy report, with Chapman's name on it, at Midland Heights headquarters the night Sharon had first left for Lake Carey. It was a blue folder, too, and being delivered to Dutton. Must have been from the Middlesex County ME's office, courtesy of East Brunswick.

But that was beside the point. I shifted back toward Kowalski. "I don't doubt that you did everything that needed to be done, Detective," I told him, and noticed Dutton nodding with agreement that I was showing the other officer the respect to which he was entitled. "But I'm telling you, I know that man"—I indicated the body—"isn't Russell Chapman."

"And how do you know?" Kowalski put his hands on his hips and glared. At me. It wasn't pleasant.

"I'll show you." I reached into my jacket pocket and pulled out a special piece of equipment I'd gotten when we'd stopped home to update Meg. Then I dragged one of the chairs in the waiting room to a spot under the monitor, and stood on it. I placed the object on the picture of the man's face. "See?" I said to Dutton. "You met him, didn't you?"

"Damn," Dutton said.

"Hey . . ." the morgue attendant tried to say, but Kowalski, who appeared annoyed, deferred to Dutton, and held up his hand: Hold it.

Dutton walked over to get a better look at the man on the slab. "You're right, Elliot. I do recognize him." He looked at the corpse, then back at Kowalski, then at me, then the corpse, then Kowalski again.

"I don't care what you say," Kowalski reiterated. "That's Russell Chapman."

"Maybe it is," Dutton said. "But with the Groucho glasses on his face, I can tell you for sure that when Elliot and I met this man, he was calling himself Martin Tovarich."

27

TUESDAY

"SO Mr. Chapman was pretending to be this Tovarich guy?" Sharon and I sat inside at C'est Moi!, our favorite lunch place in Midland Heights, and she was, at the moment, halfway through a french fry dipped in cheese.

"That's the theory," I answered. "It's a good thing you're eating for two, you know, or I'd be worried about the amount of food you're scarfing down."

Sharon dropped her voice a number of decibels and said, "Let's try and keep that just between us for the time being, all right? I haven't said anything to the others at the practice yet."

"You haven't told Gregory either, have you?"

She blushed a little. "It's not easy."

"I'll be happy to tell him for you."

"No!" Her head snapped up and she stared at me. So did a few people at neighboring tables. One redheaded guy, in particular, glared. Jeez; sorry to have ruined *his* day.

I stifled a laugh. "Okay. But soon, all right? My mother's going to be mad enough that I didn't tell her before *I* knew."

"Tovarich. Russell Chapman. Tell me what you know." She took a bite of her California burger and listened as I updated her on everything I had heard or discovered about her dead patient. Sharon listens very well, and did not interrupt with any questions until I was clearly finished with my twisted tale.

The redheaded guy kept glaring, but he seemed to have shifted his glare to Sharon. Which I could understand: if you're going to fix your gaze on someone, she's much more interesting to watch than I am.

"That's weird," she said between bites, never actually allowing anything to drip, a skill I find unnerving. "So between the first time they supposedly found Chapman's body and the second, he was posing as Tovarich?"

"That seems to be the consensus, yeah. But what purpose could that have served?"

"Beats me," said my ex, through a sip of draft root beer. "And if his disguise was so obvious that *you* could spot it in the glimpse of a photograph, how could his daughters miss it? They were both around when you saw 'Tovarich.'"

I nodded. "But I did notice that he ducked into the men's room whenever he spotted Gwen or Lillian. It just never occurred to me that he was doing it because he was their dead father, and not just a guy with a weak bladder."

Sharon put her hand over her mouth and burped, heartily. I was starting to worry that our child would be born with a tattoo. "They are a rather opposite pair, aren't they?" she said.

"Gwen's nice enough, but she seems stunned. Lillian didn't seem to care about their father being dead so much as this mysterious endowment he was supposedly leaving you in his will."

Sharon made a face that indicated her low tolerance for such suggestions. "That's absurd," she said. "I'd never accept that kind of legacy from a patient. It's a breach of so many ethics, I can't begin to imagine it."

"So you're actually less concerned about the insinuation that you would inherit money from a patient than the accusation from one of his daughters that you were sleeping with him to get the money?" I would have stolen one of her fries, but I'm way too classy a guy to take food from a pregnant woman. Besides, the congealing cheese was kind of grossing me out.

"Oh, be serious. I never would have had an affair with Russell Chapman. The man was at least thirty years older than I am, and a patient." Sharon took another swig of root beer. "I can't begin to tell you how many different ways that's wrong."

"How do you explain the PI telling me he'd followed the woman who was with Chapman at the hotel back to your house the next morning?"

"I can't," she answered. "But I know it wasn't me, and no other women live at my house."

"Well, Lillian thinks it's true, and I'm a little scared of her," I said. I looked at my own chicken Caesar salad (with low-calorie dressing) and wondered why my genes weren't as tolerant of fat as Sharon's. It's a sad state of affairs.

"The last thing I need to worry about is getting money to add on to the practice," she went on, as if I hadn't spoken. This was a heartwarming tradition left over from our marriage. "As it is, sometimes I've consulted on Lennon and Toni's patients as well as my own, and they do the same when I ask. In fact, Lennon consulted with me on Chapman. The idea that we'd want to add on a clinic is fantasy. I don't know where this stuff comes from."

"That's weird."

"What?" Sharon asked, perusing the dessert card left on the table.

"Lennon said he didn't know Chapman very well. He didn't mention being consulted."

Sharon looked up. "That *is* weird," she said.

I paid the check (granted, with money that probably came from Sharon's alimony, but let's not split hairs; I was being gallant) and Sharon asked me to walk her back to the practice, something I would have suggested on my own anyway.

Especially since the redheaded guy, now on his cell phone, was still glaring when we left.

My head was clearing from the panic-stricken mode I'd reached when I didn't know where Sharon was, and now I felt a need to talk to some of the people at her practice. The Chapman murder was going to be an albatross around Sharon's neck until someone figured out what had happened. I was feeling an increased sense of responsibility for her well-being again, and that was enough to get me curious about Chapman's strange medical misadventure.

"So let me get this straight," I said while we walked into the biting wind and proceeded up Edison Avenue. My voice fought the wind, and won by a decibel. "You told Chapman he *didn't* have a malignant tumor, and he apparently went home and wrote a suicide note, then pretended to kill himself by overdosing on Valium."

"That would appear to be the case," Sharon said, holding a gloved hand over her knit hat to keep it from blowing away and landing at Mary Tyler Moore's feet in Minneapolis. "Although the coroner's report indicates there wasn't any Valium in his body when he finally did show up dead on Sunday."

"Why did you prescribe Valium for him when he *didn't* have cancer?" I asked. "What did he have to be nervous about?"

"I gave it to him before the tests, when there was just a suspicion," Sharon said. "He was nervous *then*."

I put up the hood on my parka and fixed the Velcro under my chin. It might have made more sense to worry about how to walk into the wind, but alas, Marcel Marceau was dead, and therefore unavailable for technical assistance.

"What I don't understand is why he'd say explicitly in the note that he didn't want his illness to be a burden to his children, when he knew for a fact that he wasn't seriously ill," Sharon said.

It wasn't enough that we were walking into gale-force winds on a twenty-degree day; apparently we were being punished for even more sins, as the sidewalk took a decidedly steep upturn that I hadn't noticed in times when the climate was somewhat more forgiving. I was glad Sharon's practice was only two more blocks away.

"You're sure he understood that; he didn't walk out of your

conference unclear on that point?" I asked. If Sharon wasn't going to acknowledge our arduous trek, I certainly wasn't going to be the one.

She shook her head. "No, he understood perfectly. He was downright thrilled with it, said he'd gotten a whole new lease on life. It doesn't make sense."

We were almost halfway up the hill, which peaked at the street corner, and I was about to answer when I noticed something heading in our direction as we made our assault on the corner of East Third Street. Actually, it was the sound I noticed first: a rumbling of metal on concrete that sounded familiar and yet menacing at the same time.

With the hood on my parka pulled over my head, my vision was a little limited, but as the rumbling got louder, I looked up. Looking directly into a strong wind is like looking into a bright light: You can't do it for long, and your eyes immediately start to water. But the large, heavy, fast-moving object was unmistakable.

It was a supermarket cart, and it was headed directly at us at a very respectable speed. Sharon, looking at her feet to avoid staring into the wind, was only a few feet from it, and it was accelerating. No one was pushing it.

I reached out for her without saying anything; there just wasn't time. My arms got around Sharon, and pulled her toward me. I sat down hard on the pavement as the cart zoomed by us, but the seventeen layers of clothing I was wearing prevented any serious injury.

"You pick the strangest times to get frisky," Sharon said, entangled in my arms on the sidewalk.

"I think I landed on my coccyx," I said.

"Get your mind out of the gutter."

The cart, having reached a speed that seemed too fast even for a heavy metal object traveling downhill with a strong wind behind it, crashed into a light post about ten feet from where we sat. It hit with unexpected force, and something flew out of it and onto the sidewalk. Luckily, Sharon and I were the only two people stupid enough to be on this stretch of Edison Avenue at the moment, so no one else was in danger of being hurt.

"Are you okay?" I asked. "That thing could have killed you."

She stood up and dusted herself off, then held out a hand to help me up, which I declined for serious macho reasons. "I'm okay," she said. "How about you?"

I got to my feet and looked down. "Nothing important seems broken," I said. "How about the baby?"

Sharon smiled a smile that combined her "men just don't get it" expression with her "people who aren't doctors just don't get it" expression, to doubly make me feel stupid. "I fell on you, butt first," she said. "It was a soft landing."

"Forgive me for being concerned," I said, and marveled at how much I sounded like my mother.

"I didn't see it at all until you grabbed me," Sharon said. "You really saved me, Elliot." She leaned over and kissed me on the cheek. I held her a couple of seconds too long.

We were shouting against the wind. "Where did it come from?" I asked. "The supermarket is six blocks from here."

"People take them home for stupid reasons," Sharon said, shaking her head. "Then they abandon them in the street somewhere. I guess one just got loose in the wind."

I frowned. "It had to go uphill to make it over the top," I said. "There's no way that was a random accident."

"Elliot, you're starting to sound like Oliver Stone," she said. "It's a shopping cart. Don't get paranoid on me."

But I was already walking toward the cart. The lamppost was practically undamaged except for a scratch, but the cart had suffered a large dent right in the front, and as I got close, I could see why.

It had been loaded with cinder blocks, which had been placed at the front of the cart to weigh it down and give it increased momentum and increased impact. Sharon walked slowly over as I picked up the object that had been jettisoned, which turned out to be one of the cinder blocks, now severed in two on the pavement.

"This thing was made to cause damage," I said.

"Why do you say that?" Sharon asked.

"Because of this," I said. I held up the broken cinder block and put it back together to show her what it had looked like before its aborted journey.

Painted on the side of the cinder block were the words DOCTOR WARNING.

28

CHIEF Dutton met us at the practice after Sharon called him. We'd considered calling on Sharon's cell from the scene of the crime, but it was just too damn cold. I'd brought the offending cinder block with me, and we'd walked to Sharon's office in record time. I told Dutton where the incident had taken place, and he sent over a patrol car to investigate.

"So let me get this straight," Dutton said after we'd finished giving our statements, which sounded sillier and sillier as we went on. "You're thinking someone knew you two would be walking up that street at that time, went and got themselves a shopping cart and some cinder blocks, grabbed themselves a big black Magic Marker, wrote a message on one of them, and then pushed it up over the top of the hill at just the right time to knock you down. That's the premeditated attack you have in mind, is it?"

My opinion of Dutton was on a real roller-coaster ride these days. "I suppose you find that hard to believe," I said.

"Hard to believe? No," Dutton shook his head slightly. "I wouldn't say hard to believe. Impossible, maybe, but not hard."

"I'll admit, it doesn't seem like the most logical plan ever devised," Sharon tried, "but to be fair, you weren't on Edison Avenue just now, Chief."

Dutton sat down, and thought it over. "I'm not trying to trivialize what happened to you, Doctor," he said. "I just don't know that it falls into the category of a major crime, as opposed to a really nasty prank that went too far."

"A prank?" I said, my voice doing a really awful job of masking my impatience. "A *prank*? A fifty-pound shopping cart with a hundred pounds of cinder blocks front-loaded in it comes screaming down a hill on a forty-five degree angle, which adds momentum and creates a harder impact heading straight for a woman who's . . ."

"Elliot," Sharon said quietly.

". . . not looking, and you call it a *prank*?"

"I realize you're upset, Elliot, and you should be. Either of you could have been badly hurt. But how am I supposed to file a report of attempted murder with an unmanned shopping cart?" Dutton's manner, as it had been since Sharon's disappearance, was sympathetic, but slightly concerned, as if he thought I'd benefit from some mood-altering medication. "We don't even know that there was intent."

I held up the cinder block with the message written in thick black marker. "This means it was intentional, doesn't it? It means it was aimed at Sharon."

"DOCTOR WARNING? Isn't that a nineteen-fifties horror movie?" Dutton smiled.

I looked at him and aggressively didn't laugh.

"I've been a cop twenty-seven years," Dutton said, "and I've never before heard of people being attacked by a grocery cart. This kind of stuff usually happens to you, doesn't it, Elliot?"

"What about the redheaded guy I saw at C'est Moi!?" I asked.

"It's a crime now to look at the two of you in a restaurant?" Dutton responded. "I'm sorry, Elliot. That would have to be at least thirty percent better just to qualify as circumstantial."

I ignored that crack and asked, "What can you do to ensure Sharon's safety?"

He raised an eyebrow. "We're the police, Elliot. We're not a private bodyguard service."

"I'm serious, Chief. Someone made an earnest attempt on Sharon's life, and I want to know what's going to be done."

I swear, Dutton and Sharon exchanged a look questioning my sanity.

"We're going to do what we can," Dutton said slowly, looking at Sharon and not at me. "We'll increase drive-bys to the house and here at the office. But you have to understand, Doctor, that I can't assign you your own police officer every time a shopping cart gets loose in a windstorm."

Sharon nodded. "I understand perfectly, Chief. Thank you."

It was a good thing the blood pressure cuff wasn't on my arm at that moment. "Well, *I* don't understand," I went on. "I'm worried about your safety, Sharon. If I hadn't seen that thing exactly at that second . . ."

"But you did, and I'm grateful, Elliot, believe me," she said. "Now, you have to be reasonable and see things from Chief Dutton's perspective. All we have is a cinder block with some nasty words on it."

"I think those words are pretty specific. Someone has a real serious problem with you, and I can't always be there to pull you away at the right moment." I ran my hands through my hair, and realized the parka's hood had done it no good at all.

Dutton stood up. "Well, I'll get back to the office and see if the officers at the scene came up with anything else," he said.

My jaw dropped. "That's *it*?" I asked. "File a report and be done with it? How am I going to sleep tonight?"

The chief folded his arms and regarded me with a look that did not indicate a high degree of patience. "If you have any other ideas about what we could be doing for you, Elliot . . ."

"As a matter of fact, I do. What about fingerprinting the shopping cart handle?"

Dutton shook his head. "A shopping cart could have a hundred people's prints on it. And even if we got something, it would only help whoever did this get off with an insanity defense," he said.

"Insanity?"

"Sure. Anybody who'd go outside today without gloves on has to be crazy."

SHARON spent the next ten minutes reassuring me that Dutton was doing everything within his power to protect her, and I was just as adamant that a nationwide APB be issued for anyone seen pushing a shopping cart. But after Dutton left, I had to admit that Sharon's point of view made a little bit more sense.

Just a little, though.

Sharon had patients to see, but I wasn't ready to leave just yet. I told her I'd stick around awhile, since Comedy Tonight didn't have to open for another four hours, and she looked like she might want to dissuade me, but thought better of it and put on her white coat to go to work.

I wandered over to the reception area, where Betty was filing some medical records. Early in her employment at the practice she had been told, discreetly, to tone down her wardrobe, thus avoiding her causing cardiac arrest in some of the more fragile male patients (and to be fair, some of the female ones, too). Today she was wearing jeans that weren't quite sprayed on and a loose-fitting V-neck sweater that made me shudder to think what she'd be wearing if she *hadn't* been warned.

"How's it going, Betty?" I asked. Not original, I'll grant you, but it's an effective opener.

"Hanging in there, Elliot," she said, and wiggled back to her station. To Betty, I am Dr. Simon-Freed's ex, and that's about it. Which is fine, since she's a good ten years younger than me, and I don't actually spend my time lusting after Betty. Anymore. "How about you?"

"I'm doing better now that Sharon's back," I said.

Betty nodded. "We're all relieved." Two patients were in the waiting room: a woman in her forties and a lanky teenager utterly absorbed in his handheld video game. They were pretending to be in an elevator together, doing all they could not to make eye contact. The woman read a copy of *Entertainment Weekly*.

"Still, weird about Mr. Chapman, huh?" I asked.

She didn't blink. "Yeah. He commits suicide, then he's alive, and then somebody kills him. That's a new one."

I understand the way a doctor's office operates because I've been around one often enough. Betty wasn't cavalier about patients, and it wasn't that she didn't care. But if you didn't build up at least some protective armor, you wouldn't last two weeks in this job. People get sick, and some of them die. Those are the rules.

"Funny that you didn't recognize him when he came in dressed as Tovarich," I said, thinking out loud.

"Yeah, I thought about that. He had that coat buttoned up over his face, and the bushy eyebrows and glasses. He could have been my grandmother, and I wouldn't have known it."

"I hear some people around here knew him better than that," I said quietly. Didn't need the patients out front to hear.

Betty looked up at me. "I'm not saying anything about *that*," she said.

So there *was* something going on. Could Russell Chapman have been dating . . . Betty? Nah. Konigsberg had said it definitely wasn't Betty.

Then again, Konigsberg said it was definitely Sharon. Not the most reliable source of information, that man.

"I'm sorry if I'm saying anything that hits too close to home, Betty," I told her.

Betty's eyes widened, and she did the last thing I'd have expected: She laughed.

"Me?" she asked. "You think there was something going on with Russell Chapman and *me*?"

"I have no idea . . ."

But she was on a roll. "Forget that the guy was, like,

ninety years old. You think that I'd go after him just for his money? I don't like to speak ill of the dead, but—"

"I'm sorry, Betty, I just—"

"—who am I, Anna Nicole Smith? Is that the best you think I can do, Elliot?"

I leaned on one of the filing cabinets, as the salvo she'd fired was hitting me right in the face. "I meant nothing by it, Betty, believe me. I think you can do . . . that is, I think you could have . . . I think anybody who ended up with you would be a very lucky person."

She grinned on one side of her mouth. "That's better. No, I had no relationship with Mr. Chapman outside the office. I took his insurance information and told him when the doctor was ready to see him. That was about it."

"I'm just confused," I said. "This detective told me Chapman came here just about once a week, whether he had an appointment or not. Just about the time you locked up."

She nodded. "That's right. But it's not my place to say anything else about it."

I felt my eyebrows come together in the center of my face. "Betty, the man was murdered. If you don't tell what you know . . ."

"When the police ask, I tell. You are not the police." The front door opened, and a patient—a short middle-aged guy with a self-satisfied grin—walked over to the window. Betty turned toward him and away from me.

I walked back down the corridor toward the conference room. But before I got there, Toni Westphal walked out of one of the examination rooms and spotted me.

"Elliot," she said. "You going to take up residence here now?"

"Not if I can help it," I told her. "I've got a theatre to run."

"Good that Sharon's back," Toni said. "We were all worried. I guess you more than anyone."

"Yeah, it's a load off my mind, thanks. But Russell Chapman's daughter seems to still think Sharon had some involvement with him, and she's mad about it." I told her our Tale of

High Adventure from Edison Avenue, and Toni's mouth dropped open.

"That's crazy," she said.

"Welcome to my world. But Lillian Chapman thinks Sharon had some strange power over Chapman, and undulated her way into his will. Is there any reason she'd think that?"

"Well, I do know that Mr. Chapman used to come by at night sometimes when we were closing up, but I don't remember him looking for Sharon when he did," Toni said.

"Why not? Wasn't she his doctor?"

"Not really, no," she said. "I was."

"Then how come Sharon gave him his test results Thursday night?" Sharon hadn't told me everything about this, which was troubling but understandable. She really respects that whole thing about privacy and the doctor/patient relationship.

"She caught him the day he came in complaining of headaches," Toni answered. "I was at the hospital that day, so Sharon got him. And once you log in a patient that way, you see him through to the resolution, unless he specifically asks to see another doctor."

"He'd been coming back before then?" I was trying to get the chronology straight in my head.

Toni nodded. "Oh, long before. A few months, easy. But he wasn't seeing Sharon, as far as I know."

"Who *was* he seeing?"

Toni raised her eyebrows. "Not me," she said. "Beyond that, it's none of my business." She picked up the patient's chart from the next examining room. "Excuse me, Elliot," she said, and knocked, then opened the door and walked inside.

She was almost immediately replaced with Lennon Dickinson, who materialized from the reception area carrying a clipboard. I figured I'd make it a clean sweep and bother him, as well. How often do you get a chance to annoy an entire medical staff in one afternoon without actually being sick?

"Hey, Lennon," I said. "How's the unbridled nightlife going?" Lennon, although physically appealing to most living women, was about as exciting a personality as Millard Fillmore.

"Why do you think I have an unbridled nightlife?" he asked. See what I mean?

"Just kidding," I told him. "Listen, on that subject, I hear that Russell Chapman was . . . involved with someone here at the practice. Know anything about that?"

"I'm not gay, Elliot."

"I didn't think it was you," I said. "I thought maybe one of the women."

"I don't get involved in the personal lives of the staff," Lennon said. He started heading for another exam room.

"You haven't heard anything?" I figured I'd press the point.

"No." A man of few letters.

"It's been a blast riffing with you, you maniac," I told him as he opened the exam room door.

"What?"

I turned to go back toward the waiting room, but another examination room door opened, and Sharon walked out, with Grace the nurse, who was taking notes on a clipboard about the patient they had just seen together. The patient, I assumed, was getting dressed and ready to leave inside the exam room.

"Elliot." Sharon smiled, and Grace looked up from her writing to see me as they approached. "You're still here."

"Am I?" I looked around. "I can't seem to find myself anywhere." The Elliot Freed version of charm. It's an acquired taste.

Luckily, Sharon had acquired it a while back, and she chuckled. She stopped walking, and so did Grace. "What have you been up to?" she asked.

"Just being my usual helpful self," I said.

"Oh, dear. Did you break anything big?"

"That's very amusing, honey. I'm starting to remember why I divorced you. Or was it why you divorced me?" I reached over and gave her a hug. Lately, I'd been just a little more clingy than usual.

"Please, Elliot. Not in front of the *staff*." Sharon nodded her head at Grace, who smiled. "You don't want to give them ideas."

"Yeah," Grace agreed. "I don't want to think of you as a person, just as a doctor."

"I'm sorry, Grace," I said. "She's always been like that. But I know you're a woman with a full, full life. How's Mike?"

She grinned. "My husband's fine, Elliot. So are the kids. Mary started college in September. And she's my youngest!"

I expressed the requisite amazement that time had, indeed, passed since the turn of the millennium, and we chatted for a few minutes about families and acquaintances. But I was looking for a way to grill Grace on the mysterious affair between Russell Chapman and . . . somebody. Although she was a trusted nurse, Grace was also the most notorious gossip in the office, and would know everything about everybody. There just didn't seem to be a natural opening for the question, especially with Sharon present.

But then, my ex-wife allowed for just such an opportunity when she ducked into another exam room and let Grace know she wasn't needed for this exam. Grace started to make her way back to the office, where Betty would probably have everything completely under control. Grace, in other words, wasn't busy.

"Hey, Grace," I began, with as original an opening as I could muster, "I need to ask you a question."

"I'm married, Elliot." She smiled.

"Not *that* kind of a question." I can play along with a joke—when it's convenient. "I need some inside info, and you're the person to ask."

Grace saw the expression on my face and wrinkled her forehead, surprised. "I think the break room is open," she said. "Come with me."

I followed her into the small break room, where a coffeemaker, microwave oven, tiny refrigerator, and a table and chairs indicated this was not really what you'd call a medical procedure area. It was about as warm and cozy as the delousing area at a small prison, but it served its purpose.

She took a cup of coffee from the pot and offered me one, which I accepted. Today, anything warm was worth exploring to the fullest. We sat in the cold chairs and leaned our elbows on the Formica tabletop.

"What's our topic today?" Grace asked.

"Russell Chapman," I started.

"The poor man's dead," she answered. "Isn't that enough?"

"Not when he was murdered, and there are people who think Sharon might have been involved," I said. "There are all sorts of rumors flying around, and I'm willing to bet you know which ones are true and which ones aren't."

"What rumors?" The tone was noncommittal.

"First of all, there was a ridiculous suggestion that Chapman was having an affair with Sharon, and had left her money in his will to build a children's clinic." I watched closely for the reaction.

It came in the form of a raucous laugh. *"Sharon?"* she said. "Somebody thinks Russell Chapman was having an affair with Sharon?"

I nodded. "I'm not saying I believe it; I'm saying it was suggested."

Grace shook her head. "I'm surprised at you, Elliot. You should know your ex-wife better than that."

"I do. But I needed to hear it from you."

"Well, now you've heard it. Are we done?" Grace started to stand up.

"No," I said. "Just a second."

She sat back down. "Okay. No, there was never any suggestion I heard about that we'd be getting some of Chapman's money if he died. I can't imagine Sharon would even accept it if it were offered."

I nodded. "She wouldn't. But someone here was involved with Chapman, at least as more than a patient. A private detective saw them go to a hotel together, and saw Chapman drop the woman off at Sharon's house."

Grace's eyes widened a little. "A private detective?" she asked.

"Yeah. What do you know?"

She took a moment to think, seemingly about how much she could tell without betraying a serious confidence. "There was someone here who saw Mr. Chapman about once a week or so," she said. "I can't say how intense it got, but I know it was a regular thing. Now, what they'd be doing at Sharon's house, I have no idea."

I leaned forward. "You know I wouldn't push it if this weren't unbelievably important, but I have to ask, Grace: Who was it?"

"Don't ask me that, Elliot."

"I'm asking."

Grace's expression spoke of serious pain; she loves to talk, but hates not being trustworthy. She considered her words very carefully. "If I were forced to name names," she said, "I'd have to say it was Toni Westphal."

29

The difference between life and the movies is that a script has to make sense, and life doesn't.

—JOSEPH L. MANKIEWICZ (SCREENWRITER, *All About Eve*)

WEDNESDAY

"IT'S all tied together," said Sandy Arnstein.

Sandy, the electrician Dad had called to deal with the electrical problem at Comedy Tonight—which had resulted in three flickers and two outright blown fuses the night before—was a guy who had been an electrician since roughly ten minutes after Ben Franklin came in with the kite. He was standing in the doorway to the theatre's basement, holding a pair of wire cutters and trying (in vain) to explain himself to me in a way that my techno-challenged brain could somehow understand.

"What's all tied together?" I asked for the fifth time.

"The problems with the plumbing and the electricity," Sandy answered. "One causes the other, which causes the first one again. It'll keep up this way until someone breaks the cycle."

"So break it," I suggested.

"You can't," Sandy said, with a tone that indicated a third grader would have grasped this by now. "If I break it now, it'll just come back in the plumbing." I would have sworn I saw Jerry Lewis play this guy in a movie once.

I rubbed my eyes with my thumb and forefinger, and contemplated putting a sign on the front door that read BEST OFFER. "So what needs to be done, and how many banks do I have to rob to pay for it?" I asked.

Sandy didn't so much as smile. It was possible I really would have to go into a life of crime, after all. "I think you need a whole new electrical service, and it's possible I'll have to rewire a good portion of your theatre."

"You can't kill me with words, Sandy," I told him. "Just tell me how much time and how much money."

"Time? Impossible to say—I have to see how much wiring is burned out already. Money?" Sandy reached into a pocket in his overalls and pulled out a calculator, on which he started punching buttons. It took considerably longer to reach a sum than I would have preferred. "About six thousand dollars."

"I was wrong. You *can* kill me with words."

Dad, who had been leaning on the wall next to the men's room door, walked over. "Come on, Sandy," he said. "Give him the family discount."

"That *is* the family discount, Art," he said.

"Pretend it's *your* family."

Sandy pursed his lips, stared at my father for a moment, and said, "Lemme check." Then he walked back down the basement stairs.

I exhaled, and looked at Dad. "Thanks. But even with the family discount . . ."

"One problem at a time, Elliot," he said. "Sandy needs to stew for a while, and then decide that it doesn't need as much work as he thinks it does. But you would be better off with circuit breakers than these fuses."

"The theatre thinks it's nineteen thirty-seven," I told him. Only ten in the morning, and I was already wondering if we'd be able to open tonight. Dad went downstairs to work on his friend some more.

I went into my office to make some phone calls. Grace's suggestion that Dr. Toni Westphal had been having an affair with the late Russell Chapman threw a strange monkey wrench into the questions in my head. Toni and Sharon had always gotten along, but were never close friends. Since it seemed to follow that the person who was involved with Chapman was also trying to make Sharon look guilty, I had to know what the state of their relationship was like.

Sharon had been backlogged with patients and paperwork the day before, and still had the minor detail of informing Gregory about her pregnancy, so I hadn't bothered her about it last night. Instead, I'd come to the theatre to listen to Sophie apologize for not knowing about Sharon's disappearance, again, despite the fact that I realized I'd never told anyone on the theatre staff.

Today I sat down in the desk chair and called Sharon's practice. She was in with a patient, Betty told me, and would call back. So I decided to call Detective Kowalski in East Brunswick. Despite my telling the dispatcher who I was, Kowalski took the call.

"Got any more party favors you want to put on a murder victim, Freed?" he asked by way of a greeting.

"I put it on his video image," I said. "There's a world of difference."

"Is there a reason I'm talking to you?"

"I'm just trying to help out my ex, Detective," I told him. "What can you tell me about the weapon that killed Russell Chapman?"

"I see no reason to tell you anything," he said.

I'd been anticipating that response. "How about because I talked to Doc the night Chapman was supposed to have killed himself the first time?" I asked.

Kowalski's voice went up a full register. "You've been withholding information for almost a week, and you want an accommodation for that?" he asked. "You tell me right now what you know, Freed."

Since I didn't actually know anything, a bluff seemed the right way to go. "You get nothing from me until you tell me about Chapman. Was it really a medical instrument that cut his throat?"

There was a light moan from the earpiece. "You know, Chief Dutton warned me about you the first time he called about this Chapman thing. He said you were a pain in the ass, and you wouldn't ever let up."

"Chief Dutton is a flatterer," I said. Kowalski was lying; Dutton wouldn't use the phrase "pain in the ass," even under extreme duress. The worst he would say about me was that I was "an inflammation in the posterior." It's the same idea, but expressed in more genteel terms. That's Dutton.

There was an uncomfortable silence for a long moment. To be specific, the silence was uncomfortable for Kowalski; I could have waited all day, quite happily. I opened the file on the computer for MacBrickout. Level Eleven is a bitch.

Finally, Kowalski said, "All I'm saying to you is that it was a surgical instrument, but that doesn't mean much. That's all I'm saying."

There are these water pipes, see, that hide the bricks you're trying to hit, so sometimes you don't even know you should be aiming at something. And these annoying bubblegum balloons float in the air and gum up the works.

Kowalski couldn't take the silence anymore. "There had been a little bit of a struggle. Chapman wasn't drugged, but there were definite drag lines on the carpet, which would indicate he might have been unconscious before he was killed or moved afterward. I'll bet you it was noisy, either way."

And if that wasn't bad enough, some of the bricks are really close to the bottom, so if you don't get the paddle down low enough (which requires a special ability that you acquire through catching a black-and-green capsule that drops from the sky at random moments), you could be shooting against something that will spit the ball back at you very quickly without warning.

"Okay," Kowalski went on. "There was also blood on the carpet and on the desk, which might indicate a struggle, or that Chapman injured his killer before he died, because the blood on the carpet wasn't all his."

It was time to let him off the hook. "So he was killed with

a scalpel, but not before he tried to fight his killer off, with some level of success," I said.

"Yes or he was attacking someone who killed him in the ensuing struggle," Kowalski added.

"So Sharon would seem to be off the hook for this one," I suggested.

"Nobody ever thought your ex-wife killed her patient," Kowalski scoffed. "What was suggested before was that she wanted to drive him to suicide to get at his will. Now that's out the door, too."

"Has anyone read the will yet?" I asked. "I want to make sure nobody has a motive to hurt Sharon."

"Probate has been filed by Chapman's lawyer, but she hasn't made it public yet," he answered. "We probably won't know for a couple of weeks exactly what's in there."

"Thanks, Kowalski," I said. I was about to hang up, but he remembered how the conversation had begun.

"Now, you tell me what you know. What did Doc say to you the night Chapman was supposed to have offed himself?"

"Actually, pretty much nothing," I admitted. "He basically said that he was bringing Chapman's autopsy report, and I said I wasn't interested."

This time, the long silence was Kowalski's doing. "That's it?" he asked finally.

"That's it."

He used language not suitable for a family newspaper, re-iterated that Dutton was right about me, and hung up. I decided to get up and stretch my legs, as they seemed too short just at the moment.

But the phone rang, and thinking it might be Sharon, I turned to answer it. The caller ID indicated Sophie's cell phone.

"What's up, Sophie?" I said. "I thought you weren't supposed to call from school." There's some fascist rule about not using your cell phone during AP Psychology class.

Her voice sounded odd. "I'm just calling because . . . I

won't be coming in." I realized the problem with her voice—
I'd only heard Sophie cry once before.

"You don't have to come in; it's your day off," I reminded
her. "Sophie, tell me. What's wrong, honey?"

"I won't be coming in, like, ever," she went on. "My parents say I can't go to work anymore."

"What? Why won't they let you come to work?"

"They say it's interfering with my preparing for college,"
she croaked. "They say I won't get into the Ivies if I keep
spending my time at the theatre."

"That's silly," I said. "You've already applied everywhere
you're going to apply, right?"

"Pretty much," she agreed.

"And you've gotten this great score on the SATs, so what
else do they want from you?"

"The ACTs, or something. I don't know. I can't do it. They
want me to be perfect. They want me to stop working. I don't
know what to do, Elliot." The poor kid sounded like she was
at the end of her rope.

"Why don't you just tell them no?" I asked. "You've done
it before."

"Now they say they're paying for college, so I owe it to
them to do the best I can and get scholarship money," Sophie
answered. Her parents were using the old guilt ploy. It was a
tactic with which I had some familiarity.

"Do you want me to call them?" I asked.

"*No!*" I was getting that a lot lately. "They'd just get mad."

"Sophie, listen to me." I stood up; as I said, I think best on
my feet. But the phone cord isn't very long, so I had to lean
over. I wasn't sure what effect that had on my thinking. "Tell
them I didn't accept your resignation. Tell them I said you had
to come to work because I don't have anyone else."

"Really?" I wasn't sure if she was grateful for the idea, or
questioning my sanity.

"Yes, really. Tell them that you have to at least give two
weeks' notice, and that'll give us time to think of something.
Okay? Now, I expect to see you at work this very evening."

"It's my night off," she said.

"They don't know that."

I could hear her blow her nose. "Thanks, Elliot."

"No charge, sweetie."

Sophie is the backbone of my staff. Yes, Anthony is incredibly valuable because he can run the projector, and Jonathan can . . . Jonathan is very good at . . . I like Jonathan, and he knows his comedy, an asset in a theatre that might, on occasion, book *Sons of the Desert* (Laurel and Hardy, 1933). But Sophie is the bridge between the technical staff (Anthony) and the support staff (Jonathan), not to mention management (that's me). I could lose Sophie to Harvard, but I wasn't going to lose her to Ilsa Beringer.

This would require some thought, and I didn't have the time for that now. I had to figure out what happened to Russell Chapman. There was only one thing to do: go out and get a sandwich.

But I had barely made it to the office door when it became obvious I had something else to do first. There was a thin wisp of smoke coming from the basement door, but that didn't bother me. There was a slight smell of burning rubber in the lobby, but that didn't bother me.

It was the flames coming down one of the walls in a straight line that bothered me.

I dashed for the snack bar, where we have a fire extinguisher, and grabbed at it. I'd never actually used a fire extinguisher before, but this seemed like an excellent time to learn. So I ran with it, shaking it as if it were an enormous can of whipped cream, toward the lobby wall with the line of flames. As I ran, I yelled "Dad!" down the basement stairway.

It turns out that it's not that difficult to use a fire extinguisher. It's pretty much point and shoot, and what do you know—it extinguishes the fire. If only all things were as reliable in their ability to perform the task assigned to their names. Then we would have cough suppressors that really suppressed coughs, and public servants who actually served the public.

But perhaps that's beside the point.

Feeling pleased with myself, I immediately turned toward the basement door, from which Dad was emerging, looking a little panicked at my tone. Sandy Arnstein was behind him, holding what appeared to be the world's largest wrench.

"What's the matter?" Dad asked. Then he looked at the lobby wall—now streaked with black soot and extinguisher foam—and said, "Oh."

"This isn't anything I did," Arnstein said. Some guys know exactly how to handle human interaction, and then there are those who are more comfortable with things like wires and current.

"No," I agreed. "I'm sure the wall just burst into flames on its own, and the smoke coming from the basement where you were working is strictly a coincidence."

Dad looked shocked, probably more at my sarcastic tone with his friend than with his friend's setting my theatre on fire while Dad looked on. "Elliot," he chided.

"Why didn't my fire alarm go off?" I asked.

"I had that fuse turned off," Arnstein explained.

"I hope you have a good lawyer," I said. There went the family discount.

Arnstein said not another word. He turned and walked toward the basement door, no doubt to pack up his tools and move on. I had to consider reining in my mouth on occasion until such time as my theatre isn't in danger of being shut down by the local fire department.

"I'll talk to him," Dad said, and went to follow Arnstein.

"Tell him I won't sue him if he fixes the fire damage," I said, and Dad gave me a stern look. I thought I was being reasonable.

My day didn't get any easier when I turned to walk back toward the office. Standing just inside the lobby doors were Gwen Chapman and her sister, Lillian.

Standing next to them was the redheaded man I'd seen at C'est Moi! right before the shopping cart had tried to flatten Sharon.

I walked over to them, and extended my hand to the red-haired man.

"I'm Elliot Freed," I told him. "And you just *have* to be Wally. I've heard so much about you."

He didn't look pleased.

30

WALLY Mayer did not take my hand. Instead, he looked at me much as that big animated can of Raid used to look at the animated bugs it annihilated. "I'm not here to be friendly," he growled.

"Well, you're off to a flying start," I told him.

Wally huffed and puffed, but even given the dilapidated condition of the house was unable to blow it down. Seeing as how the house had tried to *burn* itself down only a few minutes before, it was showing surprising resilience.

"We're here to deliver a message," Wally continued, as if I hadn't spoken, which was the first sign of intelligence he had shown.

"Three people for one message?" I marveled. "That must be a huge Candy-Gram. Where'd you hide it?" I looked around the three of them, as if expecting at the very least a Whitman's sampler. Nothing.

"You can't protect your wife," Wally said.

"Ex-wife," I corrected him.

"Ex-wife," he agreed.

"I can't believe you ever married that woman," Lillian Chapman offered.

"Well, I can't believe you married that man," I countered, gesturing toward Wally. "It's all a question of taste, isn't it?"

Gwen, who had been looking like she'd rather be in Philadelphia (it's a W. C. Fields reference; Google it if you don't believe me), finally piped up, "Can't we find some common ground here? There's no reason to be so unpleasant."

"Your ex killed a very important man," Wally intoned, completely ignoring his sister-in-law. He'd learned his lines, and he was delivering them. "A very important man."

"She didn't kill anyone. And you mean a very *rich* man," I corrected.

He shrugged. "It's the same thing."

"Let me get this straight," I said. "The three of you—okay, the two of you—have come here to verbally threaten the life and health of my ex-wife? Because you still harbor some twisted belief that she drove him to attempt suicide? You haven't heard that she told him he *didn't* have cancer? And you haven't been told that he was murdered—excuse me, Gwen—not driven to suicide? Is that what I'm hearing?"

"I'm here to suggest a reasonable attitude," Gwen said. "Mr. Freed had nothing to do with Dad's death, certainly. Why are you threatening him?" But again, her sister and brother-in-law pretended she hadn't spoken at all.

"You hang in there, Gwen," I said. "In the end, you'll be proven right." I winked at her, which probably wasn't the right move.

"She told him he had cancer because she wanted his money," Lillian Chapman continued, not persuaded. "She seduced him and then took away all his hope. And she duped my poor father into willing her millions."

"Don't be absurd," Gwen told her sister. "Dad never would have invested without a prototype." Beats me; I was an English literature major.

"Man, you guys would have made great comedy writers,"

I said. "And here I am without a tape recorder to get all this down."

"You don't have any witnesses, either," Wally reminded me. "So you can't go and report us to the police. They'll never believe you, anyway."

"Oh now, stop it, Wally," Gwen pleaded. "There isn't going to be any trouble."

"That's what you think," Wally told her, betraying his third-grade level of wit.

"So, just to be clear, what kind of violence should I warn Sharon about?" I asked. "Are you going to attack her with more supermarket paraphernalia, or will one of you cut her throat with a scalpel like you did with your old man?"

And imagine this—the Chapman girls had the nerve to act offended! "How *dare* you accuse us of such a thing?" Lillian huffed. "I should have known you would stoop to this level—your kind are all alike!"

I drew myself up to my full height. "My *kind*?"

Lillian looked down the full length of her nose at me. "You know exactly what I mean," she growled.

"Lil!" Gwen admonished.

"If you guys came by looking for free movie passes, you really need to work on your technique," I told them. Then I turned to Wally. "Look, your wife was born into this family, but you chose to marry her. That wasn't a really high intelligence day on your biorhythm the day you said I do, was it?"

"Whaddaya mean by that?" he asked.

"My mistake," I said. "I guess you don't *have* any really high intelligence days on your biorhythm. Now, take your lovely sister-in-law and your fairly unappetizing wife, and get out of my theatre. The management reserves the right to refuse admission to anyone who has an IQ in the negative numbers."

Strikingly, they left, even as Gwen apologized to me a number of times.

I could hear clanking and the occasional power tool sound

from the basement, so I guessed Dad had worked his magic on Arnstein. What I couldn't decide was whether I was happy about that or not. But I did decide not to report the fire to the department of the same name, as I was tired of being shut down, and figured the fire was already out, and they'd just put on all their winter gear for no purpose. You see, it was really an effort on my part to lighten the load of the local fire department.

Fine. Believe what you will.

I could remember something about wanting to go out for a sandwich, but that seemed like a very long time ago. Since I was here, and there was little I could do while my theatre's electrical system was being dismantled—and, hopefully, re-mantled—I decided to head back to the office to get some paperwork done and try to solve a few problems. Like figuring out who killed Russell Chapman, how to keep Sophie on my staff, and whether we should name the baby after Groucho or Harpo if it was a boy.

I was planning to solve these problems by playing MacBrickout for a while (you'd be amazed how much you can think about when you're not thinking), but then I remembered there was a stack of mail on my desk that I had not looked at since Sharon had taken her little trip to the Poconos. I sat down at the desk and started sorting the mail.

After throwing away catalogs (I didn't really *need* new popcorn buckets) and stacking bills, I had a depressingly small pile of mail that actually was addressed to someone other than "occupant." I disposed of most of it quickly, and then I came across an envelope that was unusual.

It was plain, with no return address and no distinctive stationery pattern. The address was handwritten (and not by one of those computer programs that's supposed to *look* handwritten), in blue ink, to "Mr. Elliot Freed, c/o Comedy Tonight," with the address of the theatre beneath. It was postmarked in East Brunswick two days before, indicating that it had been stamped by the post office on Monday, and could have been mailed anytime between the post office closing on Saturday and sometime after it opened Monday.

The letter was strange in that there was absolutely nothing strange about it. It's rare that a business, especially, gets a piece of mail that isn't in some way generated by another business. Movie theatres don't get personal letters, and yet this appeared to be just that.

I actually used a letter opener I have on my desk, something I rarely do. Sharon had given me the opener when I started the theatre, as part of a stationery set that I almost never use. She thought it seemed "professional" to have such an item. I'm not sure I've made this clear, but I don't have use for the thing.

Unfolding the letter, I had a sense of importance; this didn't feel like a casual piece of mail. It was also handwritten, in very clear script, on heavyweight, expensive stationery. It was dated three days ago—Sunday—and it read:

Dear Mr. Freed:

I'm not sure why I'm writing to you. We've only met twice, and I know I'm not a close friend, but you have had a significant impact on my life, even if that was not your intention. In the back of my mind, however, I know the real reason I'm writing: to say that I am sorry.

My apologies for the deception I have perpetrated upon you. I hope it has not caused you any serious inconvenience, and I hope that you do not believe I have been attempting to make you feel foolish.

When we met, I introduced myself as Martin Tovarich, and that was a lie on my part. I was playing the part of Tovarich, simply pretending, and since I had not met you before, it didn't seem a terribly gross inconsideration. You were, in fact, the last person I was thinking of when I "became" Tovarich. Let me explain.

Two weeks ago, I visited your ex-wife's office, complaining of severe headaches that would last all day and make it impossible for me to concentrate on anything at all. She recommended a series of tests, and seemed concerned. I asked her what she suspected might be my problem, and she tried not to say, but rich men become used to having things their own way, and when I insisted, she told me what I didn't want to hear: that she thought it was possible I had a malignant brain tumor.

Even an old man fears death. Don't let them tell you otherwise. I was terrified, and could barely function while undergoing the tests and—worse—waiting for their results. It seemed to take forever, and I aged ten years for every day I had to wait.

During that time, I naturally got in touch with both my daughters. We've never been as close as a father would like to be to his children, but I felt it was important they know about my condition, and I suppose I hoped for some comfort and sympathy from them.

I was disappointed. While Gwendolyn was sympathetic, she was detached in her concern, asking about the state of my medical care, rather than how I felt or what emotions I might be having. Lillian was colder still. Her questions were limited to my financial affairs. This disturbed me greatly. I love my daughters, and thought they felt the same for me.

I am a very rich man, Mr. Freed. A chemist by trade, many years ago I developed a process that helped preserve certain kinds of baked goods. It worked especially well in flour tortillas, and I marketed the process to businesses that would find that helpful. When a national taco chain decided to buy the process from me outright, I became a very wealthy man. Since then, I have not worked in chemistry, which I always loved. I have instead worked to keep my finances healthy, which I found tedious but lucrative. My estate *is worth over $47 million, and my daughters are aware of that.*

But a few nights ago, Dr. Simon-Freed called to say the tests had come back, and although she said she could give them to me on the phone, I wanted to look her in the eye as she explained the results. I needed to know if she was a person I could trust through an ordeal. My late wife died of liver cancer, and I was with her every step of the way. It's an awful process. I steeled myself and went back to your ex-wife's office.

As you probably know by now, the diagnosis is much less severe than I originally feared, and I am not about to die. That new lease on life was exhilarating, but was tempered by the unsettling glimpse I'd had into my daughters' minds and how they thought about me.

I decided to test them, to see if they were truly concerned about my well-being. I emptied the bottle of Valium your ex-wife had prescribed to calm me down into the toilet, left the bottle out where it would be found, and wrote a suicide note. Then I called someone I know in authority (and I'll say no more about that) and arranged to be classified a "suicide." It was also arranged that my "corpse" would be brought to the county morgue. My daughters were summoned, and Gwendolyn identified the "body" as mine via video monitor.

I could then put on some theatrical makeup, call myself "Tovarich," and observe their reactions to my "death" and the circumstances around it. The look I got was shocking.

There was never a tear shed, no expression of concern for my welfare (whether or not I had died painfully, for example), not once. It almost made me want to commit suicide in truth. My eldest daughter said nothing about me that wasn't about my fortune. My younger one said virtually nothing at all, but she did not seem distraught, merely surprised.

Nothing can prepare a man for the realization that his daughters don't love him. Nothing. Parenthood is a huge undertaking, Mr. Freed. You don't have children yet, but perhaps some day you'll find out. And if you do, I urge you—don't be distant from your child. That bond is more important than money, personal success, or any other concern. Love your children, Mr. Freed. More than you want to.

My despair was deepening—although I found a release in playing Tovarich, as he was a very jolly man—until I happened across you at the doctor's office, and you suggested I drop by your theatre. And when I did—the film you were showing was the perfect tonic for me, Mr. Freed; it gave me insight into what really matters in this world. The enthusiasm "Tovarich" showed when we met after the showing was genuine. I really did find it a life-changing experience.

And I thank you for that.

Let me give you this one piece of advice before I close, Mr. Freed. Don't ever give up your theatre. It is your passion, as mine was chemistry. It is the purpose you have taken on while on this earth. See it through. Give the gift of laughter to more people, and leave this world a better place. I gave up chemistry, and for all I have gained financially, I have regretted that decision every day since.

Tonight I have given up the disguise of Tovarich. When I discovered that your ex-wife was under suspicion in my "death," I could not allow that to go on. I will call my attorney immediately and let her know I am far from deceased.

Now that I have told you my strange tale, perhaps I will find the courage to face you in person, instead of hiding behind a pen. But I am ashamed of my ruse, and grateful to you for all you have done for me. I would like to help you do that for more people. Perhaps I can do so. We'll talk when we meet again, and I hope that will be soon.

Sincerely, and with much gratitude,
Russell Chapman

Immediately, I picked up the phone and hit redial. When Kowalski answered his phone again, I said, "This time, I've *really* got something for you."

31

MEG appeared in the theatre perhaps five minutes later, saying Kowalski had called Dutton, who had asked her to "watch the letter" until an East Brunswick cop could be sent to pick it up. Apparently, although Chapman had trusted me with his innermost thoughts, the East Brunswick police department did not. I decided not to dwell on that for long.

Once I had realized what the letter contained, I had been turning pages with a pair of tweezers I'd found in the desk when I'd bought it. I told Meg about the tweezers, in case it had left marks on the paper. I didn't tell her that I'd used the time before she arrived to scan each page of the letter into my Mac. What Meg didn't tell Dutton wouldn't hurt me.

Tattletale that I am, however, I did tell Meg about the not-so-subtle threats Wally and Lillian had made toward Sharon. She was skeptical that it implicated them in the shopping cart assault, or even that the shopping cart incident had been an assault. But Meg did find it interesting that when I'd alluded to supermarket materials being used as weapons, neither Wally nor Mrs. Wally had asked me what the hell I was talking about.

The East Brunswick officer arrived and took the letter, giving me a form that said my "evidence" would be returned to me as soon as the court saw fit. Then the cop left, and Meg, muttering something about "real police work to do," followed suit.

At just about that moment, Sharon called back, which was convenient. She was about to take a lunch break, and I had questions. But yesterday's trip to C'est Moi! had ended badly, so we agreed to meet at Big Herbs.

Belinda had more customers than usual, but I found a table near the kitchen door and waited for Sharon. "You look better than the last time I saw you," Belinda told me.

"I am better," I said. "Sharon's not missing."

"You know, for two people who got divorced, you really don't hate each other nearly enough."

"I know," I admitted. "We're a disgrace to the institution."

Sharon walked in just as Belinda went back to get an order of tofu dogs from the kitchen for someone who, clearly, had never seen a tofu dog before, or they certainly wouldn't have ordered such a thing. My ex sat down across from me, not exactly glowing, as you hear pregnant women are supposed to do. Instead, she was all curiosity.

"So tell me about this letter," she insisted.

I did.

"That is the weirdest story I've ever heard," Sharon said when I was finished.

"And it's not over yet. After he mailed the letter, someone sent Chapman to a different destination than he expected."

Belinda came over and, seeing that we looked serious, kept the banter to a minimum while she took our orders, which I don't remember. Suffice it to say they were vegetable oriented.

When she walked away, I said, "Now that you've been back a couple of days and I've had time to think, I have questions."

Sharon's eyes narrowed. "Questions? For me?"

"Well, they're really for Albert Einstein, but your legs are cuter."

"Not for long," she lamented. "I'm going to bulk up soon."

"Don't change the subject. Questions."

"Fire away," Sharon said.

"When you got the results on your pregnancy test, you decided you had to get away and headed for Lake Carey."

"That's not a question," she pointed out.

"I'm getting there. Did you go home to pack a bag?"

"No. I had already done a home test, and I really knew what the lab test would say. I had packed some things in a travel bag that morning, and, as you know, I keep some clothes up at the cottage."

"But before you went to the lake, you were in a hotel bar in the city with some guy," I said.

Sharon's voice dropped in pitch a little. "That's not a question, either," she said ominously.

"Yes, it is."

She smiled. "It was just Lennon. I ran into him when I was getting into my car. He was going into the city that night after work, and I offered to give him a ride to Penn Station. He thanked me by buying me a drink, but don't worry, I didn't have any alcohol."

"No, you had milk and seltzer," I said. "Which, by the way, is disgusting. And if you were going to Lake Carey, what were you doing driving to Penn Station? That's completely in the wrong direction."

"Oh, I just wanted to talk, I guess, and Lennon needed the ride."

A picture began forming in the back of my head, but it was fuzzy, like an old Polaroid. I decided to press on, and give it time to develop.

"Swell. So you're all emotionally jumbled because you're carrying my baby, and your first impulse is to hop in a car with Lennon Dickinson, master of mirth."

"What?" she burst out. "Oh honestly, Elliot. You can't be jealous of every man I know."

"First of all, yes I can, and second, that's not what this is about. Chief Dutton found credit card receipts in my name in a trail that starts at that hotel bar. From there, *someone* went on quite the shopping spree, including Manhattan souvenirs, jewelry, and some very interesting lingerie."

"And you think it was *Lennon*? This is a reach, even for you, Elliot." Sharon's face couldn't decide if it was amused at my childish jealousy or concerned for my questionable sanity.

My Polaroid was finally developed, sharp and clear.

"I've been thinking about it for a while," I said. "I keep a credit card in my wallet, but I never use it. Lennon insisted on seeing it the day I came in for my physical, right before you went to the lake. I was paying my co-pay in cash, and there was no reason for him to ask for the card, but he's Lennon, and I didn't want to push it, so I gave it to him."

"And he gave it back to you, right?" Sharon asked.

"No. He gave me back a card, and I put it in my wallet without looking at it. I'm willing to bet he gave me his own, and kept mine." I told her about the waitress at the diner cutting up "my" credit card in front of my mother and me. "I thought it was because mine had been cancelled, but I'll bet you it was because Lennon's was way over his limit. Besides, Lennon never said he'd seen you that night, that you'd gone into the city with him. He didn't want anyone to connect the credit card receipts with him, even when we thought you might be in danger."

"Oh, this is absurd. Elliot, Lennon Dickinson is a *doctor*."

"So was Jack the Ripper, if you believe some of the accounts," I said.

She scowled at me. On her, it looked good. "You're being obtuse. Lennon makes good money. He doesn't need to steal your credit card to buy underwear for his girlfriends."

"How do you know it's for his girlfriends?"

"Okay, now you stop that. How do you explain a doctor stealing a patient's plastic to go on a cheap shopping spree?" Then, as an afterthought: "It was cheap, wasn't it?"

"Don't worry. Dutton and I called the company, and I'm not liable for the charges."

"Yeah, but the underwear. How cheap . . . ?"

"Let's stick to the point, shall we?" I was taking the moral high ground, which was unfamiliar territory for me.

Belinda came with the food, and we started to eat whatever it was. "I don't believe it," Sharon said. "I've known Lennon for five years. I can't believe he'd just—" She stopped, and stared ahead for a moment, not seeing the restaurant (which was just as well) or me (less encouraging).

"What?" I asked.

Sharon's eyes didn't focus on me, but she did appear to hear what I was saying. "That was the night I had the conference with Russell Chapman, where I told him that he didn't have cancer," she said. I waited, as I knew she was getting around to a point. "Naturally, Lennon and I spoke about it quite a bit in the car. When you get to give a patient good news, it's always satisfying, so we like to make the moment last as long as it can. But Lennon's questions were odd."

"Odd in what way?"

"He seemed to be curious about Chapman's business interests, like he wanted stock tips or something. He asked me if I knew whether Chapman would advise a guy on financial matters. Asked if I knew whether he'd be interested in investing in new products."

That *was* odd, and I said so. "Sounds like Lennon's interest in Chapman's state of mind was about equivalent to that of Lillian and Wally's," I said. "All they wanted to know about was his money."

"Lennon's got money to invest with Russell Chapman, but he can't afford pots and pans? What does all this mean, Elliot?"

Like I knew.

"Did you tell him where you were going? Because he never said a word, even when we were frantic."

"No. I made a point of it. Told him I was going out for the evening, and nothing more." So at least Lennon wasn't cruel enough to watch everyone squirm—he really didn't know anything.

We agreed it would not be advisable for Sharon to confront Lennon Dickinson immediately. For one thing, the evidence was entirely circumstantial, and for another, we had no idea what it meant. So the plan was for Sharon to observe Lennon for a day or two and see if she could spot any more unusual behavior.

But I had more points for Sharon to clear up. "Why was the conference with Chapman private?" I asked. "Don't you usually do that with a nurse in the room?"

"Yes, but Chapman specifically requested it be just himself and me in the room. I think he was concerned that he'd get emotional, and to tell you the truth, he did." Sharon kept shaking her head just a little. "This whole thing just keeps getting more confusing, Elliot. Chapman got a second chance at life, and someone immediately took it away from him. Why?"

"When we find out who, we'll know why," I told her. "And that's the part that's bothering me. Because I think the person—or people—who killed Chapman is the same person—or people—who tried to take you out with a shopping cart."

"I still think you're overreacting to that," Sharon said. "It was a windy day."

"You're right. The wind blew all those cinder blocks into the shopping cart, and then waited patiently until you and I were climbing up a hill against it. Yeah, that wind is a wily force of nature, all right. Besides, I saw Wally Mayer at C'est Moi! right before we left. He knew where we were."

"It's still absurd," Sharon said, as if that proved her point.

"Just as well, I'd appreciate it if you could try to keep out of the way of the Chapman women and Wally, which I believe was the name of a disco band in the seventies. Is there any way we can find out what was in Chapman's will? That could prove to them that you didn't have a motive to kill their father."

"It makes sense."

"Oh, one last thing: I talked to Grace . . ."

Sharon rolled her eyes. "You're gossiping with Grace now? Honestly, Elliot, what kind of a role model are you going to be for our"—she dropped her voice to a whisper—"*child*?"

I ignored her. "Grace said Chapman *was* having an affair with someone from your office—Toni Westphal."

"Then Grace has been drinking," Sharon said.

"What, you and Toni are such good friends that she'd tell you if she was dating an older guy?"

"No." My ex-wife grinned. "But we're good enough friends that I know Toni Westphal is a lesbian."

Oh.

Belinda came by with the check, and studied us closely. "What's going on?" she asked. "There's something new with you."

"Yeah, now we've eaten," I tried.

"No, I'm used to that. Besides, all you had was this vegetable stuff. People don't look that happy over vegetable stuff." Her eyes widened a bit, and she stared at Sharon. "Are you pregnant?" she asked.

Sharon's jaw dropped open about two feet. A snake would have been proud of her potential food capacity. "How could you know?" she asked.

"I'm a genius," Belinda said. "I just know stuff."

"Fess up," I told her.

"Okay, I heard you talking about it before. So tell me."

"Not yet," Sharon said. "We have to break the news to family first."

Belinda nodded and said, "Lunch is on me." She would hear no argument, ripped up the check, and walked away before we could protest. Sharon stood up and started to put on her coat.

"Gregory," I said.

"No, I'm Sharon," said my ex-wife the comedienne.

"What did Gregory say when you told him?"

She turned away from me and put on her scarf. I knew why she turned away.

"You didn't tell him, did you?"

The voice that came back was small and faint. "Not yet," Sharon said.

I didn't say anything. I'd suspected that this would be difficult for her, and no matter how angry it made me, I had to be sympathetic. I put on my coat and waited for her. We walked out of the restaurant together.

Without a word, we started walking toward Comedy Tonight. I had to be back to get the place into some kind of shape for the evening's showings, and to figure out a way to save Sophie's job. Sharon could walk with me to the theatre, and then continue on to her practice.

"So," I said finally, "Chapman's lawyer."

"Yes," Sharon agreed. "You should probably call her. That might help, and I certainly can't do it without breaking about seven different ethics codes."

Before I could remark about that (and it was going to be a corker, trust me), I heard a car's brakes screech, and then someone—probably Sharon—shouted, "Look out!" Then something hard hit me in the forehead.

And not to belabor the cliché, but at that moment, all went black.

32

ONE medical examination room, even in a medical practice belonging to your ex-wife, looks pretty much like every other medical examination room. But there are certain touches that, even when you're regaining consciousness, you can recognize. Sharon always has a rubber duck in her exam rooms; she says it's to amuse frightened children. I believe she considers it a talisman of some sort, and as evidence, I note that she calls the object Lucky Duck. I rest my case.

In any event, old Lucky was sitting right on the shelf, directly in my line of vision, when I opened my eyes. My head felt strange, swollen in one spot and flat everywhere else, and while I didn't exactly have a splitting headache, I was not at all anxious to touch the area just above my right eyebrow, as I had a sneaking suspicion I would find that experience regrettable.

"I don't have to ask where I am, but I'm curious about how I got here," I said. My voice sounded hoarse, and my throat didn't hurt. It also sounded like it was coming from somewhere other than inside me; I would have sworn I could hear myself speaking across the room. Closing my eyes again was starting to seem like a good idea.

Then I caught sight of Sharon out of the corner of my eye, rushing from the other side of the room to the examination table I was lying on, her face a little wet on the cheeks. "Elliot!" she barked, then tried to calm her voice. "How do you feel?"

"Like I was hit by the three thirty-five to Penn Station," I said. "What happened?"

"Someone threw a brick at you," she said, but her voice was very low, and I was confused. Then I saw Chief Dutton loom up behind Sharon. "Someone in a passing car turned the corner in front of you and threw a brick that hit you in the head," he said. "The doctor here called an ambulance, and they brought you here."

"Not to emergency?" I asked Sharon.

"This was closer," she said in her own voice this time. "I was afraid . . ." She didn't finish the sentence.

"Do I have a concussion?" I asked. "Did I concuss? Am I concussing?" I don't know why, but suddenly the word *concussion* seemed very funny to me. Sharon must have given me some very interesting painkillers.

"I'm not sure," Sharon said. "But I think you should lie still for a while."

"A brick?" I asked Dutton. "Somebody threw a brick at me?"

"I guess a cinder block was too hard to throw," he answered.

"Is it possible they were throwing it at Sharon?" I asked.

"Anything's possible. We don't even have a license number or a make on the car," Dutton said, seemingly pointing his comments at Sharon.

"It was dark blue," she said with some force in her voice. "Beyond that, I thought it was more important to get help for Elliot." It was clear they'd had this conversation already, and were now reiterating it for my benefit.

"How long have I been out?" I asked.

"About half an hour," Sharon answered. "And I want you to stay here another three hours so we can observe you."

"I can't. I have to be at the theatre. I have to save Sophie's job."

Sharon and Dutton passed a look. Maybe my head injury was worse than they'd thought. "Do you have to talk yourself out of firing her?" Dutton asked in his best "soothe the mental patient" voice.

"Her parents want her to quit, and I have to come up with a brilliant plan to convince them she can't. She's going to meet me at the theatre any minute, and I have to come up with something. I can't lie here for three hours."

Of course, the guy pressing down on my forehead with a fifty-pound mallet was making a convincing case for the other point of view.

"An hour," Sharon said. "I'm not letting you out of here for at least an hour. Argue with me, and I'll send you to the hospital. Are we clear?"

I put my head back down on the table. "I get so excited when you're all medical, honey," I said.

I don't remember a lot for some time after that.

WHEN I realized I was conscious again, there was no one else in the room. Except Lucky Duck. I discovered this by lifting my head, which was scarier than it was painful. I sat up, and again, felt better than I had expected to. I was considering standing up when the door opened and Sharon walked in.

"What day is it?" she asked.

"Buy a calendar," I suggested. Then I realized she was asking to test my brain, so I said, "Wednesday."

"What's your middle name?"

"You know I hate it," I told her.

"Who's going to hear? I already know your middle name."

I told her my middle name. Don't even dream I'd tell you.

"What's your mother's maiden name?" Sharon asked.

"Sperber."

"Okay. I think maybe you didn't have a concussion, or if

you did, it was a mild one. But I'm still not crazy about your condition."

"You liked it enough to let me get you pregnant," I reminded her.

Her face twisted around in a sour sort of way. "That's it. You're okay," she said.

She gave me the requisite lecture about putting ice on my head, taking acetaminophen for pain (apparently she hadn't given me anything for pain to this point: "You don't give pain medication to someone who's unconscious, Elliot"), calling her if I became dizzy, and having someone look at my eyes on regular occasions to see if my pupils were dilated. I promised to do all those things (although I really intended only to take the pills), got on my feet—which didn't require as much effort as I'd feared—and headed for the theatre. A quick check of my watch indicated I'd been asleep for an hour and forty-five minutes, which meant it was about the time the staff would start appearing at Comedy Tonight.

Sure enough, they were grouped together in the lobby, staring at the burn marks on the wall, still in their winter coats when I arrived. Sophie, who was there despite not being "on duty," informed me that the plumber and the electrician had apparently conspired to shut down the heating system in my absence, and were now "pretty sure" it would be on in time for the evening's showings.

I realized it was still less than a week since I'd first heard that Sharon was missing, and I felt at least seven years older.

Anthony asked me about the Laurel-and-Hardy–sized bandage on my head, and I said I'd had an accident. I'd actually had an "on purpose"—someone had deliberately tried to hurt me—but telling the truth would have required an outlay of time and energy I really couldn't spare at the moment.

I told Anthony and Jonathan to get to work setting up, reminding Jonathan that Sophie wasn't actually working tonight, so he'd be running the snack bar, and I'd show him how to work the popcorn machine at last. He nodded solemnly, as he always did when given responsibility for anything, and went about setting up. Sophie's expression was somewhere between that of a proud mother watching her son attempt the multiplication tables for the first time and a nervous bank manager handing over the safe combination to Willie Sutton.

Sophie followed me into my office, where I sat down, letting my head wound overcome my sense of chivalry. She didn't seem to care. "How are you holding up?" I asked her.

"I'm okay," she said, her tone saying the complete opposite. "I'm sorry I called up and cried."

"I don't mind. Well, of course I mind—I don't want you to cry. But we have to figure out a solution to our problem. What did your parents say when you told them you had to give two weeks' notice?"

She closed her eyes for a moment. "They said I shouldn't have to listen to you about that. They said I should tell you I'm not coming back, and that's it, because you can't sue me or anything because I'm a kid. That's what I told them I was doing today, coming to tell you I'm not coming back. But I don't *want* to stop working here, Elliot."

I sat back in my chair. "You've applied to how many colleges, Sophie?" I asked.

"Seven," she said firmly.

"You're pretty realistic. How many do you think you'll get into?"

"Seven," Sophie answered.

"What is it your parents expect from you?" I asked.

She thought for a long time. "More," she said.

"Okay. Tell them I didn't accept you resignation, and that I need to hear it directly from them. Get them to come here tomorrow before the showings. I'll work it out." I had no idea *how* I'd work it out, but I saw no reason to tell Sophie that.

She grinned at me for the first time since she'd reported her SAT scores. "Thanks, Elliot," she said. And she went out to tell Jonathan the problem was solved.

Now all I had to do was solve it.

And that's when the phone rang, and the caller ID said Meg was on the line. "We finally got Wally Mayer's cell phone records," she told me. "Over the weekend when he was supposed to be in Japan, he made seventeen phone calls, all from Newark."

"Newark! Who goes to Newark?"

"People who want to take in a hockey game or a performance at the Performing Arts Center, but nobody involved in this case that we know about," Meg answered. "There are many fine hotels, if one doesn't want to leave the room much. Idiot registered under his own name, too, and paid with his own credit card." She said she'd call with any more news, or that I'd see her back at the town house later. I hung up.

I decided not to worry about that *now*, because one must prioritize. The most important thing right *now* was Sharon's safety, and making my head feel better. Okay, the *two* most important things.

Since I couldn't do much about the pounding in my head—having taken two pills, which had the same effect as if I'd had someone blow lightly on my temple—I needed to concentrate on keeping Sharon safe. And the surest way to do that would be to find out who killed Russell Chapman.

I called up the copy of Chapman's letter I had on the iMac, and read it over again. He was disappointed about his daughters' reaction to his "death," particularly Lillian's laserlike focus on his money. What would a very wealthy man do in a situation like that?

Change his will.

There were just as many Angie Hogencamps listed under lawyers as there had been Allen Konigsbergs listed under investigators. I dialed the Spotswood number, and got a receptionist, whom I told I was calling on behalf of a party interested in Russell Chapman's will. I figured I was a party, and I was certainly interested, although I certainly didn't have any *financial* interest in Chapman's estate. Why split hairs?

It took some convincing, mostly in the area of why I couldn't tell the receptionist exactly whose interest I represented, but finally, she put Ms. Hogencamp on the phone.

"What is the nature of your interest in Mr. Chapman's estate?" she asked after we'd exchanged artificial pleasantries.

"I'm not as much interested in who was left how much, as I am in whether there were changes made very close to the day Mr. Chapman died," I explained.

"Are you a private investigator?" the attorney asked.

"I am an investigator," I admitted. Well, I was investigating, wasn't I? Nobody had mentioned the word *professional* in any context.

"May I ask whose interest you represent?" she asked again.

"I'm afraid I'm not at liberty to divulge that information," I told her. I've watched enough detective movies to have that line down pat.

"Then I don't see any reason I should give you any of the information I have," Angie Hogencamp said.

This wasn't doing Sharon any good. "Look, Ms. Hogencamp," I began. "The fact is, I'm not a private investigator. I own a movie theatre."

"I already knew that, Mr. Freed." She did?

"I'm sorry?" I said.

"You own Comedy Tonight, a movie theatre in Midland Heights that shows only comedies. I'm told it's quite a nice place to see a classic film." There was a certain amused tone to Hogencamp's voice. Dammit! Now I was starting to like her!

"How could you have known that?" I asked her.

"I'm afraid I'm not at liberty to divulge that information," she parroted back to me. "But I'll tell you this, for free: There *was* a change made to Russell Chapman's will, on the very day he died."

"He died on a Sunday," I reminded her.

"When you have a client with forty-seven million dollars, every day is a working day," she said.

"He could sign it that fast?"

"He was a very determined man," Hogencamp said.

"Has there been a resolution to Chapman's estate yet?" I asked.

"A resolution?" Now she was having fun with me. "You mean, has there been a reading of the will?"

"Um . . . yeah."

"Nobody really does that anymore, Mr. Freed," Hogencamp said. "I don't know if they ever did. The fact is, when the will clears probate, I act as executor and send out letters by registered mail informing all the heirs of their share in the estate."

"Have those letters gone out yet?" I asked.

"Not yet, no. It should be another day or two. Why the interest?"

"Just between us? No tape recorders or stenographers on the other line?" I asked.

"Oh, Mr. Freed, you really do see too many movies. Yes, we're off the record on this. I'm just curious."

I stared up at the ceiling of my office, which made my head hurt, so I closed my eyes. "Frankly, Ms. Hogencamp, I'm concerned about Lillian Mayer's reaction to his will. Someone I care about a great deal might be mentioned in his estate—although I doubt it, but Lillian thinks so—and if Lillian and Wally don't get the kind of inheritance they expect, whether it's this person's fault or not, I'm afraid they might react . . . badly."

"First of all, call me Angie. But, let me see if I'm understanding you correctly. You're worried that Lillian and her husband might commit violence on a person who may or may not be mentioned in Lillian's father's will if they don't get all the money they want?"

"That's right, Angie. And you call me Elliot."

She took a moment before speaking again. "Who is the person you're concerned about, Elliot?"

"Are you going to tell me if that person is mentioned in Chapman's will?"

"No." But she had a twinkle in her voice.

"Then I don't see the point of telling you." I was bantering with a woman I'd never met. It must have been my head hurting.

"Suppose there's no tape recorder or stenographer."

"Off the record? It's my ex-wife, Dr. Sharon Simon-Freed." Why did she want to know, if she wasn't going to tell me about the will?

"Your *ex*-wife."

"Yes."

Angie Hogencamp sounded baffled. "Most men with ex-wives would be at the very least ambivalent to the idea of violence against the woman," she said.

"I'm not most men."

"Clearly not. Well, if it makes you feel any better, everyone involved with the estate should be informed by I'd say Monday the latest."

Monday? Way too much could happen by Monday. "The latest?" I asked.

"Yes. It might be sooner. I can't say any more than that."

We exchanged genuine pleasantries before hanging up, and while I wasn't less concerned, for some reason, I felt better. Until I opened my eyes and saw my father and Sandy Arnstein in the office doorway. They didn't look happy.

I just didn't have the patience for it anymore. "What?" I asked.

"What happened to your head?" Dad asked at the same time.

"I cut myself shaving."

He gave me a look, but before he could answer, Arnstein said, "This is an old theatre."

"Thanks. I understand the earth is round, as well. Any other incredibly obvious things you'd like to point out?"

"All I'm saying is, this is an old building. There's things that go on here that wouldn't go on in a new building." Arnstein's face seemed defiant, somehow, as if I'd told him that this *wasn't* an old building, and he was proving me wrong.

I decided to slow down the conversation, under the (as it turned out, mistaken) assumption that it would make my head hurt less. "Okay. What has gone wrong that wouldn't have gone wrong in a new building?" I asked.

"There was a short in the electrical wires. For all I know, rats have been eating away at your wiring since Harry Truman was president." I felt like Arnstein had been making excuses for his work since Harry Truman was president, but for the first time in about a week, I decided to keep a thought to myself.

"So, what happened?" I asked again, my voice so patient you'd have thought I was Mr. Rogers on Xanax.

"So that ran up the wires into the lobby and made your wall catch on fire," he said.

Aha! Arnstein was asking me, in his abrasive way, not to sue him for almost burning my theatre down. Since I had to start thinking about paying college tuition in about nineteen years, I shifted my focus to the idea of saving money on the repair work. Maybe a lot of money. "So that's what caused the fire," I said. "What can you do about it now?"

"I've already done it. I ran some new wiring up through that area and put in a new electrical service where you had that ancient thing in the basement. I was afraid to put my hand near those fuses you used to have, I'm telling you." He waited, as if expecting applause, or at least a hearty "atta boy."

He got neither. "I meant, what can you do about the damage that you caused to my wall and the smell in my lobby?" I asked. Pleasantly.

Arnstein looked astonished. Here he had done me this tremendous favor, put his unparalleled talent to work for my benefit, and all I could do was remind him of a minor failing on his part (which had only narrowly escaped burning the building down)? He looked at Dad, no doubt wondering how such a fine and well-mannered man as Arthur Freed could have such an ungrateful, ill-mannered son. "What can I do?" he asked. "The damage is done."

"Yes, and it will have to be repaired. Now, would you prefer to fix it yourself, or would you like to pay for it to be fixed?" I think the bandage, which might have had a spot of blood on it, was giving my argument added weight.

Arnstein mumbled something, and slunk away. I looked at Dad, who repeated, "What happened to your head?"

"Another boy threw a rock at me, Daddy. Don't tell Mommy, okay?"

"Are you going to keep giving me smartass answers?" My father likes to assert his paternal authority from time to time. It occurred to me at that moment for the first time that I should have been taking notes for decades.

"I'm sorry. I was walking with Sharon and someone threw a brick. I got hit with it, but Sharon says I'm all right."

"Jesus! Who throws a brick at a total stranger?"

I didn't think the best strategy was to tell him it was the same person who tried to run down a pregnant woman with a frontloaded shopping cart, especially since he didn't know: (a) that the shopping cart incident had occurred, or (b) that Sharon was pregnant. There were all sorts of things I wasn't telling my father. If my kid ever tried that, I'd have to ground him for a month. "It's a crazy world, Dad," I said, and that part, at least, was true.

He shook his head at the insanity of it all, and followed Arnstein back, I assumed, into the basement. It hadn't occurred to me to ask whether the heat was going to come back on soon. I didn't care; we were having our showings, regardless.

Something had to be normal.

I went upstairs to the projection booth, where Anthony was dutifully cueing up *Sullivan's Travels* for the first show tonight. I sat down heavily in the available chair and watched him as he went about his work. Anthony was precise and focused, two things college students are not supposed to be. It was one of the reasons I'd hired him.

The other had been that no one else applied for the job.

"So, how are things in the projection booth?" I asked. Apparently, the injury to my head had inhibited my ability to smoothly converse.

Anthony looked at me. "Okay," he said. "Why?"

"I like to keep track of things," I said, as if that made sense. And then I realized why I'd come up here to begin with: for advice.

Yes, that's how bad things had gotten.

"You know about this thing with Sophie and her parents, right?" I asked Anthony.

"Yeah," he said. The kid thinks film all the time. Conversation is so beside the point.

"You're a lot closer to her age than I am," I babbled on. "What would convince *your* parents that you should stay on here?"

Anthony, to his credit, stopped what he was doing to think about it. "My parents," he said, "were so thrilled I had a paying job, I don't think they'd ask me to leave if you were a brain-eating zombie." Anthony is a gore movie fan.

"That doesn't help much," I said.

"No. I guess it doesn't." He thought some more. "Suppose you sold Sophie the theatre. Then she couldn't leave."

I pointed at the projector. "Thread, Anthony." And I went back downstairs.

The lack of heat in my office (and everywhere else in the building) reminded me that I'd seen something about the weather this morning, which seemed like it was nine days ago. So I checked on the computer, and there was, according to the National Weather Service, a forty-percent chance of snow showers around midnight. Certainly it would be cold enough for black ice. Just the thing for a cyclist on his way home.

Bobo Kaminsky is not your average bike shop owner, but then, Bobo is not your average anything. He's about six-feet-two in any direction, and lives to sell bicycles. Not long ago, he had resurrected my trusty mode of transportation from circumstances too dire for me to relate (I tend to tear up when thinking about it), and still grumbled about the fact that I hadn't simply plunked down a couple of grand on a new model. Bobo thinks I'm wealthy. I don't know why.

When I called him today, Bobo was clearly eating something, but that wasn't unusual—you don't get to be six-feet-two in any direction without fueling the fire every few minutes—and cranky. That was *really* not unusual.

"Bobo, do they make snow tires for bicycles?"

"I swear, Elliot, you sit around that theatre all day just

thinking up stupid questions to ask me, don't you?" I think that's what he said. I really didn't want to know what kind of sandwich Bobo was chewing at the moment. There's such a thing as too much information.

"Well jeez, I just thought I'd ask. So they don't make snow tires for bicycles."

His voice rose an octave and I thought a piece of some food matter was lodged in his throat. "Of *course* they make snow tires for bicycles!" Bobo coughed. "It's just amazing that it's taken you this long to ask about them. You've been riding that . . . thing . . . for years, through all sorts of weather, and this is the first time you ask?"

I decided to ignore the insult, because it saves time. "So if I get the bike over to you today, can you put them on by tonight?"

"Oh, of course, Mr. Freed. We exist merely for you, and no other customer ever darkens our doorstep. Your wish is my command."

"Great. I'll have it there in half an hour. By the way, how much are they?"

"The studded tires for a twenty-six-inch wheel are eighty-six dollars each," Bobo said.

"For *bicycle tires*? I might as well have a car at those prices!"

"So don't buy them," Bobo answered. "It's going to be twenty-six out there tonight. Enjoy the ride on the ice."

"I'll tell you what, Bobo," I said. "I'll bring the bike in. You get it done whenever you can get it done. No hurry. Is tomorrow okay for you?"

There was a long silence. "Who are you, and what have you done with Elliot Freed?" he asked.

"Exactly. I'm bringing the bike over, and I'm going to *watch* you put the tires on." I hung up before this jolly back-and-forth could continue.

The front wheel of the bicycle, which I always remove when I chain the bike up outside the theatre, was in the back of my office. My head felt well enough to ride the five blocks to Bobo's shop and then walk back, I thought. I stood up, and didn't see stars or tweeting birds. It marked progress.

Reaching over the piles of debris on top of my filing cabinets was an adventure—you always think you're going to bump whatever part of your body is already injured, because it feels like it sticks out two feet. But my head was still roughly the same size it had been this morning, and I extracted the wheel without any damage to anything but my sensibility.

I was halfway to the door when the phone rang. And sure enough, Sharon was on the other end of the phone. Thank goodness for caller ID; she was the only person on the planet I would have picked up for at that moment.

"Just checking in on your head," said my ex. She yawned loudly. "Any further symptoms?"

"Yeah. I have an irresistible urge to follow you around twenty-four-seven until that baby comes out."

"Any *new* symptoms?" Sharon yawned again.

"No, but you sound like you have Epstein-Barr virus. Am I boring you?"

"I'm sorry," she said. "The baby didn't want me to sleep last night. Everything they say about first trimesters is true. And then Grace got me out of bed at six."

"Why? Was there an emergency?"

"No," Sharon answered. "I left early and she stayed late last night, so she had some files to drop off for me to look at before I went in this morning. She does that every week or two."

It took me a second. "Oh, for goodness sake," I said.

33

I met Grace Mancuso at the Midland Heights Dunkin' Donuts. In New Jersey, it doesn't matter if your town is only a post office box number, you're required to have a Dunkin' Donuts. A version of the same law put a Starbucks on every corner in Manhattan. I was eating something on a croissant, because that's the closest thing Dunkin' Donuts has to food. Grace was drinking coffee, but she seemed caffeinated enough on her own; her hands could barely stay still for a second.

When I told her I knew it was she who had been having an affair with Russell Chapman, she blanched, but nodded her head. It made sense: Konigsberg had seen her with Chapman, and then followed her to Sharon's house, where Grace was dutifully handing over paperwork. Once I'd figured that out, I'd called Grace, made a few discreet remarks about things I knew were true, and arranged this meeting.

"It wasn't an *affair* affair," Grace said. "I mean, we didn't have *sex* or anything."

"But the detective said you would spend the night sometimes in Chapman's hotel room, and the maid told him the sheets . . ." Have you ever been halfway through a sentence when you wondered why you had thought to start it in the first place?

"I'd go to his hotel room, yes," Grace agreed, nodding. "You know, Mike travels a lot for work these days, and with the kids out of the house, I get a little creeped out there by myself. I haven't been alone for any extended period of time since we got married twenty-seven years ago."

"So then . . ." I just didn't have an end for that sentence. I was beginning to wonder if I had any future with this whole "conversation" thing at all.

"So then one day a few months ago, Mr. Chapman comes into the office, and he doesn't have an appointment." Grace, ever the charitable, was helping me out of my ineptitude. "Betty says he wants to talk to me, so I meet him in the break room, and he asks if I'd come out with him that night because he wanted to see a movie. Well, I thought he meant in a theatre, you know, like yours, Elliot, and I even suggested we go there. I think you were showing a Mae West movie or something."

"She Done Him Wrong," I said. Ask me who the president of the United States is, and I have to think about it. Ask me what I was showing in the theatre three months ago, and I can give you title, year of release, running time, and best scene. Everyone has idiosyncrasies; I just have more of them than most people.

"Something like that," Grace agreed. I felt it would have been inappropriate to insist that I was right about the title, so I let it go. "But he said no, he wanted to take me out and then we could watch some movie he had on a disc in his hotel room."

"Didn't the hotel room thing worry you?" I asked.

"Of course it did," Grace said, a little peeved, wondering who I thought she was. "But Mr. Chapman saw that right away, and he told me he just wanted some company. We'd talked a few times when he'd been in for exams, and we just hit it off, you know. He told me right up front that there'd be no funny business, and he was true to his word."

"What about the movies? Were they, you know, *real* movies?" I wasn't just asking if Chapman had shown Grace pornography. I was also asking what a rival exhibitor was programming.

"Yeah, it was all old stuff, you know, like at your theatre." Okay, so Grace isn't *always* charitable. "But real serious things, you know, mostly foreign. Fellini. Goddard. People like that."

"And you'd just sit there and watch movies?"

Grace's eyes welled up even as she nodded. "Yeah, that was about it. But now, this detective is calling up and saying he found out who I was, and do I want my husband to know I was sleeping with this old man, and what's it worth to me."

I could feel my eyebrows drop. "Konigsberg is blackmailing you?"

She nodded, then gathered herself. "He called yesterday. Said he'd just found out it was me. And he wants money."

"How much is he asking for?"

Grace stammered a bit, but got out, "Fifty thousand." A woman sending three kids to college at the same time on the salaries of a public relations executive and a nurse.

"What did you tell Mike about all this?" I asked.

It took a few moments, but she pulled herself together. "Not much of anything," she said. "It was all so . . . innocent. Or at least, I thought it was. But if this guy tells Mike, it won't sound that way."

I swallowed the last bite of whatever that was which would comprise my dinner. "Don't worry for a minute, Grace. I'll take care of it. Believe me, you won't hear from Konigsberg again." Her eyes grew. "Oh, stop it. I don't mean it like that. Who am I, Don Corleone? But if I were you, Grace, I'd tell Mike about this the way you told me. He'll understand."

She sniffed. "You think?"

"Look, I don't really know the guy, but if it were me, I'd understand. Now, I have to get going. Is there anything I can do?"

"You already did it." Grace stood up, a changed woman.

The old glint was back in her eye. I see it every year when she gives me a flu shot. "I'll be okay. Thanks, Elliot."

"I haven't done anything yet."

She kissed me on the cheek. "Yes, you have." And she turned and left.

I went back to the theatre, and immediately called Meg Vidal.

34

THURSDAY

ARMED with my newfound information, I decided on arising the next morning to list the tasks I had to perform today. They included:

Number one: save Sophie's job with a plan that hadn't been formulated yet;

Number two: protect Sharon from the Chapman girls and Wally;

Number three: stop Konigsberg from blackmailing Grace;

Number four: figure out who killed Russell Chapman;

Number five: find out who trashed my house and Sharon's (and you thought I'd forgotten about that one);

Number six: do laundry.

The laundry thing seemed least important, and while protecting Sharon was certainly my highest priority, that could probably best be served by taking care of item number four, the unmasking of Chapman's killer. It would be good to get that one off the agenda.

I wondered how one went about doing so.

The facts I had so far amounted to the following: Russell Chapman had been murdered, a few days after having staged a fake suicide, when someone cut his throat with a scalpel, which the killer had not been considerate enough to leave at the scene.

Inside the room where Chapman had been found, there were signs of a struggle. There was some blood on the rug and on Chapman's desk, not all of which was his, to indicate he might have injured his attacker. There appeared to be drag marks on the carpet, which could have come from Chapman's feet or the wheels of his desk chair.

Chapman's elder daughter appeared to be very concerned about the inheritance they might receive after his death. His younger daughter was concerned with making everyone play nice, an admirable goal that I am convinced is rarely achieved. Neither appeared to be terribly hostile toward the other, but they didn't appear to be best friends, either. Then there was Lillian's husband, a repellent man named Wally. But it's hard to be seriously concerned about a man named Wally.

It was also true, according to Chapman's attorney, that his will had been altered very soon before his death, after he had spent three days disguised as an insurance investigator for the distinct purpose of determining how much his daughters loved him, if at all.

Chapman had also been having a platonic but personal relationship with Grace Mancuso, the nurse at Sharon's medical practice. It was possible, however unlikely, that someone might have told Grace's husband about the suspicious-looking "affair," driving him into an uncontrollable rage, but considering that even the crack PI Konigsberg had thought it was Sharon until yesterday, confronting Mike Mancuso would be a bad idea. The last thing I needed to do was blow Grace's cover for her. And I'd met Mike a couple of times; he didn't strike me as the "uncontrollable rage" type.

All of which left me feeling like I was in a dark room, searching for the doorknob I couldn't see. And my head still hurt a little, even though I'd changed to a smaller bandage.

The best plan of action I could come up with—and keep in mind, eleven in the morning is early for me—was to go to Chapman's house and see for myself. I admit, it's not much, but maybe by seeing the room where the murder took place I could better picture how it happened, and that might lead to why it happened, and that might lead to who was there when it happened.

I *said* it wasn't much.

And that, finally, was what led me to Moe Baxter.

When I need a car, I go to Moe's repair shop and test drive something he wants checked. I give him a full report on returning from the trip. It's a great arrangement, unless you ask Moe.

Moe, for reasons I've never fully comprehended, believes that I am merely mooching off his business for a free ride whenever I need one. Apparently, the auto repair business tends to make one cynical. So when I approached Moe's shop, after a bracing bike ride in twenty-degree temperatures with a wind chill of four (but with snow tires), I girded myself for the usual argument.

I marched into Moe's office without knocking, and he barely looked up from his desk. "Elliot," he said. "Long time, no see, which suited me just fine."

"Where were you on August 19, 1977?" I asked him, and that made him look up.

"Probably on summer vacation from college," he said. "Why?"

"That's the day Groucho Marx died," I told him. "I thought perhaps his soul had migrated to you. You're such a wit."

Moe blew a raspberry. "I assume you're here for a car," he said.

"Yeah. And I know how you feel about this, but . . ."

"Is this about the Sharon thing?" Moe asked. Things get around quickly in a small town.

"Yeah."

"Take mine," he said.

Before I knew it, I was tooling along in Moe's tricked-out Mitsubishi Galant, enjoying the state-of-the-art sound system playing Corinne Bailey Rae. Normally when embarking on such a mission, one might contact the investigator in charge of the case, but Kowalski would only use that whole "we're the police and you're not" defense, and what good was *that* going to do anyone?

Moe's GPS told me (in a British woman's voice, which was somehow reassuring) when to turn. I became hooked on the thing during the drive, and wondered whether it was worth putting one on the bicycle I use mostly to go back and forth to the same place every day.

Probably not.

In less than half an hour, it had directed me to the large house, hardly an estate and not the kind of place you'd expect a guy with forty-seven million dollars to live. The home had no gate, but did have a circular driveway. The house was built of light-colored brick, three stories high. I parked the car right at the entrance and zipped up my parka for the ten-yard walk to the door.

I rang the bell, expecting a butler at least as formal as an archduke to answer. Instead, I got Wally Mayer.

"What do you want?" he growled by way of a greeting.

"A steady income, a warm girl by my side, and the six missing minutes of *Horse Feathers* in a thirty-five-millimeter print," I said. "But at the moment, I'll settle for being let in the door."

"Why?" Wally's conversational skills had not improved since our last meeting.

"Wally, it's four degrees out here if you count the wind chill. Even a somewhat less-evolved being like yourself must feel the cold. How about we discuss this indoors?"

He thought that over for an uncomfortably long moment, since thinking was not Wally's strong suit, and finally stood to one side so I could walk in. He closed the door behind me.

"Now," Wally said, "what do you want?"

"I thought I made that clear. A steady income, a warm . . ."

"Why are you here?" He'd made the leap of logic. If I'd had a liver treat in my pocket, I'd have slipped one into his mouth as a reward. "This is our house now, and we don't have to let you in if we don't want to."

"Wow, Wally," I said, savoring the alliteration. "You didn't wait long to move your stuff into the old place, did you?"

"He was Lil's dad," Wally said, actually trying to justify his actions. "He'd want us to be here."

"That remains to be seen, by registered mail," I told him. "I was wondering if I could have a look around."

Wally's eyes became slits. "Why?" he growled.

"I'm looking for a new place, and I heard this one might be on the market," I told him. I took a quick look around the foyer. "Do those drapes absolutely have to go with you?"

"We're not going anywhere, and neither are the drapes," he snarled. Good lord, the man was taking me seriously—what were the odds?

"Oh, that will be awkward," I said. "I'm not really looking for a live-in couple just at the moment."

"You're not moving in," he said, as if he were actually telling me something I didn't know. "So what do you want to look around for?"

"Honestly, I want to see the room where Mr. Chapman died," I said. "I think maybe I can help figure out what happened if I see the room."

"The cops have been there," Wally said. "What do we need you for? Somebody cut the old man's throat. Lil thinks it was your wife, since he was killed with a scalpel."

"There are so many holes in that theory you could fill the Albert Hall with them," I said in an obscure *Sergeant Pepper* reference. "Sharon has no motivation to want Chapman dead—she's not listed in his will." (Okay, I didn't know that *for sure*, but I was willing to bet it was true.) "Second, there was blood on the floor and the desk, and it wasn't all your father-in-law's, so someone is running around with a very incriminating wound. And third, you're stupid."

"Your ex-wife was humping the old man," he said, then did a double take Joe E. Ross would have thought was over-the-top. "Hey . . ."

"No, she wasn't," I said. "But that's not important, either way. Somebody cut Russell Chapman's throat. You're strong enough and dumb enough to do it, if your wife told you to. You know if she did it, she'll claim you were in on it, even if you weren't. Why not protect yourself?"

"Hey . . ." he repeated. The man could out-quip Oscar Wilde.

"Just let me up into the room," I said. "In fact, come with me. If I find something there, I want you to be present to corroborate."

"I'm not an accountant," Wally said. It was a miracle he could brush his teeth in the morning.

I dropped my voice half an octave. "I know where you were when you were supposed to be in Japan," I lied.

Wally's face turned white as a sheet bleached for a Ku Klux Klan meeting. "No, you don't," he said.

"Yes. I do."

"I . . . I . . . I . . ."

"Come on," I offered, gesturing toward the winding staircase.

Surprisingly, he followed me. As we climbed the stairs, he said, "I heard they let your wife walk."

"Ex-wife, and yes, mostly because she's innocent."

Wally rolled his eyes, and then, in a triumph of sensitivity on his part, said, "What happened to your head?"

"Like you don't know."

At the top of the stairs, Wally guided me to the door at the far left of the hallway. I was beginning to suspect that he'd given in a little too easily when we reached a dark wooden door. "This was the old man's study," he said.

I stood there until he turned the doorknob. I was determined not to touch anything I didn't have to touch.

The room was large, but not ostentatious. Chapman hadn't done it up in thick oak paneling, and didn't have a bear's head mounted over his desk. It looked more like the office of a mid-level executive, but for the gleaming, pristine chemistry set of test tubes, beakers, and burners sitting on a very taste-ful shelf behind the desk, which had an iMac on it. Chapman was an Apple man, like me. But his was newer and fancier, naturally.

"Has anything been moved or changed since Sunday?" I asked Wally.

"Huh?" he responded.

I started to act the movements out with my hands, and spoke *veeerrrrry slooooowwwlyyyy.* "Has anything been *moooooved* or *chaaaaanged* since Sunday?" I repeated.

"No. The police had yellow tape up until yesterday, and I don't think anybody's been in here since then." Wally was watching the office door, like it was going to do something interesting.

I looked mostly at the desk and the area around it. "Has anyone looked at his computer?" I noticed it was turned off.

"Cops took the hard drive," Wally answered. He wasn't looking at me, just the door. Either he was waiting for some-one—probably Lillian—to show up and give him his instruc-tions for the day, or that was one hell of a fascinating door.

I walked behind the desk. There was indeed a dark stain, although not a large one, on the carpet, near the right-hand corner of the desk as Chapman would have been sitting at it, if he were facing the computer screen. I looked for the other spot Kowalski had mentioned on the desk, but it wasn't there.

"The police said there was more blood on the desk," I said, not really to Wally.

"I dunno," he answered. A wellspring of knowledge, that man. It was amazing he'd found the office on the first try.

The carpet, where Kowalski had said there were drag marks, must have been vacuumed, because the marks were gone. Ap-parently *someone* had been in this room after the police had cleared it.

I sat down behind the desk. So this was what it felt like to have forty-seven million dollars. Well, not really: This was what it felt like to sit behind the desk of a guy who had forty-seven million dollars.

There was no rush of megalomania or a sudden urge to mess with the lives of ordinary people. There was no assumption that all my needs and wants would immediately be satisfied. In fact, the chair's wheels squeaked a little when I moved around. I didn't immediately feel the need to get a white cat to stroke as it sat on my lap, nor to shave my head and start wearing a monocle.

It was, however, a vast improvement on the shoebox I called an office back at Comedy Tonight. I had to admit that.

I turned my attention to the desk, which was large, possibly antique, made of dark wood, maybe mahogany (what did I know about wood?). The middle drawer, where a man keeps all the things he might need immediately, formed a picture of a terribly well-organized mind. Everything was neat, ergonomically situated, and absolutely typical. Paper clips in a box. Business cards in a folder (the one facing front was from Comedy Tonight, which I'd given him in his guise as Tovarich). Pens. Pencils. Erasers.

It looked like a sample desk drawer, furnished jointly by Staples and Mrs. Muransky, my second-grade teacher. "Everything in its place, Elliot." Freak.

But enough of this rose-colored nostalgia; there was work to be done. I turned my attention to the two larger drawers on the right side of the desk. One held hanging folders, presumably with investments, portfolios, and other words that financially astute people would understand. For me, they might as well have been in Swahili.

The upper drawer, however, seemed like the place where Chapman had kept his more personal belongings, or at least, the ones he'd have in an office drawer. These were more idiosyncratic, and therefore telling. Here, he had a compass (I guess to figure out which direction he was sitting in), a crossword puzzle dictionary (a man after Meg Vidal's own heart, no doubt), a pair of binoculars (no comment), a pocket watch, a small copper replica of the Liberty Bell, a harmonica (and a really good one, from what I could tell), and a baseball—not a special baseball, not autographed or anything, just a baseball.

There was also an object I could not identify. It was about the size of a pair of salad tongs, but narrower. The thing appeared to be homemade, with pieces taken from various objects: It looked like it had the handle of a delicate pair of scissors, but could not be made to open wide because of a strong band of black rubber, used as a restraining piece around the center that limited its range of motion. Its two arms extended out, but only for a few inches, and their tips were coated in a dull gray metal. They were extremely sharp, as if they'd been made out of the best steak knives available, but narrower. The arms holding them were extremely narrow and rounded. One of them had a red LED readout soldered onto it, for reasons that weren't at all obvious. The readout wasn't activated, and had a tape over it marked PTYPE.

I couldn't for the life of me imagine what that thing might have been, or what it might be used for.

"What do you suppose this is?" I asked Wally.

There was no answer. I picked my head up from the drawer and looked. Wally was nowhere to be seen.

I got up with the bizarre artifact in my hand and walked to the center of the room, in an insane attempt to see if there were some alcove, some hidden corner in the perfectly open space, where a man might hide and then leap out at you when you weren't paying attention. There was none.

Enough of this: I headed for the office door and reached for the doorknob.

It didn't turn. While I was exalting in my mental superiority over Wally Mayer, he had simply walked out of the room.

And locked me in.

35

IT didn't make sense. There was no upside to locking me in Russell Chapman's study. What did they (I assumed Lillian had to be pulling Wally's leash) think they could accomplish with this little ploy? Surely they weren't going to hold me prisoner and try to beat the information out of me. There was no information. There had to be some other benefit to them in my staying in one place.

Of course.

I walked back to the desk and picked up the telephone. There was a dial tone; my "captors" weren't terribly good at this game. I dialed Sharon's cell phone. She answered on the first ring, which isn't at all like her.

"Who is this?" she said. That replaced "hello," and seemed strange.

"Sharon, it's me." I hate to belabor the same point, but is there a sentence that exists with *less* information in it?

"Elliot!" she exploded. "Where are you?"

"I'm at Chapman's house," I told her. "I'm fine. Did they call you?"

"Yes, I'm in my car on the way there."

That's what I'd figured. Lillian and Wally weren't interested in taking out revenge on me; they wanted Sharon. That's why Wally had let me up into Chapman's study so easily. He figured that as soon as Lillian showed up, he could ask her for permission to incarcerate me there, then call Sharon, tell her I was being held against my will, and lure her to the house to torture her in some twisted way. It was a stupid plan, but then, it was Wally and Lillian. What should one expect?

"Turn around," I said. "Go back to your practice."

"But Elliot, they said if I didn't come . . ."

"Trust me, Shar. I'll be fine. They want you. Don't give them what they want. Call Dutton."

"They told me if I called the police . . ."

"You're listening to them now? Call Dutton or Meg. I don't know how long it'll be before they turn off the phone. Tell them to get in touch with Kowalski. This is how we get them, Sharon. The cops come and arrest them for holding me against my will. I'm going to make myself cozy in Chapman's office and wait for it to happen. But call now, and go back to the office."

Sharon thought about it, and I never interrupt when she's thinking. "Okay," she said.

"Good. I'll call you as soon as I get out of here."

Another long pause. "I love you," she said.

"I love you, too, but don't be dramatic. I'm not in any danger. It's Wally and Lil, the Bonnie and Clyde of the IQ-under-fifty set."

"One of them probably killed Mr. Chapman, Elliot."

"You had to remind me of that? Call the cops."

"I will. And Elliot? I've been watching Lennon, and you're right—he's acting strange."

"Strange how?"

"Mostly he's testy, but I heard him on the phone, and I think there are money problems. I'll tell you later. I have to call the police."

She hung up.

I went back to the desk and sat down. The left-hand draw-

ers didn't hold anything of interest, as far as I could tell.
Much of what was in there consisted of ledger books that had
nothing unusual in them—but I'm not an auditor. If I understood numbers, I wouldn't be in the theatre business.

Eventually I put everything back in the desk, careful to
replace it where it had been before; that seemed only fair to
Chapman, who had seemed like a good enough guy. Then I
sat back and considered that a while had gone by, and I hadn't
heard any sirens yet.

Odd.

I got up and walked to the balcony doors. It was gray outside, cold and windy, and from where I stood, I could see the
tops of trees farther down the hill, and part of the road leading up to Chapman's home. No police cars. That couldn't be
good.

Was it possible Sharon hadn't gotten through to Dutton or
Meg? Would she have waited to call Kowalski, or forgotten
his name? Could the cops have been talked out of the whole
thing by the wily Chapmans? I hadn't heard the phone ring,
and I hadn't heard sirens. I looked at my watch.

Three minutes had gone by since I'd gotten off the phone
with Sharon. Maybe I was just a little more nervous than I'd
thought I was.

So I watched the second hand on my watch for a while.
That didn't seem to help, either.

Standing by the balcony doors, I considered trying to escape. But there were a number of flaws with that plan: there
was nothing to use as a rope—no sheets to tie together, no fire
hose (for you, *My Favorite Year* fans), no emergency ladder
under the desk or in the closet. Besides, my being out of the
room when the cops got here was exactly the opposite of what
I needed. If I escaped and went to the police, it would be my
word against Wally's. If they came and saw me locked in
Chapman's study, that would be a different story.

Besides, I'm afraid of heights.

There was one truly demented moment when I looked
outside and considered the tiny ledge, maybe about ten inches

deep, that ran around the outside of the house. Hey, it worked for Cary Grant in *North by Northwest*. I have seen far too many movies, in case it hasn't become evident yet.

Just as I was contemplating my predicament, there registered from the corner of my eye a red light. Of the flashing variety.

Sure enough, two police cars were driving up the road toward the house. I didn't hear sirens, but it was possible they weren't using sirens; cops don't do that unless they need them, and there was no one else on the road.

I'll admit to a certain amount of satisfaction as I watched them drive up to the house. This would do it.

But before the cruisers reached the front door, the lock on Chapman's study turned, and the door opened. Wally Mayer walked back in.

"So, did you find everything you needed?" he asked, casual as a worn T-shirt.

"Are you serious?" I asked him. "You're just going to walk in here and pretend you weren't holding me against my will?"

The man had enough nerve to chuckle. "Against your will?" Wally said. "That's funny, Freed. Why would we hold you against your will?"

The doorbell rang. I could hear some activity downstairs.

"To get my ex-wife to come here. She's not coming," I responded.

"I have no idea what you're talking about," he lied through his teeth.

"Okay then, why did you sneak out of here and lock the door? How was I supposed to get out, by flapping my arms and flying off the balcony? Why did you call Sharon and tell her you were holding me here until she showed up?"

"Believe what you want," Wally told me. I heard footsteps on their way up the stairs. "Say what you want. They'll think you're crazy."

And that's when two uniformed East Brunswick officers appeared at the office door. "Are you Mr. Freed?" he asked Wally.

"I've never been so insulted in my life," I said.

The other officer, tall and Hispanic, fixed his gaze on me. "So then you're Mr. Freed?"

"That's right. And this man is holding me here against my will."

Wally did his best to look surprised. I saw Lillian Chapman Mayer hovering behind the two officers in the doorway. They walked into the office; she stayed in the doorway. "I have no idea what this man is talking about, Officers," Wally said.

"We got a call that Mr. Freed was being held here," the Hispanic cop said. "Are you saying he's not?"

"Of course not," Wally said, checking with Lillian at the door. She had the good sense not to nod, but her eyes said something to her husband. "Elliot came because he wanted to see my father-in-law's study, and I said it would be all right, since you fellers"—honest to god, he said "fellers"—"removed the crime scene tape."

The first cop, a sandy-haired white guy in his forties, looked me up and down. "Was he violent?" he asked me, indicating Wally.

"No," I said, feeling my blood pressure rise. "He wasn't violent. He locked me in this room when I was distracted, and called my ex-wife to say that he and his wife would do me harm if she didn't come to get me."

Wally's eyes widened, and he actually laughed. "Why would I do something like that?"

"Because you think my ex had something to do with your father-in-law's death, which she didn't, and you want to exact revenge." Even to me, it sounded stupid.

"Oh, seriously," Lillian said from the doorway.

"Officers," I said. "I know how this sounds. But the fact is, Mr. Mayer here locked me into this room, and didn't open the door again until he saw you guys coming. My ex did in fact receive a call saying I was here and that she had to come, or I'd be harmed. You can call her."

"I'm sure she'll back him up," Lillian offered. "The woman is capable of anything."

"You see?" I asked the cops.

"Okay," the older cop said. "Let's get Mr. Freed out of here." He indicated the door. Lillian vacated her spot to let us pass, and while she did not flash Wally a triumphant grin, she made a point of avoiding eye contact with him, no doubt in fear of something stupid he might do.

I followed the officer, protesting all the way. I said I wanted to file charges against the Chapmans, kidnapping, imprisonment, and I think I might have mentioned assault with a grocery cart. Lillian mentioned a libel suit, which I felt obligated to point out would apply only to printed or otherwise disseminated material. The cops said nothing.

When they escorted me out of the house, still screaming that I demanded my right to press charges, the cops actually tipped their caps to the Chapmans and led me away. But they didn't take me to Moe's car, nor to the cruiser they had obviously brought here.

They led me to the second police car, in which Detective Eugene Kowalski was sitting in the passenger seat.

"Weren't you supposed to have these people under surveillance?" I asked.

"Not *constant*," he answered. "Besides, you went in and stayed less than an hour. Hardly seems ominous."

"Not out here," I said. "In there, it was pretty ominous."

"You never get tired of screwing up my investigation, do you, Freed?" he asked.

"Those people . . ." I started, gesturing toward the house.

"We know," Kowalski cut me off. "They held you against your will."

"Well, it happened."

"I *know*," Kowalski said. "Didn't you hear me say that?"

"So why aren't you doing anything about it?" I asked.

"Because this is a murder investigation, and your little stunt would only get in the way. We're very close to making an arrest." Kowalski looked quite satisfied, pleased with himself.

"Who?" I croaked out.

"Why should I tell you?"

"I can't think of one good reason," I told him honestly.

Kowalski nodded. "Wally Mayer," he said.

"Much as it pains me to say it, you'd be wrong," I said. "Let's talk."

36

"YOU can't hold her here against her will," Ilsa Beringer said. "It's kidnapping."

Kowalski had let me out of the cruiser (where I'd taken refuge from the cold) about fifteen minutes after I left the Chapman house. I got into Moe's Gallant and drove to East Brunswick police headquarters for about twenty minutes, then directly to Comedy Tonight. I'd set up the meeting with Sophie's parents for just after three, and with all the errands I'd been running, it had taken me that long just to get back to the theatre. Being abducted takes up a lot of your day, I'd found.

"Believe me," I told Ilsa, "I'm familiar with the concept."

She and her husband had been waiting at the front door of Comedy Tonight when I'd arrived. I'd apologized for running late, but of course, standing in a subzero breeze tends to erode one's stockpiles of patience, and Ilsa didn't have much to begin with.

"I'll bet you are," she said. I have no idea what that meant, and decided not to pursue it.

The thing about this meeting was, I'd been planning on working up a strategy on my way back from Chapman's house. I know; it was pushing things to the last minute, but I hadn't been able to think of a strong argument to counter the Beringers' demand that their daughter quit her job except that we all really liked Sophie and wanted her to stay.

Somehow, I didn't think that would work.

Now, with my eventful morning having pretty much wiped out any cogent brain cells left in my head, I was ad-libbing until such time as a brilliant idea decided to drop in from the stratosphere, an event I was counting on occurring in the next ten minutes or so.

"I'm not holding Sophie against her will," I said. "I'm requiring that she fulfill the terms of her contract." I didn't know what that meant, but it sounded good.

Ron Beringer's eyes hardened. "She doesn't have a contract with you," he said. "She's a part-time employee, and she's underage. You never gave her a contract to sign, and if you had, it would be superseded by us, since Sophie is a minor."

I'd forgotten he was an attorney. Probably a labor attorney, with my luck.

"Okay, so maybe I didn't mean 'contract,'" I said, smiling. "But I can't simply replace Sophie immediately, and I'm asking her, as a courtesy, to stay at her job until I find a suitable employee to take over her job. Now, is that unreasonable?"

Ilsa screwed up her face like I'd just shoved half a lemon into her mouth. "Yes, it's unreasonable," she said. "You could take as long as you like to find this replacement, and Sophie would be, by your logic, required to stay here for an indefinite period of time. It's not only unreasonable, it's unacceptable."

Maybe I could distract them. "Well, why is it necessary for Sophie to quit her job?" I asked. "Is she unhappy here? Is the workload too strenuous, or taxing?"

"Sophie's not unhappy," Ron said, drawing a glare from his wife, which made him flinch. "But the time she's putting in at your . . . theatre . . . is cutting into the time she'd otherwise have to better her position for acceptance at an Ivy League school. She needs to demonstrate some community service, for example. Now, surely you can understand that."

"No, I can't, and don't call me Shirley," I tried. *Airplane!* is a little recent for Comedy Tonight, but I couldn't resist the reference.

"I said *suuuurely*," Ron reiterated. So much for lightening the mood.

"Look," I said. "Sophie has been spending all her free time while she's here studying and doing college preparation. She's been talking about nothing other than college, and how she's working to get in just to make you two happy, for a week now. I can see to it that she has more free time while she's here to do those things. But I'm asking you, on Sophie's behalf as well as my own, not to insist that she give up her job. I think that holding a paying position while maintaining the exemplary grade-point average Sophie has should be impressive to any admissions board. I don't think you'd want her to end that employment just as she's trying to stand out to them, do you? And if you like, I could write a very strong letter of recommendation for her. So please, just let her keep the job, okay?"

"No," Ilsa Beringer said.

"We all really like Sophie and want her to stay," I blurted out.

"Oh, seriously." Ilsa rolled her eyes. "Mr. Freed, Sophie will not be coming back to work. You need not worry about any salary you owe her. But don't expect to see her in this theatre again. Is that understood?"

"No!" The shout came from just outside the office door. Sophie and Jonathan, he possibly looking even more aghast than she did, stood there, mouths wide open. I was seated in the office chair, so I would have had a straight look at them, but Ilsa and Ron, who had to turn to see their daughter and her boyfriend, had blocked me out. So we were all surprised.

"Sophie," Ron said. "What are you doing here?"

"You can't do this!" his daughter wailed. "I'm already working my ass off . . ."

"Sophie!" Ilsa admonished.

"What else do you *want* from me?"

"We're just looking out for your best interests, baby," Ron said. "We just want you to be happy."

"Well, I'm *not* happy," Sophie countered. "You're making me give up something I really like doing, with people I really like seeing, and it's all for things that couldn't possibly make less of a difference."

Ilsa's eyes had hardened, and she'd looked directly at Jonathan when Sophie had mentioned "people I really like seeing." So *that* was what this was about.

"Couldn't make less of a difference!" Ilsa echoed. "It's your future we're talking about, Sophie. This is one of the biggest decisions you'll ever make. Don't you think that's a little more important than this part-time job you have?"

"No, I . . ." Sophie began.

"Besides," Ilsa continued, "we've already explained that since we're paying for all your college expenses, we really believe it's our right to advise you on how you're spending your time. Don't you agree?"

Sophie's eyes darkened and dimmed, and her head bowed a little. I knew the financial issue was one she had no defense for; she'd always been one of those kids who felt guilty about taking her parents' money. It was one of the reasons she'd applied for the job at Comedy Tonight to begin with, so she could have a modicum of financial independence.

"I dunno . . ." she mumbled. "I guess so."

Jonathan's head swiveled from Ilsa to Sophie, and back again in the time it takes a dog to not do anything. His face took on an expression I'd never seen on it before, so it took me a moment to recognize it: outrage.

"No!" he yelled. "You can't do that." Jonathan pushed his way into the room and stood towering over Ilsa, staring directly into her eyes. "You can't do that. It's not fair."

"I'm sorry if Sophie won't be able to see you as often, Jon," Ilsa said in her best corporate-executive voice. "But she has more important things on her agenda right now, and you have to understand that." Jonathan hates being called "Jon." He also, as it turns out, isn't crazy about having someone condescend to him.

"This isn't about whether I get to see Sophie," he said, his eyes afire and his mouth pretty much belching smoke. "This is about what Sophie wants, and not what you want, and not what I want. Sophie isn't your employee; she's your daughter. You should want her to have what she wants, not what you've decided she should want. There's no reason you want her to quit her job, except that you don't like her working here, and you don't like her seeing me. I don't know why you don't like those things, but you don't. And what you really hate is that Sophie doesn't just do what you tell her to because you tell her to."

I thought that had been all the words he had allotted for the month, but Jonathan went on: "You decide what Sophie should want because of who *you* want her to be. The job here is something that helps make Sophie the way Sophie is, and if you take that away, you'll be taking part of her with it. Is *that* what you want?"

Ilsa had shrunk a little, to some extent because it was a very small room and she had to bend back to look up into Jonathan's eyes. "I . . ." Ilsa's mouth opened and closed once or twice, but that was all that came out. Ron, however, was staring at Jonathan, his face registering the last thing I would have expected:

Admiration.

"If you want to know what Sophie wants and why she wants it, ask Sophie," Jonathan said. "She's smart; she can answer you really well. But don't just decide that because she was your baby a bunch of years ago that she still is, because now she's Sophie. And that's a pretty wonderful thing for her to be. You should be proud."

Sophie stared at Jonathan, amazed, and reached out an arm, and he walked to her. She put her arm around him, still gaping up at his face. She'd probably never heard him speak that much before, and certainly hadn't heard anyone say anything like that to her mother before. "Wow," she said quietly.

There was a long silence. A very long silence. And then the plan that I'd been searching for since yesterday suggested itself to me.

"Besides, I can't afford to lose Sophie now that I've promoted her," I said.

All four heads turned to me at once. "Promoted?" Ron asked.

"Didn't she tell you?" I asked him, innocent as O. J. Simpson. "Sophie is now the manager of Comedy Tonight."

"I . . . am," Sophie said, grinning. "Yes. I am. Sorry, Elliot. I'd forgotten to tell my parents."

"Oh well," I said, the very picture of appeasement, "of course you were adamant about her leaving. You thought Sophie was just our snack girl. My apologies. No, she's now the part-time manager of the whole theatre. It's a very responsible position, and I wouldn't give it to anyone I didn't trust completely. That's a remarkable girl you two raised."

"You don't expect us to buy—" Ilsa began.

But her husband cut her off. "Why, thank you, Mr. Freed," Ron said. "We are very proud of our little Sophie. And now, manager of a whole theatre, at her age! We couldn't be more pleased."

"Ron!" Ilsa said.

"We *couldn't be more pleased,*" he repeated, and stared into his wife's eyes. And there was something in his face that probably hadn't been there for years, if not decades: defiance. He had seen Jonathan stand up to Ilsa, and that had reminded him of something.

It's amazing what you can get from some looks.

Obviously Ilsa had gotten quite a bit out of it, too; her face transformed. She actually tried to hide a naughty grin. "Ron," was all she said. She almost giggled.

Frankly, it was a little scary.

"We'll be going now," Ron said. "We need to get home. Ilsa?"

She took his arm, and they left through the office door. Jonathan and Sophie had to back up to let them by.

As the front door closed behind her parents, Sophie said, "Ewwwwww."

Jonathan grinned down at her from his rangy height. "I guess you're my boss now," he said to her.

Sophie reached up and kissed him. "That was the nicest thing anyone's ever done for me," she said.

"It was Mr. Freed who gave you the promotion," Jonathan reminded her.

"That's not what I meant. But . . ." She turned her attention to me. "Thank you, Elliot."

"I meant every word," I said. "And Jonathan did, too."

She grinned.

From the lobby, I could hear Sandy Arnstein's voice getting louder. "We need a plasterer," he was saying, presumably to Dad. "These are old walls. I can't just put up some Sheetrock and expect it to look right. This is gonna cost, and I'm not paying for it. A plasterer."

"Here comes trouble," Sophie said.

"Hey," I said. "You're the manager. Go manage it."

"What? Elliot . . ."

I got up and closed the office door. I'd have to thank Anthony for giving me the idea: Sell Sophie the theatre.

That was one item off my list for the day: saving Sophie's job. Check.

Now it was time to work on another one.

37

BY the time I walked into Sharon's practice, it was just after four. Betty told me Sharon was in her private office.

I knocked on the door, and she opened it, and gave me a hug that, under any other circumstances, would have completely knocked all other thoughts out of my mind. But I tried to maintain discipline, and for once, was capable of doing so.

"We've got to talk," I said when there was air between us.

"You sound like you're breaking up with me," Sharon said, "and we're not even together."

"You could have fooled me a second ago."

We closed the door to the office and sat down, and I updated Sharon on the situation at the Chapman house. I had called her from the cruiser using Kowalski's cell phone, so she knew I was no longer being imprisoned in a posh office.

"They're really crazy," she said when I was finished.

"I thought you medical professionals were supposed to say things like *mentally ill* or *disturbed*," I reminded her.

"They're nuts," Sharon said.

"Fair enough. Now, tell me about Lennon."

"I've been keeping an eye on him, like we agreed," she

began. "And he's been nervous. Not so much mean to Betty or Grace, but dismissive. Closed off. And that's not Lennon. He's never exactly chummy, but he's not cold, usually."

I nodded. "You said you thought there were money problems."

"Yes, go figure! I owe you one on that. I heard him on the phone to his brother, through the closed door of his office, yelling that he needed that loan, and why couldn't Hendrix understand that."

I passed on commenting on the first names in the Dickinson family. It was starting to add up, but the total was a little strange. "Has he ever said anything to you or Toni about needing money?" I asked.

"Never. And we're his partners. You'd figure he'd say something to us first."

"Is he in his office?"

"I think so," Sharon said.

"All righty, then."

She looked at me with the same level of concern I'd seen when I was ranting about the shopping cart. "What did you say?" she asked.

"Nothing. I'll go talk to Lennon."

Sharon stood up. "Okay," she said.

"No. Just me."

She stopped and her eyes narrowed. "Why?" she asked.

"You're his partner. He's not going to speak as freely about his financial troubles with you in the room." I got up and headed for the door.

"I'm his partner. That's exactly why he should speak freely about his financial troubles," Sharon said.

"That's your problem," I told her. "You think everybody is as logical as you are."

I left her behind her desk. The truth was, if Lennon didn't react well to my questioning—what with his being testy and everything—I didn't want Sharon in the room. I'd been worrying about her enough lately.

Lennon Dickinson's office was two doors down from Sharon's, and when I stopped to knock, I did not hear shouting through the heavy door, as Sharon had. I knocked, and Lennon's voice said, "Come." So I went inside.

A doctor's office, I'm sure, could yield Sherlock Holmes (or even Buster Keaton in *Sherlock Jr.*) a wealth of information about the man who inhabits it. Alas, I am neither Sherlock nor Junior, so all I got from looking around was that Lennon was, in fact, a doctor. The bookshelves had medical volumes on them, and the walls had the requisite diplomas. There were no photographs framed on his desk, and no art hung on the walls. It was a generic doctor's office.

Except that Lennon Dickinson, possibly the world's handsomest physician, was seated behind the desk. And he smiled when he looked up, a perfectly rehearsed, friendly smile. I'll bet that one worked on the ladies.

"Elliot," he said. "Nice to see you. Sit down."

I did so, and smiled at Lennon. He probably gets that a lot.

"Sharon told me you're in on our little secret," Lennon said. "I'm sorry I couldn't tell you that she'd driven me to the city that night, but she swore me to secrecy, and I really didn't know where she was going."

"That's okay" was all I said, even though it wasn't.

"Are you here visiting Sharon?" he asked me.

"Yes, and to see you," I replied.

Lennon might even have really been surprised. His face registered some amazement, but not an inordinate amount. He was good. "Me?" he asked. "I'm flattered, Elliot." Damn good.

"I'm a little worried about everything that's been going on around here, and I thought maybe you could help me figure some things out." I had unzipped the parka, and was wearing it open. I put my hand in the right-side pocket.

Lennon didn't so much as blink, but he upped the wattage on his smile a bit. "Of course you know I'll do whatever I can," he said with professional sincerity. "How can I help?"

I closed my grasp on the object I'd found in Chapman's desk, which I had concealed in the pocket of my parka, and I pulled it out and tossed it onto Lennon's desk. He recoiled as if I'd thrown a live grenade.

And maybe I had.

"You can tell me what that is," I suggested.

Lennon didn't want to touch the object, although I was willing to guess his fingerprints were already on it. But he made a show of leaning over to examine it more closely. "I really haven't the faintest idea," he said. But his smile wasn't anywhere near as broad now. The ladies would have been less charmed.

"Really?" I could play-act, too, if the situation called for it. "I'd think you'd be intimately acquainted with that little doo-hickey. I'll bet you know every millimeter of it by heart."

It was a pity: Lennon's Academy Award–winning performance was already starting to show signs of collapse. (Of course, since the Academy never recognizes comedy, I don't place much stock in it—or is this not the time to bring that up?) His wide-eyed expression of confusion was too wide, and his hands were starting to tremble just a bit. The mannerisms were self-contradictory, nervous, and defiant. He looked like Carol Channing about to sing an aria at the Metropolitan Opera.

"Why would I know it?" he asked. "I've never seen it before."

I didn't hesitate. "Then I guess if I look through all your desk drawers, I won't find another one just like it, will I?" I asked. I raised myself off the chair then, as if to stand. "Let's take a look, shall we?" I suggested.

Lennon answered too quickly. "That's all right," he said, spreading his hands in a gesture of contrition. "You're right. I've seen that before. I designed it." Even in this context, there was some pride in his voice. "I *invented* it," he corrected himself.

"What is it?" I asked. "It looks like Mae West's eyebrow tweezers on stilts."

"It's a new kind of surgical clamp," Lennon answered with a condescending smirk. "I wouldn't expect you to understand the technical aspects, but this kind would be used in vascular transplants, cardio bypass procedures, and some kinds of cosmetic surgery."

"And you wanted Russell Chapman to invest in it, didn't you?"

Lennon Dickinson seemed to deflate in front of my eyes. His chiseled face sagged and his smile became a grimace. He sat back in his chair with the exhausted groan of a man twice his age.

"I thought that a man as successful as Mr. Chapman, who had made his fortune by reinventing a common product, would be able to appreciate the innovation I had achieved," Lennon said, his breath coming in labored exhalations. "I thought he'd have the vision to imagine a possible stream of income for both of us."

"What happened?" I tried to sound gentle. "Why were you so desperate for money? The practice is doing well."

He looked at me sideways, his sad smile not fading. "Yes. The practice is doing well."

"Why did you need the money?" I asked again.

"I was working with an investment counselor who was unscrupulous, and I didn't know it," he said, closing his eyes. "I lost seven hundred thousand dollars in the time it would take you to brush your teeth." He seemed to be trying to appeal to my sympathy, to make me feel that whatever he'd done had been justified by the unfair circumstances life had dealt him. "So I borrowed some money from a bank, and then some more from . . . I guess there's no term other than a loan shark."

"And those guys don't take kindly to your missing a payment, so there was a time element involved now."

"That's right. You have no idea the interest those people charge." The doctor was amazed that gangsters sometimes act unscrupulously.

"So when Sharon told you about Chapman's test results, you figured he'd be in a generous mood to anyone from the practice, is that it?" I asked. He'd asked Sharon about the old man's possible interest in "a product." You didn't have to be Rembrandt to connect the dots on this one.

"But then they said he'd committed suicide, and that didn't make any sense," Lennon said. "He'd been given a clean bill of health. Or at least, that was what Sharon had said she'd done. No one else was allowed in the conference room, so she could have told Chapman anything."

I tried to speak clearly and distinctly, so as not to be mis-understood. "But then you found out Chapman hadn't killed himself. He'd used the fact that his daughters thought he was dying to stage a fake suicide, and now he was alive. How did you discover that?"

"The police called with the news that Mr. Chapman was alive," Lennon said. "He was back in his house, having alerted his attorney after living in a hotel for three days."

"And you immediately hightailed it there before he could die again?" I said. That was probably a miscalculation, not being sympathetic to his cause. I'd pay for it with a tightening of his lip, no doubt.

But no, Lennon just said, "I thought I'd drop by and see our patient, and if he said he had some interest in a business proposition, I'd be ready."

"So you had how many of those prototype clamps with you when you went to Chapman's?"

"Three," he said. "This one, which Chapman initially said he'd keep to show investors, the original, which I kept, and the third, because I wasn't sure if other people would be in-volved." Lennon's face was sour, remembering that Chapman had slighted him.

"That was the problem, wasn't it?" I asked. "That he took a look at your design and decided it wouldn't work?"

"That was what *he* thought," Lennon spat out. "A man who invented a different type of taco shell, and he thought he knew whether an innovative medical instrument would operate."

"Tortilla," I corrected him, but Lennon was on a tear.

"Of *course* it would work!" he went on. "The whole idea is different, it's so simple that it could become a standard instrument in every operating room in America. Probably in the world. There was never any doubt in my mind."

"But some in Chapman's. So you got angry, and you cut him with something, didn't you? That was the blood on the carpet and the desk."

Lennon wasn't so far gone that he missed the meaning of that question. His gaze shot up from the instrument on his desk to my eyes. "It was an accident," he said. "The arms on the clamp were sharp—they had to be; the idea was for them to be used carefully, but to double as a very fine scalpel when necessary. And when I became a little . . . involved in my argument, I swung it too hard, and cut Chapman on the ear."

"The ear?" No one had said anything about a cut on Chapman's ear, but given the way he died, his ear probably hadn't seemed important.

"Yes, his right ear," Lennon said. "I saw it was superficial, and offered to put a dressing on it right there, but Chapman was furious with me. He told me he no longer had any interest in my work, and asked me to leave."

"And that's when you used it to cut his throat."

Lennon sat up straight, offended that I'd even suggest such a thing. "Oh no," he said. "I didn't kill him. When I left his office, he was alive, with a superficial wound to his ear."

"Then, I don't understand," I told him. "How did Russell Chapman's throat get cut?"

"I haven't the faintest idea," Lennon Dickinson said.

"Well, who else was in the house when you were there?" I asked him.

"It was a few hours after the police had called to say he was alive," Lennon said. "Chapman said they'd been there and left. No one else was there when I arrived."

"How about when you left?"

"What do you mean?" Lennon asked, as if I'd said something confusing.

"Was anyone there when you left the room? Now that the cops had called around, hadn't either of Chapman's daughters come to see if he was all right?"

"I, um . . . er . . . ah . . ." Lennon was becoming Larry Storch before my eyes. "I don't know who was there."

"Yes, you do. You had investors. You had people who were talking you up with Chapman. One of his daughters, or both of them?"

"All right. Lillian and her husband had arrived when I left the office. They said Gwen was on her way."

"So one of the daughters or Wally killed Chapman?"

"I honestly have no idea," Lennon said, but his eyes were lying desperately.

"Why didn't you say anything before now?" I asked.

"Once I'd heard Mr. Chapman had been murdered—and with a *scalpel*—there was no doubt I'd be the prime suspect if anyone knew I'd been there. And I couldn't risk the exposure of my invention, because I knew I'd find another investor for my device."

"How's that coming so far?" I asked.

"I expect something to happen very soon," he said. "But I don't understand how you found out I went to see Chapman. How could you tell that the prototype was mine?"

"You stole my credit card, Lennon. That thing is made of everything you bought in your little shopping spree in the city on my dime, which you had to have because your own have been maxed out. Blades from the gourmet cooking supply house. Electronics? The LED readout to show the angle to which the clamp had been opened. Pewter from the oversized ring you bought at the cheapo souvenir store, which you'd melted down to solder the thing together. I'll bet the rubber ring that restrains the blades was taken from some part of the kinky lingerie you bought."

"Very clever. I'm more impressed with you than I thought I'd be, Elliot."

"But you didn't just get inspired that day, did you?"

"No," Lennon scoffed. Even in describing his ingenuity in charging purchases to my credit card, he couldn't help pointing out what a clever fellow he was. "I'd been perfecting the idea for months. But when I . . . had your credit card, I had the means to buy the items I needed to create the prototypes. And I want you to know, Elliot, I got the very best prices I could on everything."

"I just don't understand about the book on Broadway musicals. How did that fit in?"

"I like Broadway musicals," Lennon said. "And I'm not gay, so don't even think it."

I honestly didn't care if Lennon was gay or not. "So if you didn't kill Chapman, all the police can get you for is credit card theft, assault on the old man's ear, and withholding evidence," I said. "Why won't you say who was next into the room after you left? That must be the person who killed Russell Chapman."

"I wasn't there, Elliot," Lennon said. "I had already left. There's no way I could know."

"Speculate."

"That's a joke, isn't it?" he asked. "You're always joking."

"And you've been lying, Lennon. You know who killed Chapman, because you were there."

"I wasn't . . ."

"Maybe not when it happened, but you saw the mood of the house. You knew who was mad. You had a sense of it, and when you left, you know who followed you into that office."

"I don't know what you're talking about."

I pressed my luck. "And the sad part is, whoever did it, when confronted with all this, will say it was you. They'll say Gwen went into the room after you left and Russell was already dead. And it'll be your word against theirs. Who do you think the police will believe?"

"It won't happen!" Lennon shouted. "I *wasn't there*!"

"Doesn't matter if it's true," I told him. "It just has to be believable."

"Lillian wouldn't . . ."

And that was enough. There was a tremendous silence in the room for a long moment.

"It was Lillian?" I asked.

Lennon nodded, and that *wasn't* enough. I had to get him to say it.

"Why?"

"The inheritance," Lennon said. "She suspected Mr. Chapman was changing his will, and she couldn't let that happen."

"And she was too late. But why would she let you in on it?"

"She was . . . *is* . . . the investor for my device. She knows it will make her millions."

"Not anymore. Now, she'll be in jail."

Lennon waved a hand of dismissal at me. "The police don't know any of this."

"*I* know," I suggested.

"It'll be my word against yours," Lennon countered. "And you're already known as something of a nuisance to the police. I doubt your word will count for much."

"Maybe not," I said, standing up. "But yours will." I put my mouth inside the parka and said, "He's all yours, Kowalski." Then I looked at Lennon and told him, "I'm wearing a wire."

He was still staring at me in amazement when they led him away for booking.

38

"And two hard-boiled eggs."
"Honk!"
"Make that three hard-boiled eggs."
　　　—GROUCHO AND HARPO MARX, *A NIGHT AT THE OPERA*, (1935)

FRIDAY

A Night at the Opera (1935) and *Diva Dan* (this week)

"WE still don't know for sure who killed Russell Chapman," I said.

Detective Kowalski stood in the lobby of Comedy Tonight, watching Sophie set up the snack bar, and shook his head. "We have a pretty good idea," he said.

The plasterer, a remarkably tall, thin fellow named Ralph, was standing on the third rung of a ladder I had a difficult time believing he needed, smoothing out a section of the wall where the electrical fire had scorched the previous plaster. His job would be to make the whole thing look seamless, and then a painter my father had hired, whose name was Milt, would paint the entire lobby to ensure that it all looked uniform.

My run-down theatre was going to start to look very nice, if I could figure out how I would pay all these contractors. I hadn't told them that, yet. Somehow it seemed the wrong time.

"What you've got is Lennon Dickinson's statement that Lillian Chapman was next into the room," I told Kowalski. "You don't have anyone in the room when it happened."

Kowalski gave me one of his patented "that's why we're the cops and you're not" sighs. "There are two possibilities," he said, and held up a finger—no, not that finger. "One: Lillian did exactly what Dickinson says she did, and we'll find out whether that's her blood on the rug once the DNA comes back in a few weeks."

"A few weeks?" I said.

"This isn't *CSI*," Kowalski said.

"What's two?"

"Dickinson's lying, and *he* did it."

I sat down on the second step to the balcony. "He has no motive."

"Fit of rage when Chapman turned his gadget down."

"Lennon doesn't have fits of rage," I told him. "He has fits of bland. By the way, thanks a million for not telling me you guys had been to Chapman's place and questioned him before he died, or that his lawyer had informed both daughters, who would have been on their way to the house."

Kowalski's face took on a horrified expression. "My lord, Mr. Freed! Did I not inform you of every detail in a police investigation that you had no business knowing about?"

"After all I've done for you," I said.

Jonathan came out of the auditorium carrying the broom and dustpan and a garbage bag. He disposed of all of them and walked over to Sophie, which appeared to be his most pressing task these days. It was enough to make you believe in the power of love, and who needs *that*?

"Anyway, that's not why I'm here." Kowalski stood over me, to better accentuate his superiority, I suppose. I didn't much care.

"I assumed you were here to experience the genius of the Marx Brothers on the big screen," I said.

"It's an interesting world you live in, isn't it?" Kowalski asked. He didn't wait for an answer. "I need to know whether you're serious about pressing charges against Lillian and Wally Mayer."

I waved a hand. "What, for locking me in a room and holding me against my will while they tried to lure my ex-wife there so they could maybe kill *her*?" I asked. "That little thing?"

"You were in a luxurious office for thirty-five minutes by yourself," he corrected me. "Stealing an important piece of evidence."

"Did I not show you said piece of evidence as soon as I was released from my imprisonment there?"

"I'm saying, is it really necessary for us to put the taxpayers of East Brunswick through the expense of an investigation and a trial over thirty-five minutes during which you were not harmed in any way?" Kowalski glanced again toward the snack bar; at first I thought he had a twisted thing for Sophie, but then I realized he was ogling the chocolate-covered peanuts. I could sympathize with that.

"That's your way of looking at it," I told him. "What about the psychological damage I sustained?"

"You were like this before they locked you up," he pointed out.

"I'd think you would want to add charges to Lillian's sheet," I suggested.

"If we could use them. Fact is, the prosecutor doesn't think he can make your charges stick."

Sharon walked in from the street, removing her scarf and carrying a small paper shopping bag from the card store. Suddenly, my interest in continuing this conversation waned.

"If I drop the charges, will you go away?" I asked.

"Sure," Kowalski said. "Can I get something from the snack bar first?"

"As long as you pay cash. We don't give out freebies just because you're a cop."

He scowled and headed for the snack bar. I got up and walked toward Sharon. We met by the office door. "I was afraid you weren't coming," I told her.

"You know I never miss *A Night at the Opera*," she said.

"Besides, I had to come and check on your head wound." She looked, nodded, and then reached into the bag and pulled out a small box wrapped in blue paper. "Happy anniversary."

For the first time since we were married, it had slipped my mind. "Oh, man," I said. "You remembered." I opened the office door so we could have a little more privacy. Sharon walked in, and I followed her.

"And you didn't, I'm guessing," she said.

"Ye of little faith." I thanked all that is good that I had remembered this anniversary over a week ago. "What's my present?"

"Open it and find out."

She sat down at the desk to watch me. I started to carefully remove the cellophane tape holding the small box together. I didn't say anything too precious, because I saw Kowalski leaving, and didn't want to deter him with an opportunity to make fun of me.

"Oh, tear it, for goodness sake," Sharon said.

So I did. There was a small white box inside with no markings on it. I dropped the wrappings on the desk and opened the box.

Inside was a plastic license plate, the kind kids put on bicycles. It was the same nondescript colors as the ones that adorn New Jersey cars. And printed where the license would be was, simply, DAD.

I started to well up. "Wow," I said.

Sharon's lower lip turned down. "You're disappointed," she said.

I looked up at her and she could see how it had moved me. "No," I told her. "I think it's the best present anyone's ever given me." And she stood up and I hugged her for a very long time until she made me stop.

"Now, where's mine?" she asked, crossing her arms on her chest, daring me to prove that I hadn't forgotten.

"Hang on," I said. "I'll be right back."

"If you're going to Tiffany's, you'll need your coat," she called after me as I left the office.

I ran up the balcony stairs two at a time and was knocking on the door to the projection booth before I could catch my breath. It's hell not being in your twenties.

Anthony was splicing trailers onto the front of *Opera*, since this would be the first showing of the Marx Brothers film this week. He turned around and saw me walk in. "What's up, Mr. Freed?" he asked. I noticed Carla, Anthony's girlfriend, in a corner of the booth, reading a magazine.

"Anthony, you remember that VHS tape I gave you last week?" I was gasping for breath. I should consider installing an elliptical trainer in the town house. Lord knows I needed to fill up space there with *something*.

"The wedding video?" he asked.

"Yeah. Please tell me you got a chance to . . ."

Anthony smiled, and reached into his backpack. "I have the discs," he said. "And they're very high quality. The part where you break the glass with your foot was especially moving."

"You watched it?" There are some things you don't want your staff to see, especially when your staff is a smirking teenager.

"Had to. I was making corrections for color and focus when I could. It'll look better than it ever has before, I promise you. But I couldn't do anything about the way you dance." Anthony has a sadistic streak that doesn't show up often, but it is real and active.

"I thought it was beautiful," Carla said, without looking up from her magazine.

"I can't thank you enough," I told him.

"No problem," Anthony said.

I took the two discs, which Anthony had put in professional cases, and put one in the drawer of the projector console (a table that holds the projector up). Then I stuck the other, Sharon's copy, under my arm, and bolted for the door.

I made it down the stairs in record time, and was saying, "I'm sorry it isn't wrapped as beautifully as—" Then I reached the office door. And I stopped short.

Inside the office, Sharon was still seated in the desk

chair, looking straight out into the runway to the lobby. But now standing next to her in the tiny office was Gwen Chapman.

And she was holding a scalpel to Sharon's throat.

39

"I don't really think she needs such a close shave, Gwen," I said. They tell you to open with a joke.

Sharon's eyes widened, but she didn't say anything; she knew what I was trying to do, even if she didn't agree with it.

"Shut the door," Gwen Chapman said.

I closed the door. "Can you tell me what the problem is?" I asked, doing my best to sound like an understanding psychiatrist.

"The *problem* is this woman you married!" Gwen spat out, exasperated. How could I not *know* that? "It's her fault Lillian is in jail!"

"I didn't . . ." Sharon attempted, but Gwen raised the scalpel again. "She followed me here," Sharon said, quietly, to me.

"It's actually my fault, Gwen," I told her. "I set Lillian up. Was I wrong?"

"Wrong! Of *course* you were wrong!" Gwen was playing with a deck from which the sevens and tens had been removed. "And I'm going to kill the woman you love in front of you."

"Where'd you get the scalpel?" I asked. Maybe I could distract her.

"At a medical supply store, can you believe it?" Gwen said. "You don't have to show identification, or anything. You just hand them your debit card."

"Disgusting," I said. "May I see it?" I held out my hand.

Gwen's face darkened faster than the sky before a summer thunderstorm. "Don't insult my intelligence, Mr. Freed," she said. "I'm going to slit this woman's throat right in front of you, and I thought it would be appropriate to do it with a scalpel, a little operation on the *doctor*."

"Are you going to kill me, too?" I asked. "Because I'll tell the police." Gwen didn't answer.

Sharon's hands appeared to be lashed to the arms of the desk chair with surgical tape (Gwen was taking this "operation" theme way too far), but I could move. Still, the office wasn't large enough, strangely, for me to just leap forward and grab the blade out of Gwen's hand; I'd thought of that. In such a tight space, though, any quick movement would require me to lean backward first to create momentum, and by that point, it would be too late.

Sharon would be dead.

I backed up against the door, in the hope that I could somehow gain speed in a lunge, but Gwen was already moving the blade toward Sharon's neck, and a tiny spot of blood showed on her throat. Sharon inhaled deeply, gasping for breath. She looked terrified.

But mostly, she looked angry at Gwen. "It was you, wasn't it?" Sharon growled. "You pushed that shopping cart at me with the cinder blocks in it, and you threw the brick that hit Elliot."

"Of course it was me," Gwen said. "Although I am sorry about that, Mr. Freed; I was aiming the brick at *her*, and I simply missed." Her face hardened again. "My sister and her worthless husband knew—Wally was driving the car, even—but they were useless. They left it all up to me, as usual."

"They left it up to you to kill your father, too, didn't they?" I said. The Lillian scenario had been too easy; I'd wanted it to be Lillian who did the killing, so I believed it when it was offered.

"Oh, they wanted it, trust me," Gwen said. "But they couldn't do it themselves. No, it was always me who did the dirty work."

"But Lillian got arrested and charged with the murder," I said, thinking out loud. "Why wouldn't she rat you out then?"

"She'll get off, and she knows it," Gwen said. "She can afford the best criminal lawyer in the world. And I promised if she keeps quiet, I'd end the affair I was having with her husband."

"It was you with him at the hotel in Newark."

She closed her eyes and nodded her head, acknowledging what I'd suggested, even while she pointed out what an idiot I was for not figuring it out sooner.

"My family is more screwed up than you can possibly imagine," Gwen said.

"You know," I said, deciding to take a more aggressive attitude, "I've had it with you and your family."

Gwen stopped, startled by my tone. "What the hell are you talking about, you're tired of us? This woman . . ."

"Yeah, yeah, she ruined your life. I should have figured it. You were the one who said your father wouldn't invest without a prototype, and that's what the PTYPE on that stupid gadget of Lennon's meant."

"Don't you call it . . ." Gwen began.

"I'm *talking*!" I figured crazy responds to crazy and Gwen was major crazy. "You were behind the whole connection between Lennon and your father to begin with, weren't you? You looked into Lennon's big blue eyes, and you wanted him to have whatever he wanted, no matter how impractical it was. So you went to work on your father, and he agreed to meet this brilliant inventor. But he saw the clamp was too clumsy, too badly designed, to be marketable, and he turned Lennon down. And you got so mad you went in there and cut your own father's throat, probably with the blade on the clamp. Right? *Right?*"

Gwen looked so stunned that I considered diving for the scalpel, but I just couldn't force myself to do it—one miscalculation, and Sharon would be dead.

Then there was a knock on the door.

Before Gwen could say anything, the hand behind my back turned the knob and I swung the office door out into the lobby. A guy in a dark blue uniform stood there, and I had a momentary sigh of relief; the police were here.

But, no. "Registered letter," he said, holding out an envelope.

"Don't let him in," Gwen ordered.

And that's when it came to me.

"Come on in," I said. "Do I have to sign?"

"Yes," the mailman said. "It's standard."

Now, Gwen would have to kill two *more* of us if she thought she was going to get away with this gambit. I'd have to keep the postal guy in the office, though, because she had seemed perfectly willing to slice Sharon's throat in front of me.

The guy walked in, but closed the door behind him, and that was a problem. It was already crowded in the office. He wormed his way past me to the desk, and held out a pen. "Sign, please?"

"Just a second. Let me get my pen."

He held his out. "I have one."

"I know," I said airily. I noticed Gwen had lowered her hand, keeping the scalpel out of sight, but she must have had it close by, and had covered Sharon's wrists, bound to the chair, with her scarf. Sharon couldn't use the wheels of the chair to escape. There just wasn't enough room in the office to maneuver.

I leaned over the postal guy and reached for a jar of pens I keep on the desk. I made a show of trying out different ones, trying to find just the right writing implement.

"Just sign for the letter," Gwen said.

But then there was another knock on the door, and I motioned to the postal guy. He opened it before Gwen could protest.

Leo Munson stood in the doorway, and I waved him in. "Leo!" I shouted in the most jovial voice I could muster. "Come on in!"

Leo surveyed the room, and asked, "Where?"

"We'll make room. What's up?"

Leo squeezed his way through the door and stood next to Sharon, pressed against one of the filing cabinets. "I just wanted to see if you were still showing the Pink Panther cartoon before the movie," he said. "I hate the Pink Panther."

"No," I told him. "We've moved on to Road Runner."

"About time," Leo answered. "Well, that was all . . ."

"Stick around," I said. "I think there's a box of Yodels in that file cabinet." Leo has a sweets fixation, and he started the tortured process of turning around to open the drawer.

Gwen was looking even more livid than before, and it didn't help when the door opened and Sophie and Jonathan appeared in the doorway. "What's going on in here?" Sophie said. "People come in, and they don't come out."

"Sophie! Jonathan!" I sounded like a game show host. "Leo, did I tell you that Sophie is now the manager of Comedy Tonight?"

Leo turned and smiled, chocolate on his lips. "No! Come here, sweetie, let me give you a hug. Congratulations!" And the two kids started to make their way into the room.

Sharon allowed herself a sly grin. She understood that I was trying to make it difficult both for Gwen to get away with anything in front of people, but also to move her arm. Sharon nodded in my direction. I made sure Sophie didn't close the door behind her.

"Anybody else out there?" I yelled.

"Stop that!" Gwen shouted, but she was being drowned out by the conversation in the room.

My father appeared in the doorway, with my mother by his side. "So this is where everybody went," he said. "What's going on? It looks crowded."

"We're shooting for the Guinness World Record for the most people in a broom closet," I told him. "Come on in!"

"Could you just sign for the letter?" the postman said.

"I thought you guys always rang twice," I told him. It didn't seem to appease him at all, but it did shut him up.

Gwen's face was as angry as I've ever seen a human look. In fact, since I've never actually been in the room with an annoyed cheetah, I was willing to say it was the angriest face I'd seen on any species.

She stuck out her lower lip and painfully raised her arm with the scalpel. "This has gone far enough," she said, loudly enough to be heard.

Gwen got her arm back in place on Sharon's throat, and a gasp went around the room. Nobody spoke.

Except my mother.

"What do you think you're doing to my daughter-in-law?" Gloria Freed shot at Gwen. She was on my side, yet my mother's voice still frightened *me*.

"I'm making her pay," Gwen said, and tried to move the scalpel, but it was difficult to move her arm.

"Pay for what?" my mother wanted to know. "Sharon hasn't done anything wrong, except scare us all to death."

"She ruined my life. I'm Gwen Chapman." She seemed to think that would cut some ice in this room, but was sadly mistaken.

"Oh, don't be an idiot," my mother said.

"This can't be the best way to solve your problem." My father. Ever the voice of reason, Arthur Freed.

From outside, I heard Sandy Arnstein's voice. "Arthur? Is that you?"

I nodded at Dad: Yes, get more people here. "Yeah!" Dad shouted. "Come on in!"

We hit the jackpot: Arnstein appeared with Milt the painter, Ralph the plasterer, and Mr. A-OK the plumber. "What the hell is this?" Arnstein asked. "It looks like the black hole of Calcutta in there."

"But it's so much *fun*!" Sharon shouted. "Come on in!"

And that was all it took—all four men started squeezing their way in. The rest of the gathering (with the exception of

Gwen, who was still trying to draw her arm back, but kept hitting it on an old projector we use for spare parts) now understood the game, and started pressing in to make room. By the time the four workmen got inside, we had created a scene around Gwen and Sharon that made *The Last Supper* look like an Ansel Adams photograph of Montana on an especially empty day.

Dad, edging toward Gwen, had his eye on the scalpel. But his arms were literally pressed straight down against his sides, and he's not that strong. I began to worry about his heart.

And that's when Gregory showed up.

He didn't even ask any questions. He just wormed his way in and tried to make it to Sharon. He got as far as the plumber and was caught in an eddy that threatened to send him back out the door.

"Gregory!" my mother yelled. "Grab her!"

"I would," he answered, "but she's all the way over there."

"Not her. *Her!*"

Bobo Kaminsky showed up in the door. "You didn't pay for the snow tires, Elliot," he said. "Hey. You having a party?"

"Yes, and there's Yodels!" Leo shouted. Bobo, all six-feet-two in every direction of him, needed to hear no more. He was on his way, and much groaning ensued.

"Give it up, Gwen," I said in as close to a normal voice as I could muster. "You're not getting anywhere."

"Yes, I am," she insisted. "I'll kill her if I have to carve through all of you to do it." *Major* crazy.

"Elliot?" When Meg Vidal's voice came through the door, before I could see her, I closed my eyes. *Please, Meg. Be wearing your uniform.*

But Meg is a detective, and only dresses in blues for cop funerals and special ceremonies. She showed up in the doorway, and stood, amazed, at the spectacle therein.

"What in god's name . . . ?"

"Detective Vidal, a woman in here is trying to commit felony murder!" I shouted. "Draw your weapon!"

"And shoot at *whom*?" Meg asked. "It's a sea of humanity in there."

"I'll show you," Sharon said. "Come to me."

"Officer, this woman killed my father! They arrested her and they let her go! And they're framing my sister for the murder!" Gwen's voice seemed to come out of the back wall. Leo was stretched out on the filing cabinets, actually eating a Yodel, and the mailman was sitting on the desk, chatting with the plasterer.

Meg considered her gun, but knew it was impossible to pick out a target. She sighed, and began squirming into the room.

And right behind her was Moe Baxter. "Elliot, where the hell are my car keys?"

"In here, Moe!" I yelled. "I've got 'em for you. Thanks for the loaner."

Moe stood in the doorway and said, "No way." Moe's a germophobe. Normally, being in a small room with that many people would be his idea of hell. But then he spotted Sharon in the room, and yelled, "Sharon! I'm so glad you're okay!" He dove into the scrum.

Still at the door, I decided to make Gwen that much more uncomfortable. I closed the door. There were groans from the crowd.

The seventeen of us, in a room built for, well, two brooms, were practically immobile. I couldn't decide if I wanted Anthony and Carla to come down and join us, but luckily, it didn't become an issue. Gregory stood on the little table I use for the spare equipment on the left side of the room. Sophie and Jonathan had taken up a position beneath it. I was not interested in finding out what they were doing.

Meg, in the meantime, was inching her way toward Gwen.

But Gwen was raising her scalpel hand over her head. I expected to hear Sondheim tunes and looked for the barber chair, but this time, the blade was headed downward, toward Sharon.

"You can't kill her!" I shouted. "She's pregnant!"

All the motion and sound in the room stopped. Even Gwen's hand halted in midair.

"Elliot!" Sharon said, annoyed.

Gregory, on the table, looked positively stricken. "Pregnant?" he asked. "But we haven't . . ." Then he glared at me. *"You,"* he snarled.

"A grandchild!" my mother shouted. "Finally!"

There were noises of congratulations around the room.

But Gregory was unmoved. "Oh yeah?" he spat at me. "Well, I was the one who trashed your house!"

Again, silence in the room. "What?" I asked.

"You heard me. You wouldn't listen to me, even when I told you Sharon was missing. Dumb old Gregory being dumb again. So I took Sharon's spare key to your house, and I went there looking for something that would remind her of how you treated her when you were married, so she'd stop idealizing you. That stupid video collection of yours—you love it more than her! So I started . . ." His voice just trailed off.

"But I thought your house was burglarized, too," Mom said.

"I made that up," Gregory mumbled.

"You *lied* to me," Mom gasped. Of all the things about Gregory to be appalled about, she chose that one.

"Let me clue you in, dumb old Gregory—and don't be so hard on yourself; you're not that old. When you trashed my living room, you yanked the answering machine out of the wall, so it wasn't flashing when I got home, and we *never got Sharon's message*." I looked at him (as best as I could through the sea of humanity). "You could have saved us all a lot of worry."

Gregory said, "Um . . ."

In the fray, Meg had inched her way to Gwen; with that as her mission from the start, she'd made sure to keep her arms free. She grabbed Gwen's wrist and halted any movement of the scalpel. Bobo reached over with the desk scissors and cut the surgical tape on Sharon's wrists, and she stood up, causing ripples in the crowd.

Gwen Chapman began to sob. "You don't understand," she wailed. "That woman . . . that woman . . ."

"That woman is the mother of my child," I said.

Meg started cuffing Gwen, and reciting her Miranda warning. Gwen was weeping and shaking her head.

I was leaning against the door, but couldn't turn around. "Can anybody reach the doorknob?" I asked.

But the point was moot. Suddenly, the world was horizontal, as the door flew open, and I fell backward. I felt Arnstein and Moe fall on top of me. Others flew in various directions, and the air was suddenly much, much cooler.

I was lying on the floor in the lobby, and looking up into the face of Chief Barry Dutton.

"And two hard-boiled eggs," I said.

Somewhere in the office, I heard Leo belch loudly.

"Make that three hard-boiled eggs."

40

"I was coming to tell you that I'd called on your friend Konigsberg," Meg said. "That, and I wanted to see the Marx Brothers."

The few of us who remained from the Horror of the Tiny Room sat on the floor just in front of the snack bar. Mom and Dad, of course, were in chairs I'd brought out, and Gwen was not there to celebrate. Dutton had called two uniformed cops to give her a lift to her new digs in county lockup.

"I'd forgotten about him," I told her. "How'd he react?"

"When I told him that I was a member of the Camden Police Department, and I'd heard he was blackmailing a woman in Midland Heights, he folded like a Japanese fan. Gave me the pictures he'd taken and the disk he'd stored them on. I watched him delete them from his hard drive. He won't bother Grace Mancuso anymore."

"You're a lifesaver, Meg," I said.

"Literally," Sharon piped up.

"I was trying—" Gregory began.

"Shut up, Gregory," my mother told him. I gave her a hug.

"I'm just glad you were here," Sharon continued to Meg.

"I was happy to—" Gregory began.

"Shut up, Gregory," Mom said. I gave her a hug.

Moe had taken his car keys, and Bobo had been paid for the studded bicycle tires, and then both had left. Leo was inside the auditorium, watching Groucho and Chico argue over a contract and declare there is no Sanity Clause.

"It's my job," Meg told Sharon. "Besides, you guys are friends." She actually leaned over and ruffled my hair. " 'Draw your weapon.' Honestly."

The workmen had all quit for the night when the theatre opened, and had packed up and left. The heat was back on and functioning, there was wet plaster on one of the walls (luckily, high enough that no one could put a hand into it), and wet paint elsewhere, with signs indicating what not to touch. The urinals in the men's room were once again in working order. The electricity would probably stay on through the whole show tonight.

It was a miracle the place was still standing.

"It's funny," I said, to no one in particular. "I've always thought of myself as kind of—well, not a loner—but the kind of guy who didn't have many friends. But I've got to say, tonight in that office, I certainly didn't feel lonely. Maybe I need to rethink my self-image."

Sharon smiled at me. "People like you, Elliot," she said. "You just don't understand why."

I didn't answer. I took a look around the lobby. Sophie and Jonathan sat behind the snack bar, which at the moment had no customers. She had her copy of some ACT book or another out on the counter, but wasn't reading it. Jonathan, wearing his finest *Simpsons Movie* T-shirt, looked into her eyes and probably wasn't hearing a word she said.

Meg, hand on her hip, was in a discussion with Sharon about what fools men are, which we are. Mom and Dad, like the king and queen, sat higher than everyone else, and beamed at their charges. Gregory lay on the carpet like a snake, minus the slithering.

Chief Dutton stood to one side, apart from the rest, as if he were trying to understand exactly how a group like this could have been assembled, and why. He had a bemused smile on his face. I wished I had champagne to give them all.

And the postman was standing just outside the door to my office, holding a clipboard and a pen.

Oh, yeah!

I got up and walked over to him. "I never did sign for that letter, did I?" I said. "Sorry about that, but I was trying to save a woman's life."

"Uh-huh. Sign here." Some people are flappable, and others, not so much. You couldn't flap this guy with a cattle prod.

I signed for the letter, gave him a twenty-dollar tip, and watched him leave. I suppose I should have asked his name, but odds are he didn't have one.

Walking back toward the group, I'd only taken a few steps before I stopped dead in my tracks. It took a few moments, but Sharon noticed the look on my face.

"Are you okay, Elliot?" she asked.

"I'm not sure," I said. If I'd been thinking straight, I might have pointed out that she's the doctor, and should have been able to tell *me* if I was okay. But again, I wasn't thinking straight.

The name on the return address on the envelope of the registered letter was "Angie Hogencamp, Attorney-at-Law."

She'd said that those who were mentioned in Russell Chapman's will would be notified by certified mail within a day or two.

It was now within a day or two.

Sharon stood up and walked to me. "What is it?"

I tore open the envelope carefully, and extracted the letter inside, which was remarkably unassuming, and only one page long. It took less than a minute to read, but I'd be absorbing its information for a very, very long time.

"Russell Chapman left me a million dollars in his will," I said.

Dutton straightened up. Meg's mouth fell open. Dad stood

slowly—his knees aren't what they used to be, either—and Mom just broke into a satisfied grin, as if to say, *It's about time.*

I was pretty sure Gregory was going to throw up.

"What?" Sharon took the letter out of my hands and read it. "He left you a hundred thousand dollars a year for ten years, specifically to run Comedy Tonight," she said.

"I know," I told her.

"Why?" Dad asked. But he was grinning. I saw Dutton approaching. Sophie and Jonathan probably hadn't heard what Sharon and I had said; they were engrossed in conversation.

"It's in a letter he sent me," I told him. "But I didn't realize it. The day he died, Chapman came here and saw *Sullivan's Travels*. He said it changed his life, and that what I was doing was a service to the community. But I guess he'd seen just how small the crowd was, and he knew I'd have trouble keeping the theatre going for long. This is his way of helping."

"What does this mean?" Dad asked.

"It means you can tell Milt to use the good paint when he shows up tomorrow."

Sharon's arms were around me, but I barely felt them. It takes a lot to stun me that much. I remember Dad taking the letter out of my hand and bringing it to Mom so she could read it.

Anthony and Carla came down the stairs, taking a break after a reel change, probably around the time Allan Jones and Kitty Carlisle were singing "Alone." They were both wearing expectant grins. Not Allan and Kitty.

"So?" Anthony said.

My mind was elsewhere. "So what?" I asked.

"That's what I'd like to know," Sharon said. It's an old joke between us. Don't trouble yourself.

"So," Carla picked up for her boyfriend, "how did the doctor like her present?"

I stood and stared at them for a moment. "Her present!" I said suddenly. Jonathan looked at me and pointed at the auditorium doors, telling me to keep my voice down. "I forgot."

"You *forgot*?" Carla asked. What could be more important than an anniversary gift, even if you're not married anymore?

"Yeah," Sharon said. "What about my present? You can afford something really good now."

My head started to clear. "I'll tell you what," I said to Anthony. "Can you work late tonight?"

It was significant that he looked at Carla first, and she nodded. "Sure," Anthony said.

"Then I'll talk to you during the second movie."

Anthony nodded, shrugged at Carla, and took her hand. They headed back upstairs. No rest for the projectionist.

Dutton, suddenly, was standing in front of me. "The letter from Chapman," he said. "May I see it?"

"My mother has it," I told him. "And it's not from Chapman, but from his attorney."

"No," Dutton corrected me. "The one you got from him, that he wrote before he died."

I gave him my best innocent look. "Why, Chief," I said, "you know I gave that to Detective Kowalski."

"You made a copy," Dutton answered. "May I see it?"

My head tilted a bit. Something was odd. "Sure. It's in the office. Why?"

"It's what I was coming to tell you," Dutton said as we started to walk to the office. "We think we know who Chapman's 'inside man' was at the morgue when he faked his suicide. It seems that today a registered letter also arrived for an assistant ME named Irwin S. Taubman, Jr., better known as Doc. He got a million dollars, too. And must have known it was coming, because two days ago he got on a plane for the Cayman Islands."

"I'll bet it's going to be a long vacation," I said.

"Chapman's lawyer says his estate clearly accounts for forty-seven million dollars, including the million to you and the million to Doc, and a little more here and there to charities Chapman supported."

"What about his daughters?" Sharon asked.

"He left them twenty thousand dollars apiece," Dutton said, and the amusement in his voice was more than even he could conceal.

LATER that night, after the audience (such as it was) left and the theatre was cleaned up, Sophie and Jonathan went home. They were the last remaining from the Great Office Pileup, as Dutton and Meg had gone out to catch up over dinner, and Mom and Dad had decided to go home, although they threatened to call me in the morning with baby names. Mom probably would have gone out and bought a crib that night, but Jewish superstition doesn't allow for any baby accoutrements to be set up until the child is present and breathing.

Nobody could remember when Gregory left. We were just happy to revel in his absence.

Sharon and I took our seats in the center of the auditorium, and I waved up to the projection booth. The lights went out, and the screen came to life.

And there we were, our younger selves looking nervously at each other. She wore a white gown with a large bow in the back that made her look like the best present a man could possibly receive. I wore a blue pinstriped suit with lapels that were now no longer in fashion, and eleven pounds less than I wear today.

The "us" on the screen gave each other a tense glance, then exhaled, and walked outside to a lovely lawn, set up with rows of chairs on either side. My college roommate, a guy named Dave, played "Here Comes the Sun" on an acoustic guitar until we reached the altar, which was really a spot on the grass we'd designated. Four of our tallest friends (okay, Sharon's tallest friends) held up a prayer shawl over our heads, to serve as a *chuppah*, or a roof. You need that.

Sharon leaned over in her theatre seat. Row K, seat 18. "Thank you," she said. "It's the best gift I've ever gotten."

"You're welcome. But it's just a DVD."

"I didn't mean the DVD," she said.

EPILOGUE

THREE MONTHS LATER

If the things you wanted to happen did not happen, think instead of the things you did not want to happen that did not happen.   —CONFUCIUS

WEDNESDAY

THE Wrong Box (1966) and *Dead Tired* (this week)

SOPHIE told me to take the night off.

Taking her position as manager seriously, Sophie decided that I looked tired, and should relax for an evening. And she was right.

The repairs had, naturally, blossomed into more repairs, and were just now being completed. In addition to a new paint job for the entire theatre, except the auditorium, we now had completely new plumbing fixtures in the ladies' room, a new electrical service, three newly plastered walls, new wallpaper, and a new neon sign that read REFRESHMENTS over the snack bar.

Russell Chapman's money was being put to good use, even though I hadn't actually received it yet.

We were showing *The Wrong Box*, a brilliant black comedy very loosely adapted from a Robert Louis Stevenson short story by Larry Gelbart and Burt Shevelove, fresh off *A Funny Thing Happened on the Way to the Forum*. But I could catch it another night. Black comedy being the crowd-pleaser it is, we could expect a relatively small crowd for the classic, and *Dead Tired*, the touching story of a vampire with insomnia, probably wasn't going to help. Sophie, having received her acceptance to Princeton University two days before, had taken the previous night off, so she decided it was my turn tonight. No doubt the staff would have a celebration after the showings, and I was better off not knowing what direction that might take.

So now, having had a sumptuous dinner of takeout Chinese food, Sharon and I were on the new sofa in my living room, ostensibly watching *His Girl Friday* (in a remake of *The Front Page* that makes you wonder why they ever did this with two men) on the flat-screen. But in reality, she was fast asleep, head on my lap, and snoring. Her growing belly rose and fell with each gorillalike emanation from her throat. I couldn't hear the movie's dialogue, but then, I pretty much have it memorized, anyway.

I'd been in touch once or twice with Angie Hogencamp. She assured me that the will Russell Chapman had left would be upheld, although it was being challenged by Wally and Lillian Mayer. Susan said their case was flimsy at best, what with Lillian standing by idly while her intensely crazy sister murdered their father, and then staying silent about it, but the money for Comedy Tonight would be delayed while the courts decided. She made a reference to Charles Dickens's *Bleak House*, which I had to look up on SparkNotes.com. It meant the case could take a long time to resolve.

Sharon had been working longer hours at the practice, since they'd just now found a new doctor to replace Lennon Dickinson, so she was especially tired, being five months pregnant. Lennon had managed to cut a deal for a lesser sentence in his case, testifying against the loan shark in exchange for the prosecutor lowering his charges to withholding evidence.

Rosalind Russell, as Hildegaard "Hildy" Johnson, was just taking the corrupt sheriff down in a flying tackle when Sharon shifted a bit, and ended up facing straight up, rather than at the screen. I'd have to wake her soon, so she could get home at a decent hour.

But not yet. Not just yet.

FURTHER FUNNY FILM FACTS
FOR FANATICS

Sullivan's Travels (1941)

Written and directed by Preston Sturges. Starring Joel Mc-Crea, Veronica Lake, and William Demarest.

- Veronica Lake's character is never referred to by name. She is identified in the cast list simply as "The Girl."
- Preston Sturges was a playwright and inventor (he invented a kiss-proof lipstick, among other things) who moved to Hollywood to make money to finance his plays. He sold a number of screenplays, but became frustrated with the way they were directed, so he sold *The Great McGinty* to Paramount for one dollar—on the provision that he direct it himself.
- Sturges, who was named the twenty-eighth best director of all time by *Entertainment Weekly*, died of a heart attack in the Algonquin Hotel in 1959, while writing his memoirs, which he entitled *The Events Leading up to My Death*.
- What Elliot was trying to say on page 10 was that the title of John L. Sullivan's intended project, *O Brother, Where Art Thou?*, was "borrowed" by Joel and Ethan Coen for their 2000 update of Homer's *Odyssey,* starring George Clooney.
- At one point in *Sullivan's Travels*, someone mentions that the novel *O Brother, Where Art Thou?* was written by

"Sinclair Beckstein," a mishmash of the names Upton Sinclair, John Steinbeck, and Sinclair Lewis, according to Sturges.

- The cartoon shown to the inmates that raises their spirits is *Playful Pluto* (1934). Sturges wanted to use a Charlie Chaplin film, but Chaplin wouldn't give his permission.

A Night at the Opera (1935)

Directed by Sam Wood, written by James Kevin McGuinness (story) and George S. Kaufman and Morrie Ryskind (screenplay). Uncredited writers included Al Boasberg, Robert Pirosh, George Seaton, and half the population of Culver City, CA. Some accounts include uncredited contributions from Buster Keaton, but it's more likely he worked on later Marx films. Starring the Marx Brothers (Groucho, Harpo, and Chico), Kitty Carlisle, Allan Jones, Siegfried Ruman, and Margaret Dumont.

- The most commercially successful film the Marx Brothers ever made, it was also the first they made that did not include the youngest brother, Zeppo, who had left the act to become a talent agent. Which probably bolstered Groucho's opinion, when asked if the brothers would want as much money for just three, that "without Zeppo, we're worth twice as much."
- Censors in each state had to decide whether to include the line (when Groucho and Margaret Dumont are walking up the gangplank to the ship and she asks, "Otis, do you have everything?") "I haven't had any complaints yet."
- The famous stateroom scene was conceived by Boasberg, who wrote a draft, shredded it, and threw it around his office. When the Marx Brothers and producer Irving Thalberg (the prototype for F. Scott Fitzgerald's *The Last Tycoon*) found the shredded scene, they pieced it back together, and cinema history was made.
- If you think the crowd in Elliot's office is implausible,

keep in mind that fifteen people and a huge (open) steamer trunk fit into the minuscule stateroom in *Opera*.

- Director Wood reportedly (according to the Marxes and others) insisted every scene be shot at least twenty times, and instead of saying "action," would start each take with "Okay, folks, let's get in there and sell 'em a load of clams."

The Wrong Box (1966)

Directed by Bryan Forbes. Written by Robert Louis Stevenson (novel), Lloyd Osbourne (story), and Larry Gelbart and Burt Shevelove. Starring John Mills, Ralph Richardson, Michael Caine, Peter Cook, Dudley Moore, Peter Sellers, and Nanette Newman.

- Plot: A tontine (a sort of morbid trust fund that gives all the money to the last surviving member) among twelve London schoolboys dwindles to the last two, now older men, who try to . . . speed up the inheritance process. On each other.
- Richardson was asked to take the part of Joseph Finsbury while he was filming *Doctor Zhivago*, and agreed on the condition that he be allowed to wear the same jacket he wore in the Russian epic.
- Gelbart and Shevelove were in London after a massive success on Broadway with *A Funny Thing Happened on the Way to the Forum* when they decided to write the screenplay. Aside from the film adaptation of *Forum*, this is Shevelove's only big-screen writing credit.
- Gelbart went on to write, develop, and serve as executive producer for the television series *M*A*S*H*; wrote the screenplays of *Oh, God!*, *Tootsie*, and many others; and has produced and directed for the stage and television as well as film.
- Cook and Moore performed as a comedy team on stage and television until Moore became a film star with roles

in *Arthur* and *10*. Cook appears as the preacher with a speech impediment in *The Princess Bride*, among many other roles. Together, they wrote and starred in the original *Bedazzled* (1967) with, among other people, Raquel Welch.

Peabody Public Library
Columbia City, IN
DISCARD